Heart of Iron

Heart of a Highlander, Volume 4

Rebecca Ruger

Published by Rebecca Ruger, 2021.

This is a work of fiction. Names, character, places, and incidents are either a product of the author's imagination or are used fictitiously, and any resemblance to actual persons, living or dead, events, or locales is entirely coincidental. Some creative license may have been taken with exact dates and locations to better serve the plot and pacing of the novel.

ASIN: B09KNGBDCZ

Heart of Iron

All Rights Reserved.

Copyright © 2021 Rebecca Ruger

Written by Rebecca Ruger

All rights reserved. No part of this publication may be reproduced, distributed or transmitted in any form or by any means, or stored in a database or retrieval system, without the prior written permission of the publisher.

Disclaimer: The material in this book is for mature audiences only and may contain graphic content. It is intended only for those aged 18 and older.

Chapter One

Near Muthill, Scotland, between Calasraid and Perth
Autumn, 1300

CAITRIN ROLLED HER eyes as her sister batted hers so cleverly at Fergus, who rode beside the cart that pulled them along. Good grief, but she'd be happy to be done with this conveyance and her sister's unending trifling with any male within shouting distance. Yesterday, as they plodded along, it was Bearnard who'd been given all of Mary's fawning regard. Mary did not harbor any affection or interest in either man. But always, she kept useful people around and flattered by her attention, alive with hope, so that someone might carry things for her and manage many unpleasant tasks that might be required of her and which she could then pass on to another.

Shifting on the hard floorboards of the wagon's bed, Caitrin realized a section of her gown was trapped under her sister's bottom. She jerked at the fabric when Mary ignored her but could not free it.

"Get off, Mary," Caitrin griped to her sister, made miserable by her own discomfort, upon the back of this rickety cart, and then by the fact that it seemed to bother Mary not at all.

There was only so much space in the wagon's bed, as it held Caitrin and Mary and Peigi, another household servant, and all that the family had packed for their journey, several trunks and satchels and two willow baskets, laden with straw-packed gifts for their hosts. Gordon Lorne and his wife sat up front, the middle-aged man advancing the pair of draft horses much as a farmer might upon his field, slow and steady. If he would speed up their pace to only twice as much, they'd still be only at a fast walk and Caitrin might know only two miserable days and not four upon the rutted lanes across the wild landscape.

They were not well-heeled, the Lornes, with whom Caitrin and Mary had lived since they'd lost their own parents when they were very small. The Lorne's lady-wife, as she liked to style herself, was fond of saying in those first years that it was the goodness of her heart that had persuaded her to take in those two orphaned girls. It didn't take so long for Caitrin to realize that the truth of the matter was far simpler and more closely related to Mrs. Lorne's laziness, and her distaste for anything that even remotely looked or sounded like labor. She was happy to have Caitrin and Mary and Peigi manage not only the entire small house but also so much of the business in which Gordon Lorne engaged. They did not live in any grand castle or keep, but Gordon Lorne was a respectable merchant and provided a comfortable home and lifestyle to his wife—and by association, to Caitrin and Mary and Peigi. As the sisters had no recollection of their own family when they'd come to the Lornes and were too young to object, they had since been known by the Lorne surname. They were not family, though. Gordon Lorne was fair and could be quite entertaining, but he was so rarely at home. Dorcas Lorne was not mean, certainly not constantly, but she could occasionally be short-tempered and heavy-handed. Still, Caitrin considered often that she and her sister were lucky to have a home and a bed and food for their bellies. There was little else she needed.

They traveled west from their home north of Perth to Calasraid along the River Teith, where they would spend the next month with Dorcas's sister, as they did every fall. As always, they moved about the country with only Peigi and two outriders, Bearnard and Fergus on this occasion, these men being more of a hopeful deterrent to anyone with an idea to accost them rather than actually having an ability to defend them if they should be set upon. Those two men regularly were employed by Gordon Lorne and within the tiny hamlet where they lived, which was a good three leagues from Perth itself, they were the only available men to make the trek, not beholden to a wife or family.

Caitrin did not dare ask again how much longer until they reached Calasraid. Already, she had asked twice today, and the sun was not yet directly above their heads.

She listened to Mary feign an interest in Fergus, supposing as she sometimes did that the Lornes allowed Mary to behave so shamelessly as it did regularly benefit them. Not a day might pass without some hopeful swain idling around their modest home, and Gordon Lorne was not above putting them to use. Lorne had once said to Caitrin, "Yer a wee bit finer than Mary to look upon. If you'd care to lose the scowls and deign to make conversation with the lads, we'd have all our labors attended all the livelong day." He'd chuckled robustly at whatever it was he found humorous about that and had sauntered away, not waiting for a reply, though Caitrin's narrowed gaze had followed him darkly.

She and Mary were not true sisters. They were related only by circumstance and not by blood. But neither of the Lornes had bothered to explain this to Caitrin or Mary, and as they'd always called them sisters, they thought of themselves as such. It was only about three years ago that the truth had come out, inadvertently, and not without much misplaced cackling from Dorcas and Gordon, who evidently had never given it much thought. As surprised as Mary and Caitrin had been to discover they were not true siblings, so great was the shock of the Lornes, who couldn't conceive how they hadn't known.

Caitrin had been riddled with guilt at that time, and sometimes since then, as her initial reaction had been one of relief. Mary was difficult to love, being as self-serving as Dorcas often was, but with a sharper tongue that cut without warning. Such relief she'd known then, her first thought being, *I don't have to love her*. She did, of course, as five and ten years of being raised together did not dissipate with only some irrelevant statement that they shared no blood. Aye, she loved her still, but only felt less guilty on those days when it proved so difficult.

Peigi had not been known to them before she'd come to the Lornes seeking work two years prior. She was pleasant but did not live with the Lornes. And she only accompanied them to Calasraid last year and now to get away from her own family and home, Caitrin believed. She'd met Peigi's father but once and that had been enough that she wished never to repeat the occasion, as he was as ugly outside as he was internally, brash and loud and stinking of stale mead and shouting at Gordon Lorne that his daughter was being cheated of wages. Gordon had argued with the man, threatened violence upon him even, telling him he paid Peigi what she was worth. He did not give up what Caitrin and Mary had immediately suspected, that Peigi was squirreling away coin for herself.

Bored with Mary's banter with Fergus and since Peigi now slept slumped against the side-rail of the wagon bed and wasn't available to pass the time with, Caitrin closed her eyes and concentrated on other sounds. The wagon itself put out several noises, dull clanking sounds of wood groaning and creaking with each revolution of the wheels. The wheels themselves made little noise as they rolled over a blessedly level field of dry, golden grass. They moved now through the wide meadow of a glen between hills that Caitrin could not name but that were not steep, which rose gently upward in a thick forest of trees. Those trees that crowded the slopes of the hills were home to many birds and critters and just now, a large group of rooks shot out from the top of the trees, as if something had startled them. The black birds swarmed up and away and Caitrin tipped her head back, watching them soar overhead and into the trees on the north side of the meadow. Supposing this lone wagon and two riders slowly crossing the meadow had not uprooted them, Caitrin assumed a larger critter within the trees must have scared them away.

As she passed her gaze over the dark green and brown of the pines and oaks, and moss and lichen, a flash of white light caught her attention. Frowning and squinting, Caitrin tried to peer deeply through the branches and leaves. But it was only a flash, seen and now gone—until it sparked again, and she realized it was sunlight, glinting off something within those woods, something shiny, metal or steel.

"Fergus, did you see that?" She asked of the youth, not turning toward him as she was dedicated to scouring the trees on the south side of the wagon.

"Eh?"

Lifting her arm off the side rail, Caitrin pointed to the trees on the slope, where the light had shone. 'Twas not a flame, as that would have been golden, neither so bright in the daytime nor so white.

An icy chill walked down her spine. "Someone is in those trees," she said, "watching us."

Gordon heard her and replied jovially, "And like as no', only hoping we dinna stop but are just passing through. I tell ye, Caitrin, you dinna bother the bees and the spiders and the critters—or those upon whose land ye travel—and they'll no' bother you."

This brought her no relief. It was a dangerous time to travel in any part of Scotland, with the English having waged campaigns steadily since the beginning of the year.

"Thirteen years we've been traveling these roads," Dorcas said over her shoulder, "haven't run into—" her own shriek of terror cut off her words as an arrow whooshed through the air and struck Gordon Lorne in the face.

Caitrin pivoted on the planks of the wagon bed, stunned speechless in the space of the second it took her to realize the arrow had struck Gordon on the left side of his face, and plowed all the way through and out the other side, so close to Dorcas that her cheek was sprayed with blood.

Fergus and Bearnard drew their swords and faced the woods and were, in the next second, brought down by two more arrows. Gordon fell forward and the draft horses jerked into four or five steps of a run, tossing Peigi off the end of the wagon. And then the draft horses stopped, and Caitrin saw mounted men erupt from those trees, cantering toward them, seemingly in no hurry to carry on with their killing. Caitrin and Mary exchanged horrified glances, and both scrambled out of the wagon, running toward the north, away from the assailants.

Only an innate sense of self-preservation allowed Caitrin to move her legs at all. Fear gripped every fiber and nerve, ringing in her veins. But she ran, pulling Mary along with her. They followed Peigi, who had leapt first from the wagon bed. Caitrin kept her eye on Peigi and the forest in front of her. They were only sitting ducks on this open field but might stand a better chance of escaping inside the thick forest of trees. Caitrin's eyes widened just as Mary screamed her fright when a rider cut between them and Peigi and gave chase to that stumbling woman. Instinct made Caitrin change direction, turning and pulling Mary toward the left, but still aiming for those trees. A yip of horror burst from her as she spied Fergus's prone body, splayed in the center of the field.

"Hurry," she called to Mary, whose steps faltered.

Both girls cried out when a missile flew by them, within only feet of the left side of Caitrin. It landed many yards ahead of them, struck into the ground, and Caitrin realized it was a hatchet. They were throwing hatchets at her and Mary as they ran for their lives.

Laughter rang out behind them, and someone guffawed loudly, "You missed. Ten pence says you miss again. Here, use mine."

"I'll use the bow."

"I'll take no wager on a bow. Any fool can plant an arrow."

Sweet merciful Jesus, they were playing games as they tried to kill them, as if they only diced on a dusty bit of earth inside a castle yard.

Fear proved valuable in that it propelled her forward more desperately, even as she suspected at any second she might be struck from behind and felled by their perverse contest.

She had a tight and sure grip on Mary's hand, and they were running as fast as they could. Caitrin thought for sure they would reach the trees before they were caught or killed. A split second later, her hand was yanked low as Mary fell. She lost her grip completely, her sister's hand going limp as she tumbled to the ground. Horrified, Caitrin stopped and covered her mouth with her hands. This hatchet had found its mark, struck nearly at the exact center of Mary's back. As she bent over her, Caitrin jerked and shook and screamed when an arrow landed in Mary's back in the next moment, finding its target just below the buried axe with an unassuming *pfft* of a noise.

"Run," Mary breathed as Caitrin bent and tried to lift Mary to her feet. "Run."

Frantically, Caitrin spared only one glance at the murderers. There were only six or seven men, and they were not chasing her. Two men were mounted yet on horseback, walking around the wagon; one reached out and flipped open the lid of one of the willow baskets. Three more had dismounted and were talking to each other, looking at the bow in the hand of a stout youth, as if it were not behaving properly. Another man pointed at her and called out something, but not with any great volume that Caitrin could make it out. He then approached Gordon Lorne, and Caitrin gasped. Gordon was alive yet, and crawling away on all fours, while the arrow that had first toppled him was yet entrenched in his face. The man gave a kick to Gordon's slowly moving body, sending him onto his back.

English, she realized, recalling their distant speech of moments ago and now noticing the familiar chainmail hauberks and tunics of red and gold.

"Go," Mary gurgled now, her left cheek planted in the brown grass, her eyes drifting closed.

Caitrin sent only one more glance to Gordon but did not want to witness what his obvious fate was going to be, as the man tormenting him had drawn a long and thick sword. She wasted not another moment, but lifted her skirts and took off, once again attempting to gain any security the trees might offer.

A call followed her swift departure. "Get on that! There she goes!"

And while it was true that fear remained a great impetus, pushing her onward, Caitrin struggled against sluggish limbs, which she dreaded only *seemed* to move swiftly while she was fearful that she was not gaining much ground. With each step, she fretted her legs might buckle beneath her. She could not control her breathing, hastened by her flight and made erratic by the events she'd just witnessed and her ongoing fear that she would be the next one—the last one—killed.

She pushed against low-hanging boughs and stumbled over exposed roots, clambering upward along the slope.

At one point, she detected some hollering below her, as someone complained she was getting too far away. A stray arrow and then another whooshed through the wooded area, striking a tree or the earth many yards away, hinting that they could not see her now within the hillside forest, but were only aiming blindly.

Caitrin continued to run, ran all the way to the crest of the flat-topped ridge and turned only once, to peer backward, below, to gauge the quality and closeness of their chase. She heard no pursuit but kept on, wanting to be further away.

ROSS KILDARE SENT ONE last look back at Blackwood, naught but a spot of red stone upon the landscape, nearly unseen now, tucked into the foreshadow of the mountains beyond it. 'Twas a fine home, a fine settlement there. Good people filled it. He would be pleased to visit there again one day. His army of not quite one hundred moved steadily west. Once they reached the flatlands of the glen near River Pattack, they would open it up, close the distance between where they were and home.

He'd not planned to stay so long away from Westcairn, but he'd left with only some vague directive that he was to meet with Lord Comyn's army and stave off the English advancement further north into Scotland. That had been more than half a year ago, in late spring. They had given up no ground but for Caerlaverock Castle, which had served in some capacity as the center of Scottish resistance. What few skirmishes followed the siege at Caerlaverock could only be deemed inconclusive. And then last month, Edward I of England had simply turned around and gone home. It was too soon to know if the Pope's open denouncement of his actions or if shortages of victuals and men and arms or if merely the coming winter had sent the English monarch home. It mattered not but that he was gone and with him, the larger part of his army. What English remained in Scotland now, in the autumn of the year of our Lord 1300, were only those with a firm hold on the castles and towns they'd seized and now held.

Ross and his men might have been sooner turned toward home and Westcairn, but he was pleased that he'd whiled away a few days at Blackwood with his friend Gabriel Jamison. He'd only wanted to give his army—those wounded specifically—time to recover, but it was fortuitous that he'd chosen to pause at Blackwood, as the Jamison laird had returned home to find his new wife kidnapped by a neighboring clan. Ross was glad to be of assistance to him in the scuffle, which had seen the fair bride of Gabriel returned safely from an inept clan of wastrels and unsavory characters.

All was well.

And now Ross was anxious to return to Westcairn. But even now, with consideration to those yet recovering and the many vehicles that transported those wounded and all their supplies, they could not rush. Almost a dozen of their men were horseless, having lost or sacrificed their steeds to battle in the last month. With a nod toward these factors, Ross instructed that they be paced at only five to ten miles a day, dependent upon the terrain.

On day three of their journey, Ross rode somewhere in the middle of his men as they walked in near silence through a forest of trees which saw little brush but only a blanket of leaves and pine needles on the ground. The sun, if any could find it, might have been directly overhead when the forward scout used his sword to poke and lift a piece of fabric from the ground, holding it above his head that all those behind could see. 'Twas a woman's piece, pale blue and decorated with shiny gold threads. The scout paused, awaiting direction, thus stopping the entire moving army.

By the time Ross reached the scout, Idgy, at the edge of the trees, he found the man slack-jawed and bloodless. Slowly, the man lowered the sword, with the fabric dangling and swaying, and pointed ahead to the open field. Pushing aside a low hanging bough, Ross's mouth fell open as well as he surveyed the heath and thistle strewn meadow before them.

A half dozen bodies lay strewn about, bloodied, cut down. Several of them were on their stomachs, suggesting they'd been running for their lives, felled from behind.

One body looked to be sitting, curled up, the face bent over the knees, very close to another woman sprawled out on her stomach.

Jesu.

Another quick scan of the area said whoever committed this atrocity had fled, was gone now, and Ross slowly walked his horse out into the open field. He thought to instruct another who stood nearby. "Fingal, run on back, bring up the rest of the army. Set them here at the edge of the woods." He didn't wait to be sure Fingal would do as instructed or wait for the army to come forward so that he might know greater ease for their numbers.

Unsheathing his sword, Ross kept his steed to a quiet walk, watchful, alert. His younger brother, John, walked with him. When Ross reached the first body, he found a young woman, a servant mayhap, dressed well but not fine. She was flat on her belly, her face turned toward him, her eyes unseeing. The middle of her back showed a pool of blood surrounding the hole just the size of the width of a Scots' sword. He did not touch her but kept on, past an older man, mayhap in his late forties, dressed well, his tunic made of red linen and covered with a fur-lined mantle. The man was on his back, his hands sliced and cut with telltale defensive wounds. He'd faced his attacker head on, had possibly gripped with both hands the very blade that had cut him down. An arrow was lodged through his face, having entered one side and exited the other, between his nose and mouth.

Ross glanced over to where John maneuvered his horse around another body. John met Ross's gaze and shook his head. That woman was dead as well.

Ross blew out a harsh breath for this travesty, hoping that what he'd come upon had been mercifully quick for these travelers. Clucking low at his destrier, he moved to the pair that were closest together, not scattered about so far apart as were all the others. He was still a good fifty feet from them, he and his brother, when that curled up body jerked and moved.

Surprised, Ross reined in. 'Twas a woman, and she was clearly not dead.

She'd just come to as if she'd been sleeping, stirring sharply. But she did not turn to them, hadn't been wakened by the silent men walking among the dead. She was in profile, her flaxen hair falling all around her, only one clump of it yet held by a thread of yellow ribbon which at one time might have contained all her thick hair, mayhap when the day had begun. While Ross approached again, with a more pronounced slowness, she clawed at the earth. She used both hands and reached far ahead of her bent knees, pulling at the ground, bringing clumps of it toward her, which she scooped away to her side at the last second before it might have piled up at her knees. She moved frantically, breathing harshly or weeping softly. Each forward reach of her arms came with a wretched sound and each shoveling of dirt away was made with a strangled cry.

It wasn't until he was closer that he realized she was trying to dig a hole in the earth. A grave. She had a good portion of dirt removed before her but had very far to go yet. He wondered if she had passed out and had only just woken and gotten right back to it. Having witnessed plenty of war and death, mostly of late, Ross already recognized that these people had not been killed just today. Mayhap as long ago as yesterday, said the condition of the bodies and the vultures circling overhead. He saw no evidence of a fire or any signs of a camp that he surmised they'd not been surprised from their overnight camping but had been found and slaughtered while they'd traveled. Perchance their carts and horses had been stolen.

As quietly as he'd come, Ross dismounted, sheathing his sword smoothly to make no sound. He held up a hand at John so that he would remain still.

"Lass," Ross said softly, approaching cautiously. She gave no sign that she heard him. She kept on burrowing in the ground, all her motions unsteady, frantic.

Ross walked around the front of her so that she might see him and not startle. He held his hands up so that when she noticed him, she would not be alarmed; he brandished no weapon. But she did not see him, though he was well inside her periphery.

"Lass," he said again, and when she still did not acknowledge his presence, he went to his knees in front of her, across the hole in the ground. He didn't want to frighten her. Gently, he set his hand over hers until her fingers stopped scratching in the dirt. Her head moved, mayhap she nodded, understanding that someone had come, but the movement was jerky, not entirely discernable. It was a moment before she looked up. Her eyes were magnificent. Magnificent in the quality of the green of her gaze, even as he wasn't sure she saw him, or anything at all. At the same time, the haunted emptiness of her stare stirred him, that Ross found himself mournful for her, that she only looked through him, saw only horror.

With greater firmness, he circled his fingers around all of hers and dragged her hands away.

"No more, lass."

"Aye, I must bury them." She whispered with some scratchiness, as if her voice were rusty, or battered from her wailing. Her eyes and nose were red, horrifically so, that he thought her sobs must have been powerful, that she must have keened for hours and hours and recently. Otherwise, her face was a mixture of dirt and streaked tears with one cheek having a smudge of blood. Likely she had held a body close to her, mayhap had wept against it.

"And we will. Bury them," he assured her evenly. "Come away."

She allowed him to pull her to her feet, even as she said, "I must cover Mary before the rains come. She doesn't like the rain."

"Aye, we'll get it done in time." With some consideration for her ghostlike mien, for his suspicion that she wasn't right at the moment, Ross put his hands on her shoulders and turned her around. More riders had come, his men. He inclined his head for Tavis to collect her even as he walked her forward toward that lad. When Tavis was close, on foot, Ross gave a little push to the small of her back, propelling her toward the wincing and sympathetic Tavis.

He watched for several seconds until she was further away. She kept her elbows bent, tucked against her sides and held her hands in front of her, trembling. He didn't know where her gaze was—on her hands, on the army or the trees ahead of her, on the ground watching each plodding step—but he might have imagined that she saw only these dead bodies still.

An hour later, Ross stood beside her again, standing above six mounds of freshly turned dirt.

She'd come woodenly to the graves, rigid and yet wraithlike. But now she sank to the ground, fell so smoothly, so swiftly that as Ross reached for her, meaning to grab an arm to break her fall, his hand met only with air. She was on her knees before he might have brought her upward again. He let her sit, felt the sinking of everything inside her while her bloodied and muddied skirts settled about her in a near perfect circle.

Her shoulders slumped.

Ross glanced around at the few men gathered. Most of them had their gazes trained on her and her reactions, the ethereal quality of her shock and mournfulness, and not on the even drifts of freshly turned dirt in front of them.

"I should like to stay awhile," she said. She was not of this world at the moment, her spirit gone with them. There was a long pause before she added, "With them."

Though she was seated, she swayed a bit, all her attention given to those mounds of earth. Ross went to his haunches and put his hand on her upper arm to steady her.

"I don't want to be alone," she said. Not to him. She was only bringing out her thoughts, was not speaking to anyone but herself.

Or so he imagined.

She finally turned her head and pierced him with her green-eyed gaze. "Is that all right?"

Jesu. "Aye, lass."

Chapter Two

The rain came then, more a mist of water drifting downward than an actual dripping or pouring. But it put a chill in the air and quickly laid a fog over the crime scene in the meadow.

"Get her a plaid," Ross said to no one in particular when she shivered and hugged her arms to herself.

Someone moved at his directive. He did not know who, his gaze holding hers as she stared through him again.

After a few minutes, he said, "It's done, lass. We have to move now. We are only targets for whoever—"

"I will stay," she said in that same flat tone.

Scowling, exchanging an impatient glare with some of the men gathered round, Ross persisted, "I canna allow that, lass. They might still be near, the ones who did this, whoever they might be—"

"English," she said softly. "They were English."

"English?" He repeated. "Nae, lass. There are no English in these parts. And those...wounds were made by wide blades—Scots' blades," he told her, though it pained him to do so, imagining the type of man who would do this to his fellow countrymen.

"They were English. I heard them. I saw them."

"Aye, verra well," he said then, not wanting to argue with her, or cause her grief on this account.

It was Tavis who returned with a plaid, which he handed to Ross. Standing, Ross unfolded the large piece and draped it around her slim shoulders, wrapping it around her twice so that it was secure. "C'mon then. We'll move now." Gently, he found her hands beneath the plaid and pulled her to her feet. "Your name, lass?"

"Caitrin," she answered mechanically.

"I am Ross of Westcairn, and you'll come to no harm now, lass. I promise you this."

Lifting her face to him, she implored, "Can I not stay with them?"

Ross shook his head, belatedly easing his scowl. "You ken the why of it. You'll no' be safe. You will come with us now."

She did not give any indication of her acquiescence but then she did not resist when he steered her away from the graves. "She can ride with Mercer in the cart," he said to Tavis, who stood near and ready, and who then led her away.

John walked forward, his hand on the hilt of his sword. "All Scottish: the tracks, the weapons, the arrows."

One might never suppose they were related at all, Ross and John Kildare, let alone that they were brothers only two years apart. Ross was tall and wiry with square broad shoulders and corded, muscular arms. His hair was blond and his eyes blazed bright blue in fine sunlight. John Kildare, in complete contrast, was several inches shorter with a square face and body, bulky as opposed to lean, but possessed of a similar strength; his eyes were gray and though he'd once been as fair-haired as his older brother, his locks were now the color of the red deer and normally left untrimmed, brushing across his shoulders.

"She said English," Ross advised his brother and captain.

John shook his head. "Nae. Unless they've stolen all these things. No' impossible, but unlikely."

Ross sighed, even as he agreed with this assessment. Planting his hands on his hips, he turned and considered the east, from where they'd come, and then the west, the direction in which they'd been headed.

"What now?" John asked, wondering the same as Ross.

Ross chewed this inside of his cheek for a second, contemplating their options. He said to his brother, "Further backward to Blackwood, but that crew there—the Jamison's wife and Cal's wife on the property—might suit her better right now. There're no women at Westcairn, none to... get her through this."

"And yet Westcairn is considerably closer," John mentioned, meaning it certainly would be easier to bring her home with them.

Ross scowled and he and his brother exchanged similar grimaces, though neither was willing to admit they were thinking selfishly of expediency and what was most convenient for them, and not the lass's grief and horror or what was best right now for her well-being.

Uttering a mild curse, Ross couldn't allow his own want to take precedence over hers. "Let me find out where she was headed," he then suggested to his brother and strode away toward the wagon in which the lass had been situated. He had only a hope and not much else that wherever she and her party had been destined, it was not too far out of his way. He had no intention of bringing her to Westcairn.

Schooling his face into an indifferent mien, Ross approached the young woman where she'd been settled in the back of one of the three supply wagons. Huddled inside the overlarge plaid, seated at the end of the cart with her feet dangling but motionless, she lifted her still-haunted gaze to him.

"Lass, from where do you hail?"

She blinked twice, possibly having to concentrate to understand his words, that he was speaking to her, seeking a response. She spoke first without sound and was forced to clear her throat. "Near Perth. We...." Whatever else she might have contributed remained unsaid, mayhap unthought.

Of course, she could not assume the home or the land herself; a female could hold no deed, unless she were a widow.

"Have you more family there? Someone who can—"

"This is—this was all of them," she said, her tone as wooden as her posture.

"And where were you destined when your party was... attacked?"

She nodded mutely then, watching him with greater interest now. A sharper focus seemed to overtake her bonny features, her trancelike state overtaken by curiosity.

Stepping closer to her, though still allowing a foot or more of space to separate her knees from his waist, he explained, "I had it in mind, lass, to take you somewhere safe, where you might... convalesce, and be warmly received. Likely your original destination would be such a place."

Tiny drops of the dewy mist clung to her hair, where shorter tendrils curled around her winsome face. She bobbed her head again, just once, seeming to understand. But it was another few seconds before she told him, "To Calasraid, at the River Teith."

He knew the burgh. It was not so far out of their reach along the road to Westcairn. Nodding, he advised, "If you are ready to depart, we can be on our way, have you delivered there by day's end."

Her gaze skittered away from him, around his left arm, to where those graves sat so prominently upon the north side of the meadow.

Ross said nothing but had to imagine that she was reluctant to leave her family here. Basic human compassion urged him to suggest this new graveyard was not but a half day's ride from Calasraid, that she might visit if she were so inclined, but he said nothing.

"I-I do not have anyone else," she said, her voice as small and slow as she'd used thus far. After a space of several seconds, she added, "I haven't anywhere else to go, I suppose."

Ross accepted this as her consent, nodding, about to turn away and inform his brother of their next destination when she asked, "Might I ride?"

When he didn't answer immediately, sparing some time on surprise that she could ride and then wondering why she might not prefer the ease of the wagon, she added, "I can manage a palfrey. I would prefer to have..." she let that thought trail off with a sigh, though she held his gaze with her imploring green eyes.

I would prefer to have an escape available to me, Ross thought she might have meant to say.

They were a moving army who had, for the last nine months, followed one directive after another, so that by the time Ross had found a palfrey for Caitrin to ride and had helped her gain the saddle, John had advised the officers of their plans and the news likely traveled on down the ranks as it normally would. Thus, the army moved again in the same direction as it had earlier, before they'd been stalled these last two hours. They would continue westward until the River Teith was just north and then shift in that direction. It would not take them so far out of their way, and they might find respite for the night just outside Calasraid. From there, Westcairn would be but another day's ride.

The army settled into their usual formation, mounted scouts and a dozen foot soldiers leading them on. John and several other mounted knights and men led the main line of the army, with Ross riding just behind Caitrin, wanting to find out that she could manage the horse capably, which she did, he concluded. Her gown was of good wool and her boots not cheaply made or worn beyond repair, which led him to suspect she was of a middle-class family, but not a lady. That she'd taken the saddle astride and not sideways and showed no concern for how much of the creamy skin of her calves and shins were put on display, bolstered his suspicion.

He needn't have suffered any concern over her state or any need that she might have. Over the first few hours, while he watched, one after another of his men made their way to her side as they rode along. They offered condolences and inquired if she were warm enough or if she'd had anything to eat. Mercer, a fastidious middle-aged man who had served Ross's father, spoke to her the longest, but in hushed tones that Ross was not privy to the conversation. After a while, Tavis nudged his steed next to hers and tried to improve her mood with some inane chatter about the dreary weather and then about the age and provenance of the mare on which the lass rode. To any and all, she responded with monosyllables, barely lifting her head, that one after another, they eventually ambled away, fruitless in their attempts, whatever their objective had been.

The army trudged along, going only so fast as they had for days now since leaving Blackwood, which was as fast as the infantry would or could walk all day. Only treks through rocky terrain where a horse could so easily lose its footing or greater consideration needed to be given to the carts and wounded slowed them down. Thankfully, the mist never materialized into a full rain, thus abetting their want of a good, brisk march across the region.

Caitrin began to cry again when they were a good five or so miles gone from those graves. Having been watchful of her—to be assured that she was steady on the horse, he told himself—Ross knew exactly when fresh tears came. He thought if she didn't need to be attentive to her riding, she'd have dropped her face to her chest and wept fully. Instead, her lips quivered, and her shoulders shook and, riding only a half a length beside and behind her, Ross saw the new tears that streaked down her left cheek.

She was remarkable, he'd already decided, that she was not yet catatonic with her shock and despair. This had him wondering about the timing of the incident—how long before they'd arrived had the killing taken place? How long had she sat all alone with those dead bodies?

Ross let out a three-note bird call, which effectively slowed the entire party. His brother cast a glance backward and Ross subtly inclined his head toward the woman, indicating his wish to slow their pace. Gesturing his understanding with a nod, John continued on, leading the pack in a slower walk now.

Ross positioned his destrier directly alongside the brown palfrey, where so many others had walked today.

"Dinna cry, lass. You're almost there."

Her impassive response, the way she turned her face so slowly toward him, suggested she was more withdrawn than he'd imagined. She appeared now surprised, because he rode so close or that he had spoken to her, as no one had for nearly thirty minutes by now.

"There?" she repeated, her voice cracking. "Where?"

"Away from it," he explained. "Further away, enough to be done with the shock of it, that you can start with the mourning."

For a moment, her expression showed only a mute wretchedness. And then she asked, "You've done this? Lived through... something like this?"

"Something similar."

"I'm sorry."

He nodded, accepting this. "You will no' ever forget how they went, but that will fade further and further. You will get to a point that you only remember them, how they were."

The glassy-eyed look she gave told him she couldn't imagine how that was possible. She nodded, but only barely, and put her gaze over the horse's head again, her shoulders yet slumped.

SHE'D NEVER PARTICULARLY cared for visiting Dorcas's sister, Eskaline, except that it was a removal from the mundane of their normal life in the house near Perth. Eskaline Canyart herself was a robust woman in both appearance and manner, much harsher than her sister Dorcas—which was saying quite a bit. Caitrin and Mary would still be expected to labor all day, 'twas not meant as a break from their work, but certainly there was less to do than at home. Often, Caitrin wished she'd had Mary's cool head and swift rebuttals to Eskaline's sometimes severe directives and criticisms.

She realized when they'd moved several miles away from the massacre that she would have to make her home with Eskaline—if that woman would have her—as she hadn't any other options for either shelter or employment. She lamented that she'd left what few coins she'd saved over the years wrapped discreetly in a linen cloth and affixed to the underside of the crude bedframe she'd shared with Mary in the house that she might never see again. She was now not only bereft of family and home, but the means to improve at least the latter, or any part of her current pitiful circumstance.

When they came upon the small burgh of Calasraid, Caitrin advised Ross Kildare that the Canyart homestead was beyond the burgh itself, on the opposite side of the river. There was then some discussion with the man called John and a few others before the Kildare warrior walked his massive destrier over to her again.

"We'll go on, just a few of us," he said. "The army will stay here."

Nodding, Caitrin further advised, "There's a wooden bridge—wobbly but passable—a bit ahead."

The army dug in then while a half-dozen men, including Ross and the one named Tavis, accompanied Caitrin to Eskaline's home. They came upon the aforementioned bridge about a half a mile further and crossed the river without incident. Within minutes, along a well-rutted lane angling northwest from the bridge, they found an area with three different homes. Caitrin could not remember the names of the Canyart neighbors but thought she would recall faces if presented with them.

The Canyart house was one of the larger structures in and around Calasraid, a two-story wooden and stone longhouse of a cruck frame, having a curved timber ceiling and a slate roof, with a small stone tower on the east end. Immediately, as they trotted into the yard of the house, Caitrin spied Eskaline's husband, Tàmhas, turning with a cautious eye to the armed men coming toward him. He was a big man and of a natural inclination, his hand settled on the sword at his hip as he squared himself to face the visitors. Tàmhas spared not a glance to Caitrin but kept his narrowed gaze on Ross, who led them into the yard. Had Tàmhas observed her among these soldiers, she wasn't sure he would have recognized her, as he'd taken scant note of her or Mary over the years.

Lest the man become overly concerned with the party coming toward him, Ross called out before they'd reined in, "Ross Kildare, of Westcairn, sir. I bring news of your kin."

This brought only slight ease to Tàmhas's stance, that they were not here with any nefarious intent. Ross dismounted directly and spoke in low tones to the man, his back to Caitrin, still mounted but stopped with Ross's men. Tàmhas's face effectively displayed his reaction to the news Ross delivered. First, his brows lifted high into his forehead while his jaw gaped. After only a few seconds in this pose, a frown overtook him, his gray and unkempt brows dropping low. He sent his gaze beyond Ross's broad shoulder and over to Caitrin, huddled in the Kildare plaid.

She heard him ask of Ross Kildare, "Which one is that? I canna recall the names of those lasses."

Ross cocked his head, as if surprised by this revelation, and said, "Caitrin has survived. Her name is Caitrin."

Nodding quickly and waving his hand, Tàmhas spoke rapidly then, "Aye. Aye. That's it." He blew out a breath and sent a curious glance to Caitrin again before saying, "Aye then, give us a minute, will ye? I'll deliver this sorry tale to my wife. Wait, please."

Of course, she had given no thought to what her welcome might be, other than shock for the news that she brought with her, but Caitrin was imbued with a sense that Tàmhas only appeared inconvenienced by the situation. But she was weary and did not put too much stock in her own judgement now, and she dismissed her vague worry.

Caitrin only discovered now how weak and exhausted she was, when she tried to dismount while they waited. Slackening her rigid grip on the reins, she realized all at once how drained and feeble she felt. Twice she tried to loosen her foot from the stirrup before she could pull the heel of her shoe off the metal bar. Her movements were sluggish, and she did not even startle when Ross appeared at her side, waiting for her.

"Caitrin?"

"Aye," she said mechanically as she tried to swing her leg over from the far side of the horse.

"May I?" Ross inquired when he realized her struggle.

"I...nothing seems to work," she said, hating the pitiful sound of her voice.

He murmured something she could not understand and took her waist in his hands, easily bringing her to the ground. She faltered just a bit, unsteady on her feet after so many hours in the saddle.

His big hands stayed on her waist, until she gave him a nod that she was stable. He kept one supportive hand on her elbow as they both turned toward the longhouse when a long and powerful wailing erupted from inside. Only seconds later, a figure appeared in the open doorway. Eskaline Canyart stood there, her gaze locking instantly on Caitrin in the foreground.

Dorcas's sister was broad and red-faced, unconcerned that her pained grimace showed she was missing so many teeth. Eskaline charged forward, stomping across the damp yard to Caitrin. She braced herself as the woman waved her arms and cried out, thinking she meant to engulf her in an embrace of shared sympathy.

But no. Eskaline's words penetrated. "Why do you live, and they do not? How selfish have you been, to have saved yourself and no other?" She curled her fingers into claws, intent on striking out, Caitrin realized belatedly, too late to lift her own hand defensively. She had time only to wince and turn her face to the side.

But the blow never came.

Opening her eyes, Caitrin saw that Ross Kildare had caught Eskaline's arm in his hand before her blow might have landed. Caitrin's now wide-eyed gaze moved from Eskaline's startled and angry expression to the promised menace of Ross's clenched jaw.

"You will rethink your approach, woman. Now," he suggested, gritting these words through his teeth, his voice dangerously low.

Eskaline whimpered and dropped her shoulders so that when Ross released her wrist, her arm fell limply to her side. And while the older woman's lips trembled as she met Caitrin's gaze, she let Caitrin see she harbored much resentment still in her seething gaze.

Without another word and offering no apology for what might have only been her overwrought emotions and not any genuine hatred of Caitrin, Eskaline Canyart whirled around and trudged inside her home.

"People... react differently, lass," Ross supposed softly after a moment, in some attempt to lessen the effect of that dramatic greeting.

Nodding, pretending she believed this as well, she forced a wan smile of understanding and squared her shoulders. Ross's hand at her elbow propelled her to follow the woman inside. As with the yard itself, naught had changed inside the dwelling that they stepped directly into a room that would have served as a hall in a greater house, but that was too small to be named such here. A flat and low ceiling of timber hung over a trestle table and benches, which were positioned to the right of the door. The wall behind the table showed one arched doorway that led to the kitchen on the right, and the rest of that wall housed a modest stone hearth. A poorly crafted tapestry hung proudly on the back wall, covered now with many years of grease and smoke, that the inferior quality of the threads and the artistry were barely discernable now.

The lady Canyart had flopped down onto the bench, her arms on the wood top, her head buried, her sobs muffled. Her husband stood near, awkwardly rubbing the top of one shoulder, as if he'd never had cause to provide a similar comfort, his fingers patting and rubbing at the same time.

Without invitation, Ross led Caitrin to the far side of the bench, gently pressing her to take a seat across from the weeping woman. With her back to the hearth, Caitrin held herself stiffly and glanced at the door, where two of Ross's men hovered. The man named Tavis, who was not much older than Caitrin, and who seemed rather clumsily put together—his face was not naturally symmetrical but appeared to be thicker and lower on the right; his red hair was shaggy and his clothes, including his plaid, might not have met with a washing in quite some time—stood with his thumbs hooked into his worn leather belt while he chewed the inside of his cheek and frowned at Eskaline's show of grief. She did not know the other soldier's name, but he was thick all over, from his head of black hair to his wide face and hulking form; he ducked his head under the doorframe while he tossed his eyes all around the room and then sometimes outside as well.

"I am sorry to have to bring this news," Ross said. His gaze shifted between Tàmhas, who nodded at this, and Eskaline, who only wailed louder for a few seconds. "We found evidence of the perpetrators but not the assailants themselves."

They didn't seem to care. At least they made no comment about this.

It was a full two minutes before Eskaline lifted her teary-eyed face from her arms. In that time, aside from her keening, the only other noise was that of a door shutting somewhere else inside the house and then a whinny from a horse just outside the door.

"So," Eskaline said when she met Caitrin's gaze. But she stopped to give life to another sob that bobbed her head for several beats. When she gathered herself again, she said, "So you've come to us."

It was several more seconds before Caitrin nodded, not quite sure what response she expected.

Eskaline sniffled and used her knuckle to push against her nose to stifle further wailing. "I suppose we always have need of extra hands here." She glanced up at her husband, whose reaction was more a shrug than an assent.

"But how did this happen?" Eskaline wanted to know, with a fresh wave of grief heard in her bawling tone.

Swallowing—and somehow shocked that she'd given no thought that she might be called upon to relive it—Caitrin told them what she remembered. "We... we were just going along. I spotted a flash of something—sunlight glinting off a sword, I suspect now—in the woods next to us. I had barely mentioned it when... when Gordon was struck with an arrow. Dorcas screamed. And...and Mary and Peigi and I ran. The outriders, Fergus and Bearnard, were... killed next, immediately. Um... they chased Peigi. I..." she swallowed again, and her chest heaved, even breaths hard to maintain, "I... didn't see what happened to Dorcas and Peigi until I'd come back," she cleared her throat and added, "when they were all gone. But Mary," she said and blew out a slow and steadying breath through pursed lips, "they cut down Mary while we ran, while I... I was holding her hand. She... she just fell, her hand was gone."

"And you just ran, didn't see what you might do—?" Eskaline started. The veins in her neck were noticeable for how tightly coiled she held herself.

"Was the right call," said the beefy Kildare soldier in the doorway. "Lest they all be dead."

"I should have stayed," Caitrin uttered tonelessly, only now realizing her error. Staring at the deep wood grain of the smooth table, she said in a small voice, "I don't know why I ran. I knew they were all dead or about to be. Why didn't I just wait for my end to come? I could have been with them now." A hand touched her shoulder. Ross Kildare's hand, she presumed, but gave it no other thought, so perturbed now with regret, that she'd missed her opportunity to have escaped this, the grief, the fear of going forward without them. "Oh, I should not have run," she breathed raggedly while fresh tears pooled in her eyes.

"That's right," Eskaline concurred harshly, fisting her hand on the table across from Caitrin.

"You did what was right," Ross said at the same time, his tone implacable.

Tavis spoke up next. "'Tis only natural, lass, the survival instinct."

No one spoke for many long seconds. Mayhap minutes, Caitrin did not know, so lost in her shame, how poorly she'd conceived her escape.

Tàmhas was the next to speak. "Who did this?"

Ross cleared his throat now. "Caitrin... supposes it was English, but it's too far north—"

She didn't bother to bolster her belief again but was surprised when Tàmhas unwittingly supported her claim. "Heard just last week there are pockets of them nearby."

Talk continued around her and over her, but Caitrin ignored all of it now. She felt eyes upon her and lifted her gaze to Eskaline, who was regarding her still with a hostile expression.

I should not have run, she thought again.

Chapter Three

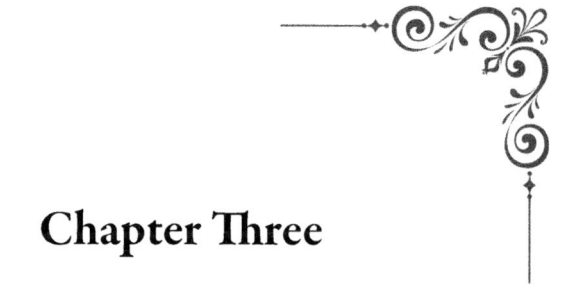

He passed a wretched night.

'Twas not the hard ground nor the sinister cold that snaked all around him that kept him wakeful throughout the night. Perhaps it should have been the news that Tàmhas Canyart had shared, that he'd heard the English had seized Muckart Castle not more than half a day from Calasraid, that quickened his pulse and had him on edge—but it was not. Truth be told, the image of Caitrin haunted and taunted him, so desolate and anguished that she had saved herself.

Her regret had not come until she'd met with that awful woman, and to a lesser degree, her husband. They had made her feel evil for having survived, which didn't need to be thrust upon her so soon. Like as not, she'd have developed survivor's remorse in her own time. People usually did.

He rarely suffered guilt himself, but it did not sit well with him to leave her there. Yet despite her despair—including the absurd shame Eskaline had heaped on her—Caitrin was an intuitive, sensitive person, that she'd assumed a valiant if stiff effort to project a calm that she might never know. He read more than that, though, resignation and hints of despair, which she'd struggled to reject.

"Thank you," she'd said when it was time for him to leave. "For all you have done for me."

She'd looked at him with an unfathomable light in her gaze then. Looked through him, he'd thought at the time, wondering if it was such a good idea to leave this pitiable creature with the harridan.

But he had left her.

He'd wished her well, proposing she would be safe there, so close to Calasraid. He'd offered a few other needless platitudes while pretending he did not imagine that she was about to cry again. Her eyes brightened, but did not pool with tears, and thankfully so, as that might have proved his undoing.

He'd held his teeth clenched, lest he do something foolish like offer her respite at Westcairn. That would not do; Westcairn was largely a garrison of hardened soldiers, not truly a family home. Since his mother had passed—his father had been gone for more than a decade now—the keep housed only Ross and his brothers, John and Robert, the latter who'd been left in charge in Ross's absence. Though several women came daily from the village to work inside the keep, there were no females in residence. Until and unless he or either of his brothers wed, it would remain essentially the domain of men. Ross preferred it that way. They had much to do upon their return. He wanted his army in fine shape, ready to make war when the next call came. When every last warring Englishman was banished from Scotland was soon enough to get on with making marriages and families.

The entire Kildare army had camped on the south side of the river, where they'd waited yesterday while Ross and the others had escorted Caitrin to the Canyart house. Ross had made his bed beneath a tall pine, the ground covered in a carpet of needles that he would likely spend days picking out of his plaid. The sun was not yet risen, and a low hanging fog hovered all around, shrouding the area in a blanket of gray. It would be hours before the sun, if the sky was clear, would chase the fog away.

Giving up on sleep completely now, he pulled himself up to a sitting position, leaning his back against the trunk of the tree. The camp of almost one hundred men began to stir, bodies rising from the cold, hard earth, eager to get on with the day, closer to Westcairn. A frisson of intuition made him still, and he scanned the surrounding area, moving his eyes but not his head. Sensing that someone watched him, he slowly reached his hand out along those cool needles of pine to find the hilt of his sword, which had lain next to him all night long. Just as his fingers closed around the icy steel, he saw Caitrin sitting near another tree, not ten feet away from him, cloaked so heavily by the morning fog that she appeared only a wispy figure, though unmistakable all the same.

"Caitrin?" He said, releasing his sword, sitting straight, away from the tree.

"I did not want to startle you," she said. Her voice was stronger today, even as she kept it low in deference to any who might yet be slumbering. She did not stand, but stayed there, her arms hugging her knees while the haze of the fog barely moved around and between them.

Ross got to his feet, taking his sword with him, tucking that into the sheath on his belt. He was only curious and not so much alarmed by her presence, as she'd given him no reason to be so.

"You did no' startle me. But did you come all this way by yourself?" Plucking his plaid from the ground, he began the daily necessary task of folding all the pleats into the length of it. He would not rush her but would let her announce why she'd come when she was ready.

"Aye. 'Twas hours ago."

"Were you no' afraid to be about the road and river by yourself?" After what she'd been through, he thought, but did not say. He did not ask if she'd sat there, wakeful for those hours, watching him struggle to sleep as well.

This prompted her to unveil the reason for her arrival, why she'd trekked through the dark and cold night by herself to be here.

"I know it puts a burden on you... that it would be inconvenient, but I... I would rather stay with you if that would be all right."

Ross's hands slowed with his present surprise but did not stop in their efforts to arrange his plaid.

"I do not know them," she said, obviously referring to the Canyarts. "And they do not want me."

You dinna ken me, was his first thought to this request.

He nodded, but it was only to buy time, while he thought about this. He'd already decided that Westcairn was no place for her. Mayhap back to Blackwood would be the best position for her. Still, she wasn't his responsibility and despite the wretched night passed, he had been pleased to have the matter settled, to have dispensed with the basic duty of delivering her to her kin. He assumed he'd be haunted a wee bit by those stark green eyes of hers, but otherwise had considered the affair concluded.

Flipping the plaid over his shoulder so that it hung a few inches longer down his back than his front, Ross unbuckled his belt and reattached it over the plaid and tunic. When this was done and the creases neatened across his shoulder and chest, Ross went to where Caitrin sat and extended his hand to her.

Her fingers were small and as icy as the steel of his blade when she placed them in his much larger hand. Instinct bade him squeeze her fingers a bit, with some half-conceived design to warm them. He pulled her easily to her feet until she stood directly before him, having to tip her face up to him.

Her green eyes glistened as she set her gaze so stonily upon him, though no tears fell. "They... might soon be kind, but I want to be with you."

Later, he would think he did a bloody fine job of keeping his shock from overtaking his expression. But his jaw did tighten as he considered this. She wanted to be with *him*?

Bravely, she answered this before any wild ideas might have taken flight in his brain to resolve the why of it.

"You are the only connection I have to them—my family," she explained, and when he frowned before he could control that response, she added in a small voice, "such as it is. You are the last to see them and know them. I don't want to be away from you."

She did not jerk her gaze away then but moved it slowly from his face and his scowl and set it on his shoulder, waiting, her free hand now wringing in the folds of her skirt.

She was different, transformed since he'd left her yesterday. Even inside the misty morning grayness, he recognized the changes. The transformation was not subtle, not something that might have been overlooked. The blood-stained and muddied gown was gone, replaced by a too-short and too-wide léine of plain blue wool, likely loaned—grudgingly, he had to assume—by the Missus Canyart; she'd had a bath, her hair and face and hands now scrubbed free of all the grime and blood and any streaks of her tears, though her eyes and nose were yet red-rimmed; her long hair was only a wee bit damp yet—the cool air of night would not have helped to dry it—darkened to a golden wheat color, closer to the shade of her curved brows, and pinned loosely to the back of her head.

He couldn't name or identify what he felt, what his exact response was to the way her hand felt so natural in his grasp. She met his gaze again now and regarded him steadily, though without even the slightest hint of pleading. She did not give attention to the growing noises coming from the waking camp only a few yards away, did not explore her surroundings, only held his gaze with her unblinking green eyes. Her regard was compelling, if only for the humblest explanation of it, that she'd sought him out as something familiar. *I don't want to be away from you* was a powerful inducement, if only for the feeling it invoked of some connection between them, which they truly did not, could not, know. Whatever the whole of his reaction was, it made Ross decidedly uneasy. A woman simply had no place either with his army or at Westcairn, and that was fact.

A flash of color on the ground caught his attention. There sat the plaid he'd given her yesterday, folded neatly, not used throughout the night to ward off the cold that she surely must have felt.

"Put that on," he said. "It will no' get much warmer today."

He watched as she bent to retrieve the plaid but then only hugged it to her chest, while she waited his answer. Her nostrils flared a bit as she stared at him, while her nerves were likely on edge and not to be appeased anytime soon.

"I'll have someone escort you back to your kin, lass," he said flatly. "We are a moving army and no' simply an itinerant camp.

We canna help you." Her shoulders fell at the same time her lips parted with her dejection. Resolutely—before the sudden misery in her green eyes undid him—he said, "You're better off—safer—there with those people."

For one brief moment, she looked as if she might argue or beg him to reconsider. She would not, he knew. She was not anywhere near her stupefied and withdrawn state of yesterday, but she was a pale and frightened thing still, another reason she would not fare well among his men. And, too, there was the fact that she would likely only prove a general distraction to the army. There were few women at Westcairn, but not one of them could claim a beauty to rival Caitrin's. She would only cause trouble, he predicted.

"Aye, and good morrow to ye, lass."

Seething through his nose, Ross turned and found Tavis striding toward them. The lad seemed not to recognize either Ross's implacable mien or the lass's crestfallen expression but asked with some excitement, "What brings you around before the sun, lass?"

God's blood, this was exactly what he feared. A distraction, indeed. And worse, following in Tavis's wake was Idgy, who also looked pleasantly surprised to discover Caitrin here.

Ross didn't allow her time to answer, but said brusquely to Tavis, "She'll need an escort back, to the house across the river."

"Aye and I'm happy to oblige," Tavis responded.

"But you're here now," Idgy supposed, "might as well break yer fast with us."

"She needs to be returned now," Ross said curtly. Before she got too comfortable.

"I'd asked to travel with your party, but he refused," Caitrin shocked him by saying. She'd rushed out the words, desperate to be heard, afraid he would see her gone before she'd truly pled her case to any who might know greater concern than he had.

Pivoting, he turned his steely gaze onto her and said slowly and without any remorse, "As stated, we are a moving army, no' equipped to house and entertain an orphaned female."

While she stiffened at his callousness, Tavis chose to ignore it, declaring in a hopeful tone, "She willna be a nuisance, Laird. She's only one lass."

"Aye," chimed in Idgy, the foolish old goat, "she's no' a child who'll need minding."

Ross wasn't so sure about that and was about to say as much when his brother entered the discussion.

"What's this?" John asked, scratching his head, his eyes yet puffy from his comfortable sleep.

"Lass wants to get on with us," Idgy informed him. "Yer brother says nae, we're no' an orphanage."

Hands planted firmly on his hips now, Ross said pointedly to John, "We can no' afford distractions—and, as discussed, Westcairn is no place for a woman."

Tavis barked out a laugh. "Aye, and mayhap that's what's wrong with it."

While Idgy chuckled his response to this, both Ross and John leveled Tavis with dark glares until he had the good sense to give all his attention to the ground.

"It doesn't have to be forever," Caitrin decided to add now, into the silence.

Spinning only his upper body and hot gaze over to her, Ross demanded, "Until when? What would change that might take you away from Westcairn after you'd landed?"

"Well, I don't rightly—"

"Exactly. Nothing."

Even John frowned at his brother now for his harshness, that Ross felt compelled to explain his position fully. "We are no' set up to house a female. We dinna even provide for the servants we already have inside the keep. We've got to recover from half a year away, keep up with the fields and the plowing and whatever else they dinna manage while we were gone. We've got to get healthy and train harder so that we dinna lose another bluidy battle to the bluidy English. Aye, she's quiet now, still crazed with shock and grief. But when it's done, what then?" He threw a hand out in Caitrin's direction. "Look at her. You dinna think she'll be a distraction, cause no trouble among the ranks? You're naïve at least, and an idiot at worst if you think any good'll come of it. Even now, these two are tripping over themselves. Later it will be two more making fools of themselves over her and tomorrow yet more. She has a home, a place to stay—it's no' with us."

John almost looked as if he might smirk. At the very least, a jovial light shone in his gray eyes. He shrugged carelessly. "Dinna matter, no' anymore."

Ross threw up his hands again. "Why the bluidy hell not?"

John did not respond with words but inclined his head over his brother's shoulder.

His ire risen, and with the day barely begun, Ross pivoted once more, just in time to see the back of Caitrin melt further into the trees as she walked away. Good, he thought. Perfect. Solves all this fuss.

The relief he should feel did not come, and he felt like a greater monster when he saw that she'd dropped his plaid once more on the ground, leaving it behind.

Determined not to give leave to any doubt or allow guilt to assail him, Ross told himself he'd made the right call. He wasn't running a monastery at Westcairn, and any man was welcome to bring home a wife and start a family, but as of yet, few had. It was hard to meet a wife if you spent your days laboring at Westcairn where there were so few women, or waging war against the English, which always took you away, further afield, but presented very little opportunities to meet a female.

Still, he'd always thought the keep functioned so well, so effortlessly, because there were so few women to cause a man trauma. Caitrin of the green eyes had a look about her that suggested trouble would follow her wherever she went.

SHE HADN'T CONCEIVED the idea that she might prefer to be with strangers rather than a quasi-family that had no use for her and certainly held her in some contempt merely for surviving, until she tucked herself onto the pitiful mattress with the Canyart's kitchen girl, Clara, and wondered what the morrow would bring. All the anxiety over so simple a thought—the coming of another day—had been what sent her from the coarse and lumpy bed and out into the night. Aye, she'd been terrified, but at the time, had been also imbued with that sense of remorse that she shouldn't have survived, that it didn't matter what might become of her. In hindsight—now—she could attest that her true, underlying thinking had been much different: she'd chased and found the Kildare army because she wanted to live and live well, and that would never be possible with the indifferent Tàmhas and the unforgiving Eskaline.

Alas, 'twas not to be. Ross Kildare had apparently exhausted his limited supply of kindness by seeing her safely to her kin, a distinction that was tenuous at best. She was not angry at him. His reasons were his own, and while she didn't understand them, he'd been attached to them, quite passionate about them, that she supposed it wasn't her place to question his ruling. If Mary had lived still, she'd have turned his mind around; she'd have charmed him into compliance as she so often did so many others.

Still, Caitrin wasn't quite sure what to make of his statement, where he'd demanded that the man, John—his brother, she now understood—look at her, and had predicted that she'd prove a distraction if she were allowed to leave with them. A distraction how? From what?

Sighing as she trudged along, she decided it didn't matter. She was, at least for now, stuck with the Canyarts. *One day at a time*, she cautioned herself, lest she become too distraught at the idea of weeks and months and years stretching out in front of her, all of them lived wretchedly inside a home with Eskaline.

At the house near Perth, the only home she could recall, Caitrin and Mary and sometimes Peigi walked back and forth from Perth to their home, running errands for Dorcas or sometimes about some business for Gordon. They'd used the well-rutted road for all those miles and never once had they known fear or anxiety for walking by themselves. Caitrin wondered now if she would ever again know such freedom, such ease. Presently, she walked parallel to the path she'd used to find the Kildare army, but not directly on it. She kept herself concealed many yards inside the trees that swelled around the path, at one point wishing she'd not childishly discarded the Kildare plaid since the air did not grow warmer as the morning lengthened. She guessed upon her first trek along this path that the distance might only be a mile and a half, no more.

Despite her efforts, she could not prevent herself from considering Ross Kildare and his indifference when he'd refused her. Actually, it was only indifference to her plight, but not his desires. She did not know Ross Kildare, not any more than she did any of his men or Clara with whom she shared a bed or any person she might pass on the street. And she couldn't have explained why she believed she would have been safe and protected with him and his army, and not made to feel things she should not. *Would have been*, she mused, allowing the dejection to take hold. Possibly, she had misread what she supposed was a softening of Ross Kildare's hard gaze whenever he set those blue eyes upon her.

Her muddled and miserable thoughts were interrupted by a noise that was incompatible with the quiet of these woods. Instinct, born only a day ago, made Caitrin duck low behind a scratchy-barked tree. She stayed bent on her haunches, ready to spring into a run if necessary, and did not put her knees to the ground. And just like that, her blood rioted inside her and her heart pumped furiously in her ears, it seemed. Fright was a peculiar mechanism, wielding so much power.

She stayed very still and listened and decided fairly quickly that the noise she heard sounded similar to a crackling fire, but on a much larger scale. Inhaling deeply, she smelled it, too, smoke and burning wood. Caitrin dared a glance around the tree. The woods were yet dark with morning gloom but quite a distance ahead, mayhap hundreds of yards, she spotted flashes of orange and yellow.

Her jaw gaped, trying to determine if the Canyart house was on fire—was she that close? Could it be one of those neighbors whose names she could not recall? Screams and shouts sounded out, but seemed very far away, drowned out by the oddly loud roar of the fire. Without conscious thought, but with an instinct that she should do something, give some aid if she could, Caitrin leapt to her feet and ran toward the bright fire and muffled wails.

She struggled enough to make good time inside the woods that she changed direction, making for the narrow lane so that she might move faster. As she drew closer, she saw that it was not the Canyart house on fire but that of their closest neighbor. The scene, a slim vista presented to her with the trees crowding left and right, showed people scurrying about in plumes of smoke and dust. A mounted figure charged across the narrow panorama, likewise appearing as a ghostlike gray figure inside the cloud of smoke.

At the end of the lane, where the trees cleared completely, her view expanded. The whole of the two-story structure was engulfed, the hot flames streaking high above the house while smoke billowed and plumed all around, at twice the volume of the flames themselves. To her left, well down the road, smaller fires burned in and around the Canyart house. Her pulse pounding, Caitrin ran toward that blaze.

She was brought up short by a person emerging from a cloud of dust and fumes to her left. It was a man, running, chased by another on a horse. At the very same moment, someone howled, "Peter!" and then another voice shouted, "Run!"

The fog of her brain cleared in an instant.

The English had come to Calasraid. The mounted man, sporting an open-faced helm, wore the same hated red and gold as the ones who'd murdered her family. He chased the peasant man around to the back side of the house, the two figures swallowed up inside the haze of smoke..

Breathing a shaky breath that was half a cry of disbelief, Caitrin was frozen in place by fear.

I am dreaming, she thought. *I must be. This cannot be happening again.*

A wind burst onto the scene then, briefly dispersing so much of the smoke and dirt clouds. Trembling, she was shown that there were many English, closer to the house itself, on foot and on horse. One stood over an unrecognizable body, stabbing repeatedly with his sword, using two hands in his zeal to end that life, while Caitrin watched in horror, her hand covering her mouth.

She might have collapsed then, might have been dropped to the ground by the surely fatal beating of her heart or because her limbs turned once more to pudding. But there came some shouting from the English and one of them pointed a red-smeared sword at her, calling out, "Get that one there!"

A noiseless cry burst forth and for the second time in two days, Caitrin turned and fled, running for her life. She retraced the steps that had brought her here, turning the corner at the narrow road, running for all she was worth back along the path. She tripped once and caught herself, her tears blinding her and then stumbled again, but fell this time.

When she planted her hands on the ground to push herself up, she felt a vibration beneath her palms and fingers. Neither the ground nor her fingers stirred, but she could feel that something large and powerful was moving over the earth.

Horses, she decided. And not only the few that were chasing her.

Please be Ross Kildare and his army, was her next thought.

Hope blossomed inside her chest, warring with the fear that twisted her lungs that made it difficult to breathe. But she bounded to her feet and ran hard again, too afraid not to look behind her even as she knew it slowed her down. Three Englishmen chased her on horseback; a fourth man ran lazily on foot toward her. Facing forward again, she knew some relief when blurry figures appeared on the horizon at the edge of the thin path. She could not make out faces but could distinguish the green and gray and blue of the Kildare tartan. They came swiftly, dozens of them, barreling over the ridge and down the treeless path. However, as much hope as their nearness gave her, she was frantically aware that the ones pursuing her were actually closer. She had no choice but to duck into the woods again, as she was too easy a target on the open lane.

Never before had she paid so much attention to noise. She did now, hearing the hoofbeats of pursuit over her own ragged breaths and what disturbance she made as she dashed about the woods, slapping at branches while her leather-shod feet crunched on leaves and twigs. Noises thrummed inside her head, creating a cacophony of pressure that was nearly unbearable.

Someone shouted her name at a deafening volume. "Caitrin!"

Breathless and running still, she scanned the trees ahead of her and cried tears of joy when she recognized Ross racing toward her, inside the woods and not on the path. Several Kildares followed in his wake, at the same furious pace. She only needed to shift her direction a bit, sprinting now directly toward the Kildare laird. He was still too far, she knew, hearing the unmistakable sound of pounding hooves and jangling harnesses closing in on her from behind.

A larger panic engulfed her, fearful now that Ross Kildare would be only seconds too late to save her. No sooner had she thought this than she was startled by fingers clasping in her hair. She screamed immediately as she was lifted off the ground, her feet skipping and dragging along the floor of the woods as her captor's horse still raced forward. Lifting her hand, she tried to claw herself free, scratching at the hand that pulled her hair. At the same time, she met Ross Kildare's blazing blue-eyed gaze across the remaining distance between them and felt no shame for the silent torment she let him see, expecting that her life would end now.

Ross charged still, his sword drawn, his face a mask of brutal rage. His massive destrier was sure-footed and swift and Ross rose up in the saddle, his feet dug firmly into the stirrups. He drew back his arm and bared his teeth and just as he was nearly upon Caitrin and her captor, he swung his mighty blade with a ferocious roar and Caitrin was dropped to the earth.

Something dropped with her, bouncing off the back of her thigh and rolling to a stop several feet away. Two horses flew past her, so close that leaves were stirred up around her face. Metal clashed with metal above her head and a strangled grunt was followed by a thump as another body landed on the ground.

Her hands and arms failed her, that she could not lift herself, could not rise at all. With her cheek laid against the cool, damp earth, she saw that an entire arm, detached from its body, stared back at her from a dozen feet away.

That's what had bounced off her leg. Ross had cleaved the man's arm from his shoulder.

Caitrin gagged and retched and then screamed when hands touched her arm and her back. She jerked around onto her back, lifting her hands to lash out at this new attacker.

"Lass—Caitrin!"

Ross.

She let her arms drop, felt all of her body sink and liquify as fear oozed out of her, even as she met the feral gleam in his stone-cold blue eyes.

"Get up," he urged, his fingers circling her arm. She did, or rather was pulled to her feet and then tugged along behind him as he ran to catch up with his steed. She caught a glimpse of a headless body but did not let her gaze linger. Ross easily gained the saddle again and reached a hand down to her, lifting her up. Caitrin scrambled to stretch her right leg over to the far side of the horse, which proved easier than she might have imagined.

"Hang on tight," Ross called back to her. "Dinna let go, no matter what! Keep your head down!" And with that terse command, he gave a sharp, "Yah!" to his steed, who leapt forward immediately with a burst of speed.

She didn't need to be told twice but wrapped her arms around his solid midsection. Not ten seconds had passed since he'd pulled her up onto the horse with him before he unsheathed his great sword again and they burst from the woods just in front of the burning house.

War cries sounded all around them. The Kildare Scots were a raw and wild herd, charging enthusiastically into a fray with the more circumspect English.

Caitrin curled her fingers into the bottom of Ross's leather breastplate, near his waist, while her chest and forehead were pressed against his back. She squeezed her eyes shut, not wanting to witness more brutality and death.

When the first clang of steel sounded from Ross's sword, she winced and shriveled against him but held on tight. Turning her face to the right, she flattened her cheek against his broad back, aware of every one of his movements by the shifting and rolling muscles, undulating up and down. Every clank and growl and curse from Ross only made her squeeze her eyes tighter.

She'd have kept on this way, until it was done or until they were dead, but that a blade sliced across her left forearm and stayed there, leaning against the cut it had made. Horrified, Caitrin turned her face against Ross's back, opening her eyes to see a thin English blade laying over the top of her arm, impaled into Ross's side through his padded leather armor.

Without preamble, Ross grabbed at the weapon embedded in his side and ripped it out, tossing it away, before he charged forward to meet the next opponent.

Some desperate impulse, fueled by panic, made her slide her hand under his armor and tunic and onto his warm skin. She flattened her palm over the hole in his side, hoping to keep his blood within while the rigid leather breastplate at the back of her hand effectively kept her hand in place. And she slumped against him, going numb for the shock of it all while Ross continued to take on several more English antagonists.

Chapter Four

Bluidy English infidels!

His jaw was still clenched, even several long seconds after he'd determined no Englishman remained alive or worthy of his fight. Slowly, he turned his destrier in a circle, surveying the damage. He saw none of his own men fallen, but counted, just here immediately surrounding him, eleven Englishmen. And three more were dead inside the woods where he'd recovered Caitrin.

Flexing his fist around the hilt of his sword, he shifted his steed once more, until he met the gazes of Samuel and John, equally as breathless as Ross, their poses similar, alert, sword-ready, waiting.

It was done, then.

Ross relaxed his shoulders, which shifted Caitrin's face against his back.

He remained still for a moment, taking stock of them both, not at all unaware of the hand that covered his wound or how warm and soft her fingers were against his flesh.

"Caitrin," he said, still a wee bit winded, his voice hoarse.

Her voice was decidedly in worse shape, almost unrecognizable. "Aye."

Gently, he reached around to tug her hand away from his wound. "Leave it," he said. He came away with her fingers, bloodied now, and pulled her hand outward that she might dismount. "It's safe now, lass." He kept hold of her hand, lowering her to the ground when she'd swung her leg around, and then easily alighted himself.

They faced each other, standing beside the horse.

"How did you know they were here?"

"We saw the smoke," he answered simply, and then frowned, lifting her wrist now to inspect the gaping cut across her forearm. Cursing under his breath, Ross bent and tore a strip from the hem of the linen kirtle she wore beneath the wool gown—to which she barely responded— and wrapped the soft strip around her arm, tearing the end of this smaller piece to make a secure knot.

"Send up Gideon," he said to John, who was walking toward them.

"Your side," Caitrin said, lifting the arm he'd just wrapped to indicate the blood seeping out under and around his leather breastplate.

"Is fine for now," he said.

He looked over the whole of her, discerning there was no other obvious injury. Even her fright—that startlingly placid horror he'd glimpsed in her gaze when that brigand had carried her along by her hair— seemed to have faded to a bland and blank stare.

It stayed that way, her gaze, when she said to him, "You said I'd be safer with them."

Aye, that was the first thing he'd thought when Samuel had spotted the smoke rising over the trees, coming from the direction of the Canyart house. He'd sent her into danger. And now, because of him, she'd barely survived another massacre, and was again reduced to this fragile and waiflike creature.

There were no words he could give to justify his reasoning that would make sense now. All of it was trite and selfish, in hindsight.

"Aye. I was wrong."

She blinked, her gaze vivid for its unnerving serenity, but otherwise did not acknowledge his admission.

"Come," he urged, taking her hand once more, walking with her up the lane, to where the corner of a small livestock fence jutted out in the road. "Sit here," he said, indicating the short grass there. The swelling smoke blew in the opposite direction, away from the back of the burning house. The house itself, or what remained, was yet twenty yards away.

She sank to her knees, as he'd watched her do once before. He did not move away immediately, though there was plenty to be done, as Caitrin still held his hand. When she realized this, she lifted her fingers slowly from his and lowered her hand to her lap.

"Stay here, Caitrin," he ordered her.

Her response was unexpected—she made a snorting noise and wondered, "Where would I go now?"—but it was neither unwarranted nor unappreciated, the latter at least showing a presence of mind.

There was nothing to be done about the fires, nor those Scots who were lost, which included seven people here, and then, they learned later when Idgy and Tavis returned from scouting the area, sixteen more souls from Calasraid proper. And the lad,

Louis, who'd made his first foray with the Kildare army only this year, was in rough shape, Ross was informed.

Ross first saw to Louis, as he was carried on a litter and placed on the surgeon's cart, which forced those already occupying that vehicle to make room. The entire army, from that camp a mile away, had since come forth and were now stationed in the fields adjacent to the burning house.

They had no surgeon, not anymore, not since their expedition near the River Cree in early summer. Surgeons rarely found themselves in harms' way unless a retreat was ordered and the whole army scrambled to escape. That had not been the case when Hugh was lost. He'd only been tending the slice across Samuel's thigh when a stray arrow had glided through the air and into the tent he'd used as his office of operation. By Samuel's report, Hugh had given him a startled look before he'd collapsed to the ground, the missile sticking straight out from his heart.

Thus, Arailt had been tapped to assume the position. He was no surgeon—knew very little about healing in general, he'd be the first to tell you—but he was of a mature age, had known many battlefields and operating tents that he was tasked with doing whatever he could until they returned to Westcairn.

At Louis's side, Arailt had only shook his head sadly at Ross's inquisitive stare. The lad was unconscious and deathly pale everywhere but for the gaping wound in the middle of his belly, where blood made a bright, circular pattern all around the fissure.

"Make him comfortable," Ross intoned, setting his hand on the lad's forehead for a moment.

"Aye, I'll send someone back up to the village," Arailt said, "Might be able to find willow bark or henbane, as our supply has been depleted."

Ross nodded and left, and then met with John and Samuel, sharing a weary discussion about the English being so far north, and why they might remain when Longshanks had taken his royal army home.

"Might have been left specifically to do this," John supposed with a shrug, "wreak havoc far and wide so that we've no chance to recover or regroup 'fore they strike again in the spring."

"But Christ," Ross complained, challenging this idea, "why so few to see the job done? Caitrin said there were but a half dozen the other day. Today—what?—two dozen total, if a few escaped?"

Samuel proposed a different theory. "Might have a larger army camped nearby, and these units are sent out to subdue smaller populations?"

"They're no' subduing," Ross clipped with a rabid irritation. "They're annihilating."

Samuel shrugged. "Same goal met, different fashion."

John mentioned what they were all thinking, "Muckart taken, and that's naught but forty miles west. Westcairn is no' so far from that, though strictly northwest."

"We need to move, and swiftly now," Ross decided, "and make straight for Westcairn."

John sighed and glanced around, "But no' until this is cleansed."

They would at least need to watch the fires burning, make sure they didn't spread rather than only die out. And they would bury the dead. Again. And see what might be salvaged for those who'd survived.

"And get that taken care of," Samuel said, his gaze upon Ross's side.

"Aye."

It wasn't until an hour had gone by that Ross finally returned to Caitrin. He was just now feeling the effects of his own wound and knew that needed tending. Might as well have Caitrin's arm looked at as well.

Idgy stood near her, his wide frame blocking all but her feet and the bottom of her skirts from Ross's view. When he was close enough, he saw that Caitrin handed a flask to Idgy, which he must have shared with her. She held a chunk of hard bread in her hand in her lap, but it didn't look as if she'd taken even one bite.

Idgy greeted him with a nearly defensive, "I was only making sure she dinna faint for all the excitement, since she dinna have no meal this morn."

If he detected any censure in his lieutenant's statement, Ross ignored it, giving only a nod that he heard and understood. He studied Caitrin more thoroughly now, with an eye toward her well-being and not only searching for injuries as he had earlier. As she had been yesterday when they'd stumbled upon her, she was again roughed up; her face and hands were streaked with dirt and grime—the blood which covered all of one hand was likely his; a long but shallow scratch marked her left cheek, from just below her eye to the corner of her mouth; and her hair, which had intrigued him this morning for being so neat and shiny, was now untidy, one side being tousled and snarled to twice the width of the other.

To Caitrin, who responded to his scrutiny with a still-bland gaze, Ross once more held out his hand.

"Come. Let's wash up," he said.

She complied instantly, if slowly, placing her less bloody hand in his.

He led her first toward the outbuilding that was the family's barn, and which now housed the English horses as well as whatever livestock had been enclosed there. Just beyond that was a tributary of the River Teith, a small and winding creek with a flat bank of grass at the bottom of a minor decline.

"We'll clean up here," he advised and began to unlace the blood-crusted leather breastplate.

Caitrin nodded mutely and crouched at the creek's edge, splashing water over her face several times before she began vigorously scrubbing her hands. Standing a few feet behind her, Ross lifted the untied armor over his head and dropped that onto the ground beside him, where it stood on its own for the stiffness of the piece. He paused a moment, his hands on his tunic, about to pull it out from where it was tucked into his breeches, as Caitrin loosed the ribbon that held her hair in that knot at her nape. Inexplicably transfixed, he watched as she shook out the length of her long hair and ran her clean fingers through it, spreading the wealth of thick flaxen hair over her shoulders. The sparse wind kicked at the curls and danced them across her back and Ross's mouth opened, though he did not investigate his response to so simple an action, why the graceful swaying of her hair should rouse so much interest in him.

Giving himself a mental shake, he returned to his own business, removing his tunic, which he draped over the standing armor. He squatted beside Caitrin, doing as she had, washing his face and hands.

When his face was clean, he rested his elbows on his thighs and thought to inform her, though he was not surprised that she had not asked, "Your kin survived. Apparently, they were on their way to town when they saw the fires there and took to the woods to hide. A young lass was with them, safe as well, though they suspect their farm hand was lost." He had all this from Tavis, whose regular prying often yielded much information, and who'd run into the couple and their servant on the way to Calasraid.

A lengthy pause preceded her response, which was softly given while she kept her gaze on the slowly running water. "They are not my kin." Clearing her throat, she then added, "But aye, all is well then."

They stood at the same time then. Ross meant to splash some water on his bloody side but was brought up short by Caitrin's gaping astonishment as she stared at him, so much so that he glanced down over his bare chest, wondering if he'd suffered some other injury of which he'd not been aware. He found no other wound and lifted his mystified gaze to her.

After what felt like an eternity, but was likely only seconds, he sensed that she focused, and now her brow furrowed as she stepped closer, reaching out a hand to his injury.

"Oh, it's still bleeding a bit," she said. She touched her fingers to the area, moving the pooling blood around, trying to determine what was fresh, and how much it still bled. Earlier when she'd touched him in the same place, her purpose had been completely utilitarian—as it was now. But now, well, now there was no fighting army to draw his attention. Now, he was standing half-clothed, and she faced him with her hair loose and incredibly attractive for the way it fell around her face and shoulders. Right now, though it wasn't her intent, there was an intimacy to her touch—one that Ross knew he would do well to ignore.

Having made some determination about his wound that she did not share with him, Caitrin busied herself with unwinding the linen he'd wrapped around her forearm. She bent and scoured her bloody bandage against a jagged rock in the creek. Her movements were mechanical, not imbued with any urgency, her posture as wooden as her words.

Ross tried to recall what they'd been talking about. "I'm sorry. I thought we had delivered you to your kin here, with these people."

Standing before him again, having wrung out the linen strip, Caitrin said, "You did not. They are not kin. I have no family, even before Mary and the Lornes were murdered yesterday. I am an orphan. I always have been."

All of this was delivered in a cold, flat voice and without looking at him at all. She bent her face close to his side—Ross found himself lifting his arm to accommodate her ministrations—and wiped carefully at the remaining mess.

"This will need stitching," she supposed.

For a moment, she laid her entire hand over the hole in his side—to test its warmth, he had to assume. And for that moment, until she pulled her slim fingers away again, Ross held his breath.

"As will your arm," he said, when he allowed himself to breathe again.

Straightening, she lifted her forearm to him. The cut was not very deep, running diagonal across her forearm, but it was not currently bleeding. "This is fine."

She tipped her face up to him. He thought maybe she expected some argument from him.

Instead, he heard himself say, "Perchance it would be better—after all—for you to travel on with us."

He would forever be transfixed by the green of her eyes, how transparently they displayed her emotions and reactions. Right now, he was fairly captivated by the quality of her regard, in that her eyes—along with the proud lifting of her chin—demonstrated some spark, the most spirit he'd witnessed thus far from her.

Her green eyes probed his, searching deeply within. "Guilt is a funny thing, is it not?" She remarked.

"It's no' guilt that—"

"But misplaced at this moment, and with this intent," she went on, cutting him off, as if he had not spoken.

Bending once more at the narrow creek, she scrubbed the ripped linen again.

Planting his hand on his hip, Ross said, "Lass, like as no' you might find a better time and place to choose to be defiant as retribution."

A humorless laugh was barked out over her shoulder. She stood and wrung out the linen a second time. Facing him again, she said, with only a wee bit less spark, "I do not play at retribution, sir. Thank you for your offer, but I will head on back to the Canyarts."

Where possibly you might once again be vilified for surviving today's brutality, he thought but did not say. Grinding his teeth with this new annoyance, Ross watched her walk away from the creek bed for several seconds before he growled and chased after her.

"Caitrin, wait!" He called, but she did not. "Wait." He pulled at her uninjured arm, which turned her around and showed her pinched-lip expression. "I did wrong by you today and I—"

"I do not desire your apology."

"And I dinna desire your pardon," he snapped. "But I owe you a better opportunity than what they'll give."

She shook her head and favored him with a sad, barren smile. "You owe me nothing." A sudden frown came to her. "Why would you think you owed me anything?"

"Because you asked it of me."

She sighed at this, thoughtful for a moment. "I had no right to ask anything of you."

She might have left again but that he still held her arm. "You ken it'll no' be good with them. Caitrin, I canna promise you what Westcairn will be to you, but there'll be no disparaging, nor any abuse. Why did you beg it of me this morning but refuse it now?"

"Because I do not believe now that it will be any better with you."

His answering scowl was instantaneous, since she'd just compared him—unfavorably, it seemed—with that awful Canyart woman. Later, when sleep eluded him for the second night in a row, he would be able to pinpoint exactly what it was that made him press and insist now that she must come with him to Westcairn.

"Caitrin," he said, the bite gone from his tone, "dinna be foolish. You ken it's what you want."

More toneless words were given. "Want has nothing to do with my choices."

"Aye, it does," he refuted hotly. "I've given you a choice now. Which will you choose?"

It was odd. He'd employed more passion now in his attempts to woo her into compliance than she had earlier when asking the same favor of him. He had a suspicion that while she'd engaged with responses, if he were to wave his hand in front of her face, she would not blink or move her eyes. Still, she met his sharp gaze without flinching and he knew that yes, she'd been laid low today and yesterday, but that she was alive with spirit, or could be if others stopped beating it down.

"I ken you are brave, lass," he prompted.

At that blatant provocation, she squared her slim shoulders and swallowed. "Very well."

And that was that.

He nodded at her and unclenched his jaw, allowing her to pull her arm from his grasp. With one last sideways glance at his chest, she slipped away, marching up the slight embankment.

Ross breathed out a heavy breath laced with some lingering frustration. A moment later he swept up his tunic and armor and leisurely followed her, turning toward where Arailt was near the wagons.

Oh, the reason he'd persisted so relentlessly that she must come to Westcairn?

It was the baffling but irrefutable terror that had clutched his chest when he'd turned at Samuel's urging this morning to see the smoke wafting ominously over the tree line in which Caitrin walked. And as much as that had terrified him, it was nothing compared to the heretofore unmet horror he'd known when the Englishman had clutched at her hair and she'd sought out his gaze, her own so disturbing for her acceptance, believing she would die then.

Aye, guilt might well be a funny thing.

But distractions, those with green eyes, were something else altogether.

DINNA BE FOOLISH. YOU ken it's what you want, he'd said.

How she ever kept herself from releasing the words that had come to her head, she would never know.

Do you know, do you have any *idea, what it's like to be unwanted, everywhere you go, all your life?* Mayhap that was one more reason she'd fled the Canyarts' home in the middle of the night and why she'd turned her back on Ross after his refusal this morning: she'd long ago given up trying to force herself on people who did not want her, trying to win them over and fill that constant barrenness. True, she'd never been unwanted at the Lornes, not any more than Mary had been, but she and Mary had not been loved and coddled, had known so little joy save for with each other. The Lornes had taken them in much as they'd taken on Peigi, as able bodies to provide labor at so small a cost. She didn't bother chastising herself for thinking ill of the dead; she did not think ill, she thought only of the truth.

Aye, but she was pathetic enough already, she didn't need to be more so, certainly not to the likes of Ross Kildare. But certainly, she wasn't so stubborn or foolish to be ruled only by pride. Aye, she had no idea what a life at his Westcairn might be made of, but she did know that life here in Calasraid, with Eskaline, would afford her less joy than the little she'd known thus far.

Yet another shock for today: when she'd stood from the creek and had come face to face with Ross Kildare's half-nude body. Good grief, but would she know any peace at all?

In truth, until that moment, Ross Kildare had been rather a hazy figure of piercing blue eyes and blonde hair. Possibly, she'd entertained some thought that he was far too young to have such a commanding presence, to be leading an army of almost one hundred, half of whom might be well older than he was. He couldn't be more than ten and twenty, but was so at ease giving orders, taking charge, making the world around him move at his command. Of course, it had not escaped her notice that he was handsome, but her mind had been beset with larger concerns since meeting him that she'd given it scant thought. At best, he was only a means to an end—escape. Safety, even. Nothing more.

But that was before he'd stripped away his tunic and armor. At that moment, he was a man, and a beautiful one. Possibly, the grander appeal of the man might be attributed to the sum of his parts—his merits and aesthetics—that he was so confident and sure and strong and then so unbelievably handsome while being so.

She stopped suddenly, realizing she had no destination, that she'd only been walking away from Ross. Glancing around, she saw that his army had come, all of them, and they were establishing themselves here, in the fields to the north.

She saw Ross, still bare-chested, being treated by a middle-aged man who was dabbing some yellow substance on Ross's injury. She avoided that direction and then saw four men lifting an inert figure out of a wagon. The soldiers carried him by the heavy tarp beneath him, walking him toward what might be the center of the impromptu camp, the flat area where already another man was down on one knee, etching out a spot in the earth where a fire would likely be built. Caitrin skirted away from all of this, angling toward some privacy in a spot further away, having no wish to witness any more bloodshed or death this day.

"Lass!" Called one of the men transporting the lifeless man.

Stiffening, Caitrin turned and faced him. They'd just set the wounded soldier and his tarp on the ground. Before the man might have explained why he'd called to her, she stated brusquely, "I'm sorry. I do not know anything about wound care or things of that nature."

The man's thick dark brows slashed downward over his dark brown eyes. He scratched lazily at his coarse beard, in which there were two braids of black and gray hairs. She recognized him as one of the men who'd ridden with her and others to the Canyarts homestead near Calasraid yesterday, the one who'd stood hulking in the doorway.

"I'm no' asking ye to save him," the man said with a wee bite to his tone. "But can ye spare a few kind words and soft voice to see him to the other side?"

He'd asked this so plainly that it took Caitrin a moment to understand he wanted her to comfort the man until he died. Biting her lip, dismayed at the very idea, Caitrin opened her mouth to refuse. No, she could not do that, sit with a stranger and what?—tell him everything will be all right?

"Will no' cost you nothing but your time, lass," the man said.

And suddenly she was uneasy for a different reason, riddled with a new guilt that she had to be talked into performing this basic kindness. Nodding tightly, but still too disembodied to suffer any embarrassment for her selfishness, she marched forward and slowly went to her knees beside the youth on the tarp. He was covered with a Kildare plaid from the top of his stomach down, and though his chest was bare, his shoulders and arms were still covered, as if they'd torn his tunic open.

The dark-eyed man who'd challenged her stayed near, hands on his hips, watching, as if he suspected she might only sit and not provide any comfort at all. "'Tis Louis," was all he said.

Still unsure what was expected or hoped of her, she reached out her hand and laid it over Louis's forehead. She gasped when the heat of his skin warmed her fingers so quickly and spared a glance away from the dying soldier. And, as if her touch had roused him, he whimpered and writhed a bit, his youthful face pulled back in a mask of pain.

"Is there nothing that can be done?" She asked the one standing over her. "Or given to him, to ease his suffering?"

The man shook his head, resolute but not without sympathy, his marble-like gaze on Louis. "It will no' be long," was all the comfort he offered Caitrin.

Shoulders slumping at this sorry news, Caitrin shifted to a place of comfort on the hard ground and gently took up Louis's hand, holding it between both of hers. She'd never done anything like this before, and thus had no idea what *kind words* she should put out, had no idea what she might possibly say to make the going easier. "Shh," she said, feeling conspicuous and silly for so lame an attempt, and under the big man's gaze. But the watching soldier was quickly forgotten when she saw that Louis responded, albeit scarcely. His eyes were closed and had been since she'd taken notice of him, but at the sound of her voice, his brows lifted, almost as if he recognized her voice, or had been waiting for her to speak. Of course, he had not, 'twas only the fever or pain reacting, but it encouraged Caitrin to talk more to him.

"I'm right here, Louis," she said. "I've got your hand in mine. I am holding tight. I will not let go."

Louis's lips moved and Caitrin had to lean over him to hear what he said. The single, hopeful word he spoke was scratchy and weak. "Sylvie," she thought he said.

"Aye, Louis, I'm here." And she caressed his pale and clammy cheek.

"I'd be Samuel, lass," said the watchful soldier with the cheerless mahogany eyes after a few moments. "I'll be around should ye need me."

She only nodded a response, bent over Louis, intent now on his welfare.

It was nearly two hours later when Caitrin released his hand, many long minutes after he'd taken his last breath. Gently, she pulled at the wide and folded tarp beneath him, intent on covering him, surprised when hands joined her efforts. The big man, Samuel, had returned. He shifted the dead weight of Louis's young body so that Caitrin could get at the canvas, drawing it out from underneath and folding it over the body.

She smoothed it neatly over him, making sure to cover all of his face and head, having laid his hands over his midsection. She hadn't realized how stiff she was from sitting so still over the lad, not until she straightened now and exchanged a mournful look with Samuel, who was on his haunches at her side.

"I've less right than these men to feel sorry for myself," she said carelessly, just putting out a thought she'd entertained for the last few minutes.

"I dinna ken that, lass," Samuel said. He used a softer tone than he had earlier, when he'd been fairly aggrieved at her, and rightly so, for nearly refusing his request. "They've trained all their lives for what they're about. Ye were no' prepared for what you endured, what befell ye."

"But do they, any of them, have any more choice than I?" She wondered of him, turning her face on her shoulder. He was close enough now, next to her, that the massive size of his arm was inescapable. She'd been cold for days while wrapped in a plaid twice the size of her, but this man wore no sleeves under his leather breastplate and seemed unaffected by the damp chill in the autumn air. And while she first made note that no gooseflesh rose on his skin to announce that he did suffer from the cold, she could also make out every last scar and bruise and mark on his huge, muscled arms. Everything about him was gigantic, she realized: his brows were as long and thick as her thumb mayhap; his nose was large, hanging down a wee bit over his mustache and mouth; his neck was corded with veins and wider than any she'd ever known; the leg folded next to her was enormous, stretching the fabric of his wool breeches; the hands that hung over his knees now were those of a giant, likely capable of snapping a neck only using one of them. Only his eyes were normal sized, set deep under those brows with so little white showing.

"What are ye asking?"

Caitrin blinked, brought back to their conversation. "Does a man grow into adulthood hoping he will make war and wage war, kill or be killed?"

"Nae, I guess no'. Like ye, some of them haven't much choice in the matter. It happens to them and not because of them or by them."

"Aye, and there's the travesty, that we truly have so little control over our lives."

"And haven't ye been through enough, but lass, that's dangerous talk, being so downbeat."

He was right. "Just for another day or two," she said, without giving a true defense for her attitude, "and I'll...move beyond it, I'm sure."

"Aye, and that's a good lass then," Samuel decided.

"Caitrin," she informed him. "My name is Caitrin."

"Aye, I ken." His black brows lifted, and his expression lightened, if only marginally. "But dinna speak to me about having no control. We left ye yesterday with those nasty folks and here ye are today, traveling on with us. Dinna believe those who tell ye, *it is what it is*. Clearly, ye ken it is what ye make of it. Aye, Caitrin?"

Chapter Five

He told himself that he wasn't her keeper, that she'd chosen—nearly begged at one point—to travel with them. She would have to keep up and make do and learn how to go about within the confines of a marching army by herself, or at this point, a stationary army. But then he found himself constantly swinging his gaze around, to make sure she sat still with Louis, that she hadn't wandered off. Before the poor lad was gone, Ross thought he should fetch her something to eat, if she weren't going to abandon the lad, but sit there all evening with him. He resisted the urge to cater to her, unwilling to set a precedent.

As he did almost every time they made camp, Ross let the others settle while he scouted the area, circling their makeshift camp in wider and wider circles, wanting to know everything about the area and who—if any—might be about in this rugged landscape. Specifically, he wanted to make sure no other English soldiers or units might be found in the area. When he returned from this, Caitrin was no more at Louis's side and the lad was shrouded fully in the same canvas they'd used as a litter for him earlier.

Ross left his destrier with the lad, Roland, and spotted Caitrin sitting against the trunk of a tree at the edge of the farmer's field, separated from the bulk of the army gathered near a blazing fire that would have to be tamped when night fell. She was wrapped tightly in another Kildare plaid, a good section of it covering her head and hair, and Ross thought her eyes might be closed.

He let her be now, and sat with Louis's body for a while, saying a prayer for his soul. They were close enough to home now that they needn't bury him out here. He would be interred with honor at Westcairn upon their return. Ross was thankful that two nights ago, the night before they'd discovered Caitrin, that he'd spent some time with the lad, that he'd praised him for how hard and bravely he'd fought.

When he stood again, Caitrin was gone from where she'd rested near the tree. He spun around, looking for any sign of her, her trim figure in the oversized plaid, or any trace of her long, flaxen hair.

"She will no' be long."

Turning yet more, he found Samuel watching him. The goliath was stretched out on his back, his big arms under his head, his feet crossed at the ankles. A long blade of wheat grass hung out of one side of his mouth, and he pulled one hand from beneath his head to take the grass from his mouth to add, "She dinna go far."

Ross gave him a curt nod and dropped his saddle bags on the ground near another tree a good distance from Samuel, close to where he'd last seen her. He sat with his back against the rough bark, using it as a back-scratcher for a moment before he dug into the leather bag for his flask. He was whipped today and looking forward to a quiet night. By God's grace, they'd be home on the morrow. He couldn't deny that he was fairly enthused about meeting up with the firm and sweet feather mattress of his own bed inside Westcairn—it had certainly been too long. He cocked his head and drank deeply of the warm ale, making note of Caitrin's return out of the corner of his eye while he did so. She walked silently and cautiously through the camp, more around the perimeter actually, hugging the wool plaid tight around her. She did not seem to specifically be searching him out, mayhap was only looking for that same tree she'd reclined against moments ago, but her gaze locked with his when he brought the flask down and blindly affixed the cork stopper while he inclined his head at her.

Without a word, she sat again, leaning her head back and closing her eyes.

He still didn't know if she were quiet by nature, or if some other motive kept her so reticent. She had a few good reasons, he supposed. Either the horrors she'd witnessed or her present circumstance, the lone female with an army of men, strangers really, might easily quiet a normally gregarious person. And she had just watched another person die this evening. Aye, she had plenty of reasons to be withdrawn if this were not her natural state.

"We'll reach Westcairn by day's end tomorrow," he said to her.

She might have nodded, he could not say since he was trying not to frighten her with any piercing stare.

A full minute passed before her soft voice reached him. "Is your Westcairn very large?"

"Aye, houses dozens of souls inside the keep," he answered, "and these men in the barracks if they dinna have families in the village or nearby."

She said no more, asked no other question, but burrowed further into the plaid and closed her eyes.

He might have suggested to her that the plaid was large enough that it might serve as both pillow and blanket at the same time but decided against it. It wasn't his concern, how comfortable she made herself, or if she chose not to bother with it.

AFTER A WHILE, SHE did separate herself from the tree and laid down on the forest floor. It was cold and hard and the area immediately around the tree was uneven and harder still for all the bared roots. Thus, Caitrin was forced to move away from the space directly under the canopy of the tree. To her left was some tall and bristly shrub that she didn't want to be anywhere near and to her right was Ross. Luckily, he was not so close that scooching over several feet, away from those roots, still left a good yard of space between them.

She thought of poor Louis and was sorry that she'd not asked if or when they would bury him, and that was the last thing she knew or remembered before she was woken by a firm hand clamping over her mouth.

"Dinna move," was hissed at her.

Her instant fright was waylaid as she recognized Ross's voice. Her eyes were wide though and her body was stiff. He must have crawled over to where she slept as he was on his belly and not bending over her. Slowly, he lifted his hand away from her mouth. Something moved against her hair, and she realized it was his other hand, on the ground above her head. She saw only the underside of his jaw as his attention was not on her but on something or somewhere over her head, into the woods.

In the same whisper, minus the hiss, he explained, "Something's out there, mayhap only a beast and no' a man. Tavis and Gideon went to check."

On her back, Caitrin tried to lift her head and follow his gaze.

"Keep your head down," he whispered against her. "The moonlight is bright upon your hair."

So she remained perfectly still and waited, listening though she heard nothing, not even Tavis and Gideon in pursuit of whatever had startled more than them.

After a moment, she was unable to ignore her position, or rather their position, with Ross Kildare's upper body draped so intimately across hers. Of its own accord, the image of his naked chest rose in her mind. He'd planted his right elbow into the ground next to her and that hand now rested against the side of her head. He'd used his left hand to cover her mouth and now, having removed it, it laid over her midsection with more familiarity than they should know. His proximity was unsettling, and Caitrin was, in the quiet and stillness, made aware of the feel and the scent of him.

Ross Kildare was not so big as that giant, Samuel, but he was indeed a very large man, long and hard and sinewy and bursting with so much strength and power, in the hand that stifled her scream, in the solid thigh pressed against her leg, in the square and broad turn of his shoulder, lifted above her while he continued to scan the darkness for any danger.

And the scent of him. Caitrin closed her eyes and inhaled slowly, drawing it in again, his distinct aroma of man and horse and leather. It should wrinkle her nose, but it did not. He was as fresh as cool water running over mossy stones, as unpretentious as fallen leaves upon the damp ground, and Caitrin was inexplicably calmed by his earthy scent and then stirred to know it more.

In the next instant, her eyes opened wide as she began to understand that her reaction to him was not only about this situation and how familiar he'd made himself with her or how pleasant and soothing was his scent. It was more than that—it was about a woman responding to a man. At that moment, every part of her body where he touched began to burn, as she was sure her cheeks did, suddenly cognizant of her reaction to him as a man. She held her breath then, as if breathing against his chin or cheek would somehow inform him of what she was experiencing. It did not escape her thinking that she'd never before responded to any man, in any manner.

And as quickly as it had come, her reaction to him, so then did the guilt, that she should feel anything so trivial as this, being attuned to a man when Mary and Dorcas and the others were not yet cold in the ground, miles and miles away, without even a marker to say who they were. And while she couldn't keep blaming her recent known horrors for her emotions now, she knew she was fragile-of-mind yet, which might well explain why she felt as if she were about to start crying.

But her growing guilty despair was interrupted by noises coming from the woods. Ross's entire body went rigid, poised it seemed to react at the same time Caitrin's welling tears were forgotten as she turned her face away from him, as if she might see beyond the nearby tree and into the darkness.

"Must have been a critter," Tavis announced to any who might be watching or awaiting his determination as he returned to camp.

"Was no wee critter," said another, who must be the Gideon Ross had mentioned. "That noise was too loud for raccoons or possums."

Whatever it was, it was gone or at the very least, not troubling to these men that Caitrin realized at least one concern was expelled. Ross relaxed as well; there was nothing soft about him, to be sure, but she felt the lessening of the tension in his body, in those parts that leaned against hers. And yet he did not move away from her directly but turned his face down toward her. For all of those few minutes, he'd been watchful of their surroundings, had not spared a glance for her, she thought, until now.

She only knew that his eyes moved over her face because the whites of his eyes, all that she could really see, shifted in front of her, only inches away from her watchful gaze.

"Why tears, lass? You dinna need to be afraid."

Stiffening once again, this time with mortification—until she realized she needn't have wasted that response; he didn't know that she cried for her disloyal and poorly timed reaction to him—she murmured, "I...they just came."

He didn't believe her. She wasn't sure how she knew that. His response to her explanation was mild, one brow lifting ever-so-slightly, but he didn't move yet, stayed leaning over her, their faces inches apart, as if he only waited for the truth.

"Dinna be afraid now, lass. I'll no' let any harm come to you."

She knew that much about him, that he was generously protective of those in his care. She gave the nod she supposed he expected, too tired to counter his statement with the truth she knew, that no one was safe.

AS EVER, ROSS'S MOOD improved with each mile put behind them, and each step closer to Westcairn they achieved.

This last jaunt, in service to the common army of Scotland, had been difficult, and mostly because they'd gained no ground. Or rather, they'd taken none of their own back from the English. To lose good and able men and not be able to claim even a small victory always sat unwell with Ross. As he'd discussed with Gabriel Jamison and Calum MacKinnon in those recent campaigns, there was a general feeling among the patriots that no good fight would be made until a greater man than any presently in service to Scotland empowered the armies with a larger zeal than what the present leaders could produce in the ranks.

They needed William Wallace.

Ross, himself, shared Wallace's passion, but had not his eloquence of words. He could not, as Wallace so effortlessly did, convince a man to give all, everything he owned and treasured and adored, to the cause of freedom, He felt it, but he did not know if he could imbue that same ferocity in others. Not the way Wallace did.

Though rarely a good idea, it was easy to let down their guard as they got closer to home. But they knew these glens and hills and lochs as well as they knew their own steeds and swords and hands. Thus, when they were only a few leagues from Westcairn, they were cleverly surprised by a band of men charging from the dark Rosyth forest just south of Westcairn.

The palfrey on which Caitrin sat was not a war horse, not accustomed to such excitement, that it reared sharply. Quickly, Ross guided his own destrier closer to get a grip on the reins while Caitrin's eyes widened and she clung to both the leather ribbons and the horse's mane, trying to keep her seat. Several others, John and Samuel included, positioned themselves defensively around Caitrin. Using a calm voice to soothe the mare, Ross yanked firmly but smoothly down on the reins, bringing the animal onto four hooves instead of only two. He met Caitrin's gaze, her green eyes alive with a fright that faded quickly when her horse's uneasiness and the attack itself settled to nothing. He kept his hand near hers on the reins while he turned his attention to the abruptly halted attack.

The wild cries and the swift eruption from the trees had stopped all at once. Almost twenty men stumbled to a halt in the tall golden grass, their weapons—some of which appeared to be farm tools—dropping as they lowered their arms. Ross recognized each and every face of the thin throng as residents of Westcairn, these men plagued by advanced age or old wounds or some other reason that kept them from joining the main army. He latched his severe gaze onto the foremost attacker, a burly man of great height who sported a shock of shoulder length white-gray hair—though he was naught but a decade older than Ross—and only one arm, the other left on the battlefield at Falkirk.

"What the bluidy hell are you about, Hamish?"

The man's entire posture shifted. His only hand, holding a hatchet yet chest high, fell to his side. His shoulders and the features of his ruddy face suffered the same decline, slumping as if they were one unit. He shook his head and announced in a pained voice, "Och, Laird, we've seen some troubles."

Ross's blood went cold. He dismounted and strode toward the big man, calling out, "What troubles, Hamish?"

The two parties converged, Ross's army closing in on the standing group, forming a larger circle of men and horses.

Still shaking his head, his face now contorted with regret for the news he must give, Hamish answered, "English, Laird—come to Westcairn."

A collective round of gasps and curses sounded out from the mounted army.

Ross's cold blood heated to boiling. "When? Where are they now?"

Hamish winced at the dangerous tone of his laird. His mouth opened and closed while he lifted the hatchet, conveying some helplessness. "They're here now, Laird. They'd come several weeks ago. They've taken the keep, have it as their own."

Through clenched teeth, Ross asked after his youngest brother. "And Robert?"

Hamish's mien only grew more distressed as he pulled his lips back into another aggrieved scowl. He gave no words to accompany this, but shook his head slowly, his gaze locked on Ross's unblinking blue eyes.

"They came out of nowhere, Laird."

Ross turned to find who said this, seeing Simidh step forward. The lad was as thin and fragile as any lass, mayhap more so, not quite capable of lifting a powerful Scots' broadsword; he was better used inside the tithe barn as he had a good head for figures and cyphering. Ross lifted his brows at Simidh, silently asking him to continue.

The lad pushed around two other men with whom he'd come and stood before Ross.

"Dozens and dozens of them, laird, razed the village first," he told. "Aye, and praise St. Andrew, so many were gone to the north fields sowing the winter crops. And more were gone, Agnes's entire brood over to Kipern for her sister's wedding feast.

They scattered... most of them. They caught some... cut them down as they fled." He paused, waiting for Ross to digest this before he spoke of the bulk of the account. "They had no time, no' really, inside the keep—barely enough to close the gate."

"Aye, and dinna they put up a good fight?" said Uilleam, a middle-aged and gapped-tooth man, giving a solemn nod to underscore this.

"Aye," said Hamish, "held them off for two whole days—"

"And with only a score of men inside," Simidh added, "against hundreds of them, including two dozen archers who wreaked some havoc, aye."

Ross took it all in. There was much to sort through, losing his brother being foremost. Later, he would wonder how he managed to stay on his feet, how the mournful news of his brother's demise had not sent him to the ground, collapsed with his anguish. Turning his head, he met with John's stark-eyed gaze. The look they exchanged was one of shared grief and the promise of retribution. They would mourn Robert properly, but first they would take on the ones who'd murdered him.

Facing Hamish and Simidh and the others once more, Ross asked, "So what have you? Just this?" He waved his arm to include the full number of men who'd come from the forest.

Straightening to his full height, which was considerable, Hamish said proudly, "We've nigh on thirty, Laird, hiding in the forest. Made a little site there. Intercepted Agnes and her brood 'fore they might have strolled on in to the..."–shuffling a bit, Hamish let that trail off.

Chaos. Massacre. Bloodshed. Ross guessed any of them might have gone through Hamish's mind.

"And now," John said from behind Ross, "we've that number plus one hundred, give or take."

"Enough to take back Westcairn," Ross imagined. Whether or not it was would remain to be seen, but he'd die trying if need be, wouldn't let them take it without a fight—another fight, he amended, giving silent praise to Robert, who'd held off the enemy ten times the size of what had been left with him for two entire days. When next he put his gaze on Hamish, his eyes were bright with a furious determination. "Lead the way."

Ross gained the saddle again, catching sight of Caitrin's sorrowful expression.

"What now?" She wondered quietly as they followed the group into the forest.

"Now I will wage my own war," Ross told her.

CAITRIN FOLLOWED BEHIND Ross's huge destrier as they were led deeper and deeper into the forest. These woods were so dense with thick-trunked pines, and tall birch and aspens and oak trees that the sunlight of midday was left behind. The forest floor of pine needles and exposed roots, with nary a trail in sight, was mostly obscured by heather and creeping lady's-tresses orchids and so many feather mosses.

The entire army moved silently through the forest, following the band of men who'd thankfully found them before they might have gone on to the keep itself. She'd watched in fascination as Ross's entire façade had shifted earlier, from angry surprise at being set upon, to that fierce and savage expression that foretold of a great retribution, to that ever-so-brief moment where he'd seemed so bereft. Having only a profile view of him at the time, she couldn't be sure, but she thought that for one fleeting instant, his face had been arrested with an incredulous grief. Whoever Robert was, he was—had been—important to Ross.

Considering the whole of her brief contact with Ross Kildare, Caitrin understood she knew him not at all. She couldn't say if he liked to laugh or if he were wed and mayhap a father to a large number of bairns; she didn't know if he generally practiced such kindness as he'd shown her or if he'd only reacted to how pitiful she must have been. Thus, she couldn't be certain, but she was fairly convinced she'd been witness to a rare weakening in him, that anguish he'd exhibited and extinguished so swiftly.

It was gone now. And as she rode behind, she could not say now what expression he wore, but she supposed it might yet be chock full of that resolute grimness that had overtaken him, when he'd said he'd wage war now. She'd shivered at the icy tone and the flash of steel in the gaze he'd sent her. That look, though brief, had been enough to discourage her from asking any of the many questions swirling in her brain. What was his plan to wage war? Would they call other armies to their side and their cause, to fight against the English perpetrators?

All that fled her mind, as quickly as it had come, when they reached an area inside the forest populated by a large herd of people, who gathered round as the entire Kildare army approached their camp. There was no clearing, no central area in this camp, 'twas naught but ramshackle tents strewn about here and there. What might be a communal fire pit was set into the earth in a flat and brush-less space of about ten feet square; just now the fire was tamped and only a light wisp of whitish smoke curled around it. A line of rope was suspended between two trees and was draped with tunics and kirtles and gowns, freshly laundered, Caitrin assumed. A splash of color above her head drew her gaze upward, where a dark linen cloth of considerable size was creased and folded as a tent over a slapdash platform, constructed around the tree, made of crudely formed planks. The platform was several stories high in that tree and possibly wide enough on one side to hold two sleeping bodies. Upon further inspection, Caitrin saw that short thick chunks of wood had been nailed to the tree itself, steps to that elevated housing, she supposed.

Three wagons were lined up, end to end, laden with cloth covered supplies or possessions, and standing between these hidden people and who—or whatever—might come from the north. Several children, lads and lasses, toddling and older, watched with wary eyes as their laird and his army walked among them. Few people gave any attention to Caitrin, their gazes fixed so steadily—almost hopefully—upon Ross Kildare. Their faces were not passive, there was no indifference or resignation, but some did light now with hope, that their laird would set things right.

Ross Kildare did not address the group at large, did not ascend to any high ground or remain risen on his steed and give any praise that they had escaped or promises that he would exact justice and revenge. He dismounted effortlessly and greeted people one at a time, murmuring to the individuals. Occasionally, though not often, he touched them. To one ancient man, whom Caitrin decided might be sightless as his eyes did not follow Ross's movements properly, Ross wound his fingers around the man's neck and touched his forehead to the wrinkled one of the old man, whispering words that had the old man nodding slowly while his expression eased.

Samuel appeared at her side, sans his own mount and took hold of the palfrey's reins, indicating she should dismount as well.

"Home for now, lass," he said blandly, his mien dark as well for the tragedy that greeted them.

The men of Westcairn, Ross and his officers and several from this concealed camp, met for some time, discussing the crime against Westcairn or a strategy to take it back, she had to imagine. Caitrin, with no idea what she should or could do, where she might make her own shelter or with what, and then a bit overwhelmed by not knowing how to occupy herself, removed herself from the immediate area. She wouldn't wander far, of course. She was not that brave. She never had been, not even before the English had made her even more fearful.

She found a swollen creek, where she supposed they might have done their laundry earlier, and sat high up on the grassy bank, near the edge of a row of pines, drawing her knees up to her chest.

She sat for quite some time and then startled when she heard a rustling of noise, brush and branches being shoved aside as another came to the creek, rendering her immobile. Relief was followed by surprise when she saw that it was Ross and that he was alone. Opening her mouth, she meant to announce her presence, but stopped before she made any sound. Here now was a different Ross completely. He strode up and down the bank, back and forth over a length of about twenty feet. He'd planted his hands on his hips and seemed at times to be talking to himself. His expression was yet grim. Intrigued, as much as she could be by anything right now, Caitrin studied his behavior.

And then he stopped.

He faced the swift-moving clear water of the creek and inhaled deeply, lifting his head and shoulders with that action.

"How different are we?" she said after a while, by way of announcing her presence.

He turned, looked at her, only mildly surprised by her presence, it seemed. "How so?"

"I have only me to consider," she said, "only my sorrow and grief and worry. And I am wretched. But you...you have to consider all of them, do you not? How...exhausting that must be."

Ross snorted out a curt laugh that contained no humor and let his hands fall from his hips as he strode toward her.

While he surprised her by sitting next to her, Caitrin said formally, "I am sorry for what has happened to your Westcairn...and to Robert specifically."

He turned his blue gaze onto her, studying her.

"I sensed the news of his demise caused the sharpest pain," she said, answering the question in his gaze.

Another sigh preceded his response. "Robert is...was my youngest brother."

How tragic. He offered nothing else, and Caitrin did not press for more.

After a few minutes, while they only watched the water ripple and bubble over mossy rocks and plain brown stones, Ross rubbed both his hands vigorously over his eyes and face, as if he might erase more than only travel grime and dust.

"I've lost my brother, among others, and you've lost everyone you've known, as well," he said then.

"They weren't mine," Caitrin told him once again, which swung his face toward her. "Not really," she furthered. "Gordon and Dorcas took in Mary and me when we were bairns. I have no idea who I am or where I come from. Mary was not truly my sister and sweet Peigi only served with us some of the time. But aye, they were all I ever had, all I'd known."

She didn't want to say that already it hurt less. She didn't think that was true, but decided it was only easier to talk about it now, that was all. Her chest still burned with thoughts of them, how they died.

When she felt his gaze still attached to her face, she swallowed and turned attention away from herself. "But you've lost your brother and your home—"

"I've no' lost Westcairn," he interjected with some sharpness. "I'll reclaim what's mine." Another space of quiet passed between them until Ross spoke again. "Tis no' a spitting competition, lass, to see whose grief might go furthest or be most severe."

Taking no offense at what he suggested, she countered evenly, "I was commiserating and not competing or conceding."

Once more, he turned toward her, his chin resting on his wide shoulder. He sent his blue-eyed gaze over her face, from her surely messy hair to one eye and then the next, down over her nose and mouth and then back to her eyes.

She looked at Ross, really looked at him for the first time, at more than only his striking blue eyes.

"Why...why do you wear your hair shorn so?"

Only a flash of a surprise for her query showed on his face before he answered frankly, "I once watched as a man was wrenched from his steed by a brigand lucky enough to catch hold of the length of his hair. At the time, I thought mayhap he'd no' have been killed, but for his hair."

She continued to stare at him, though showed no reaction to his reasoning or the image that it kindled in her mind, of her own hair being used against her so recently. "War is cruel, is it not?"

"It is, lass." He nodded his chin against his shoulder and said, "And it's no' done yet."

Chapter Six

Ross thought she might have come to life—or returned to life—if he'd been able to bring her to Westcairn, to the keep itself, and to the security it should have provided. And what distance he'd hoped to preserve between them, thinking she would have to learn to get on by herself, was rather lost in the upheaval of this present circumstance so that Ross found himself fashioning a crude but serviceable tent for her, tucked under the lowest boughs of a majestic pine. Another tree, a diminutive but leafy hazel, bracketed one side and would serve as a windbreaker, if any stronger wind should find its way so deep in the forest.

By necessity, the current home of what remained of the Kildares here in the forest, was rather a scattered assemblage of make-do shelters. It was unwise to crowd all of them together: if they were discovered and set upon, it would make destroying them too easy, naught but penned sheep to be slaughtered. Thus, her nearest tented neighbors aside from Ross sleeping close under the canopy of trees would be Uilleam and his wife, Ida, fifty feet to the north. To the southwest, he saw that Gideon, who'd been reunited with his wife, Fiona, had erected a similar structure, using stakes and rope to fashion a simple triangular shelter.

As dusk settled, Caitrin returned from where he'd left her down by the brook a short while ago. She exhibited little curiosity for what went on around her, only walked toward him once she'd spotted him.

"It's still a hard-ground bed, lass," he said, having just pounded in the fourth stake to secure the tent, "but there's privacy and a wee bit of refuge from the cold."

"Where will you be?"

Ross didn't suppose that she asked this out of any concern for his comfort but rather in consideration of her own security. She wasn't about to lose her fear all at once, or anytime soon.

Turning, he considered his own options. Under the branches of the hazel tree might suit him just fine. He pointed to that spot with the mallet in his hand. "Just there, but no' yet. I'm taking a unit out now to spy upon Westcairn, see what goes on there."

As bland as all her actions were, she nodded but then said quickly, "But please tell me when you return."

At his quizzical expression, she added, "I won't be able to sleep otherwise."

Again, he didn't think this was borne out of worry over his well-being.

"Aye, I will."

She glanced around now, possibly considering the distance between her and the next closest tent. "Is this...safe?"

"We've claimed about an acre, all of us," he told her, "with soldiers creating a perimeter around that area. No foreigner—any no' familiar with the landscape—would likely be found within this forest at night. It's safe lass, until they know we're here."

At her vaguely satisfied nod, he left her. John and Samuel and a dozen more waited for him. They would go on foot, only meaning to survey the keep from a safe distance to make determinations about the number of English and how well-secure they'd made Westcairn.

They walked across the few miles until the keep came into view, the setting sun and the glorious sky it painted being a fine backdrop to home. Standing above the narrow glen, with yet hundreds of yards between him and his keep, the view was bittersweet. It'd have been perfect if he could continue, could walk through the open gate and into the great hall, could be greeted by his always-buoyant brother, Robert.

But the gate was not open. And the wall was manned by many more sentries than Ross had ever commanded to hold watch. It was well-lit, orange glowing torches now spaced as close as ten feet apart on the outside wall, where previously they'd only employed a half dozen torches inside at nighttime.

More than two hundred years ago, Westcairn was constructed as a timber house surrounded by a wooden palisade, the home of Peile Cill Dara, late of Ireland, and his growing family. It had evolved since then, mostly at the turn of the last century, into the magnificent stone fortress it was today, sporting two towers connected by the keep itself. There was little damage done to the façade. The English hadn't need of a trebuchet, which might have leveled parts of the thick curtain wall and had apparently started no fires as no part of the blonde stone was darkened and charred with ash. Nae, they'd simply outnumbered the Kildares within. As the fortress had never been attacked before, and as the Kildares upheld rare, congenial relations with their Highland neighbors, Ross had—as he'd done before— entrusted only twenty soldiers to Westcairn's safekeeping, under Robert's direction. He placed no blame on his brother's shoulders. That was his alone, for becoming complacent, that he'd not have foreseen the trouble that had come to Westcairn.

"She is gorgeous," said John at his side, his gaze also upon Westcairn.

"Aye, she is." He thought briefly of Robert, of the fight he must have put up—the lad was the most easy-going of the three brothers, but his loyalty to Westcairn and all things Kildare was as fierce as Ross or John's. He'd not have gone easily, would have fought until he drew his last breath.

If he had been alone, feasibly Ross would have taken time to mourn his brother right here, upon the rise overlooking what was now his tomb. But they had an agenda, and Ross separated the men into two groups and advised they should move closer.

"We are only about surveying," he reminded them. "Dinna be seen or engage. They should no' be made aware that our army has returned."

John appended, "We want to ken numbers and procedures and movements."

The evening then, and all the hours before midnight were spent only getting closer and watching Westcairn, the men spaced about every thirty to forty feet. The gate never opened and the soldiers atop the wall were quiet and mostly still, as there were enough of them that there was no need to prowl the wall.

Several hours later, Ross put out a quiet bird call to round up his men and they convened at the ridge again. No one had too much to offer other than estimates of numbers, based on those employed in one shift on the wall. Thus, Ross wouldn't have said they'd learned anything greatly useful. But it did cement in his mind what his strategy should be.

"We canna hope to storm the keep to any success," he said as they walked back to the forest. "But we can keep watch, and take out a few here and there, as they come and go. Our only hope is to diminish their numbers, so that when we do attack the keep, odds are weighted in our favor."

Tomorrow would be soon enough to organize everything that required his attention: posting and scheduling sentries for this temporary settlement; setting up a raiding party that would be charged only with reducing the number of Englishmen at Westcairn, one by one if need be; sending out scouts and foragers to the now desolate village to plunder useful items and tools; making this space run efficiently for over one hundred people, expecting that recovering Westcairn will not happen in only a day or two.

But for now, he was exhausted, the last few days—indeed, the last many months—taking its toll.

Traversing the forest at night under a clear inky sky forced a man to move slowly and carefully, conscious of each step, eyes always moving. But he found Caitrin's tent easily enough and, squatting next to the closed front flaps, said softly through the canvas, "I am returned, lass."

No sound but her voice greeted him, so that he knew she was still, possibly waiting for him.

"Thank you."

He stayed there a moment. Why did it always seem he wanted to say more, or have her speak more, so that there was reason to stay close?

"Goodnight then," he offered after a moment.

"And to you."

THE NEXT FEW DAYS PASSED in a blur of quiet activity around what was now referred to as Little Westcairn.

Ross kept one eye on Caitrin most of the time and noticed that Samuel and Tavis, among others, were generally solicitous of her as well. He didn't like that she kept so much to herself but imagined that people grieved in their own ways. He would give her a bit more time.

She was only getting increasingly bedraggled, her lone léine, the blue wool still blood-stained and with a muddy hem, only getting dirtier. She must have braided her hair at some point since they arrived at this location, but it was clear she did not attend her hair on a daily basis, as it was ever untidy. Her face was still streaked with that long scratch, with bits of dried blood scabbing away from it. There was yet no sustained spark to be found in her gaze, and somehow she managed to bewitch him and possibly several others even as she was yet lost in her own world. Still, none could look at her and not first notice that she was bonny, and then wonder how breathtaking she must be when in the right frame of mind, not lost in this trance of grief.

Their first full day here, she'd found a spot near her tent, upon a soft carpet of pine needles, where the sun poked through a rare hole in the cover of trees. By Ross's reckoning, she followed that around for almost an hour with some hope to warm herself. The forest was always many degrees cooler than outside it; in the mornings and the evenings plumes of gray-shadowed breaths danced all around people talking.

Caitrin rarely talked to anyone, had yet to make any overture to any of the half-dozen women in the camp. She'd watched

Agnes chase one of her bairns yesterday morning, had even turned her head to follow their progress while Agnes hollered at the lad to be still so that she might dress him properly. The wee lad, Isaac, with no more than four or five summers to his name, giggled and ran around in naught but his tunic, eluding his harried mother for more than a minute, amusing many.

On their second day at Little Westcairn, Ross and half a dozen men returned from their early morning jaunt to the presently abandoned homes in the village. They'd managed to surprise three Englishmen—the first they'd come upon outside the gates of the keep—and lure them into the nearby woods where they dispatched them with quiet efficiency. They'd not wanted to leave any evidence of bloodshed inside the village, or in any place that other English soldiers might discover it. Best they imagine they were only lost or had deserted. When that was done, they looted several homes, fetching requested items from those that were still with them, and agreeing that their only thoughts should be of expediency when plundering homes of those that had lost their lives when the English had come. Nothing should be wasted.

Thus when they'd returned to Little Westcairn hours later, Ross was pleased to present to Caitrin a straw stuffed mattress and a soft wool blanket.

Seated almost exactly where she'd been when he'd left earlier, she watched him come and watched him lay those things down on the ground between where she sat and her tent. But she said nothing, and asked nothing, which compelled Ross to explain, "You might want to change out the straw, mayhap wash the linen cover, but you've a nice soft mattress for your bed now."

Her lips parted as she stared at the gently used piece and the blanket folded atop it. "That was kind of you."

Tight-lipped, having expected mayhap a little more brightness from her over this boon—he was not looking for gratitude—Ross sighed and left her once more.

He did notice, however, that she spent all the rest of the day doing as he'd suggested, first discarding all the old straw and then laundering the long linen sack at the stream. At one point, he saw her plucking dried grass from where ever she could find it, but never so far away that she was not within sight of her own tent. After a few hours, she had a substantial pile of straw drying out, stashed next to her humble lodging.

Over the next few days, they did as they'd set out to do. The English did, a few at a time, come and go from the keep. The gate opened only long enough to release or welcome any soldier coming or going. Groups of ten or more were not disturbed, Ross explaining to his men when they questioned this that the larger parties would indeed be missed, or they might assume the Kildares had amassed larger numbers than what had initially survived. He didn't want the English to know he was out here, stalking and waiting and planning, until it was too late.

At one point, Samuel suggested that they might need to start breaking necks rather than using swords and lances, thinking that they might want to make use of the despised English uniforms at some point, but that bloodied garb, if employed eventually, would draw too much attention.

"Aye, and ye better start exercising your English speak," Idgy teased. "We ain't gonna get in with only the right togs, no' the numbers we'll want to enter all at once."

They were careful with their fires. None were allowed here inside the forest on calm, clear days as the smoke, even a thin plume, might give away their position. Fires were best employed at night but were instructed to be kept low. The forest was thick and likely no fire would ever be spotted from the few miles between them and the keep, but it wasn't a chance Ross wanted to take, that some eagle-eyed Englishman might never detect an orange glow illuminating sections of the forest or the night sky.

On the fourth day since Ross and his army had returned, he put Arailt in charge of making arrows.

"The women can help," Ross told him. "Give each of them a task, collecting and stripping the yew twigs; feathers; and they'll need to make glue. We found plenty of silk thread inside Mungo's croft." Westcairn's fletcher, Mungo, had made bows and arrows for three Kildare lairds, including Ross. They'd found him in his workroom adjacent to his croft. His throat had been slit and his body so badly decomposed that he was only recognizable by the scruffy saffron kerchief he'd forever worn tied around his wrist, which he'd regularly used to wipe sweat from his forehead.

"The lass from Perth as well?" Arailt asked, lifting his brow at Ross.

"Aye, Caitrin can help," he decided. It was time.

CAITRIN WALKED THE now familiar path from her tent to that section of the forest where the ash trees were plentiful. She rather enjoyed this chore, which she'd been about all day, having made several trips back and forth. And as she was still within shouting distance of Little Westcairn, she knew no tangible fear.

She'd been tasked with collecting ash wood for the fires that would be needed. Arailt had approached her this morning and laid out both his goal and his plan to achieve it over the next few days.

"Now the laird wants arrows, lass," he'd said after he'd introduced himself. "Aye, and we'll leave all the security and defenses to the army, but we—you and I and several others—can take on this task. Make good work of it, I'm thinking."

"I thought you were the laird's surgeon and not a fletcher," she'd said to him.

Arailt was middle-aged, mayhap twice her own age, with a long, lean figure and friendly brown eyes. Somehow, he managed to appear very fresh, his tunic and braies unblemished, his face clean-shaven and his hair combed and tied in a neat queue at his nape.

"I am neither, lass," he'd replied with a kindly smile, "but as you ken, we are what we need to be. So you and I and some others'll be fletchers right now, aye?"

"All right," she'd then agreed, expecting there was more to come, specifically what he needed from her.

Pleased with this—so much so that she had to wonder if he expected that she would refuse—he went on with a bit more enthusiasm. "Aye, and we'll need a good, hot fire to boil the hides for glue, that's first. Do you ken the ash tree, lass? The wood of the ash?"

"I would know an ash tree," she'd said.

"Verra good. It's a steady hardwood, but dinna smoke so much, though it makes a fine heat. So I'll ask you to collect as much as you can. That'll be your task for today, though if you should come upon any hides—squirrel, rabbit, or larger—we'll make use of those as well. Aye, and stones lass. We've no smith, no' out here, nor the tools, so we'll be forced to fashion the arrowheads from stones. That'll be on Oswald and me, who have some experience. But the wood for now, aye?"

He'd then pointed her in the direction he promised she would come upon many ash trees within the forest and cautioned that she should only collect broken or downed limbs, nothing green. It had taken her nearly thirty minutes just to find the first ash tree but when she did, she then spotted so many others, easily to distinguish by the paired leaves on the slim branches. Her first forays were poorly planned and saw her struggling to haul armloads of felled ash limbs back to the camp. By her third trip, she'd wised up and had laid out her borrowed plaid, loading that up with so many more pieces, which was then easier to drag along the forest floor.

She did not mind the work at all, was actually grateful to have something to occupy her. She also did not mind that she worked alone—preferred it actually. She didn't want to know these people, didn't want to form friendships or become attached to any. She had no reserves left and feared she would not be able to mourn them when they died.

Curiously, she did not fear Ross's death. He would not die, she believed. He was too strong, too brave, too...alive to be killed.

She'd watched him most of all over the last few days. He came and went, by himself or with others, all throughout the day and night. To his credit—and Caitrin's relief—he was considerate of her anxiety and continued to sleep outside her tent every night. She found that she couldn't quite relax until he settled down for the night.

He'd left this morning atop his big destrier, as he rarely had since they'd come. Mostly, all his expeditions, whatever they were about, were on foot. As Caitrin returned to the camp with yet another haul of broken ash limbs, she saw that he'd returned, but only just, as he was still seated upon the horse. He was talking to his brother, who was not mounted, but lifted his gaze from John when he spied Caitrin coming through the trees. He continued to speak, she could see his lips move, but he did not take his regard from Caitrin.

Caitrin held a wadded end of her plaid in one hand and pulled the loaded fabric around trees and brush to deposit it with all the others, near where Arailt had said they would make the fire tomorrow. She hadn't seen Arailt since he'd given her this task and so wasn't sure how much was desired or needed but knew there was yet plenty of fallen limbs that she might bring back and so until she was told differently or had exhausted the available supply, she would continue.

She was a hundred feet gone into the woods again when someone called out from behind her.

"Lass! Wait!"

Turning and peering through the trees, she saw a young soldier dashing through the woods toward her, hopping over ferns and then the larger trunk of a fallen pine. When he was close, he stopped suddenly and announced, "Laird sent me, lass. I'm Oliver. Says you're no' to traipse around by yourself."

Oliver was a soft lad, mayhap not even as old as Caitrin, with large teeth and hands so plump that nary a wrinkle could be found. Two bright spots of red dotted each cheek, but she thought he was not blushing, might only be one of those persons whose cheeks were perpetually flushed.

"But I have been for several hours now," she told him, not wanting company. "I do not ever stray too far, not any further than a scream might be heard."

The lad shrugged, adjusting a strap that crossed his chest diagonally and held his sword at his back. "It's hard to scream if you're felled by an arrow, or by surprise."

She hadn't thought of that. Sighing, she gave him a curt nod and continued on her way, while he followed close behind. It was soon apparent that Oliver was much more eager for her company than she was desirous of his. And while she hadn't anticipated any help, she almost found it humorous that he didn't offer any. He talked incessantly, interrupting himself here and there to point out more fallen ash limbs that she might gather. He pointed, that was all, never lifted a finger to aid in any way. However, Caitrin could find no fault with his company; his unending prattle served as a nice din in the background of her own thoughts.

SHE WAS EXHAUSTED BY nightfall but happy to be so. Huddled in the plaid she spent the last hour picking clean of bark and other debris from the work it had seen today, Caitrin waited for Ross to come so that she might go to bed. There was no fire tonight, nothing but darkness all around but she knew when he walked her way, recognized the lazy grace of his walk in the gray shadowed figure heading her way.

When he stood only a few feet from her, he said, "I canna be here tonight, lass. Like all the others I've got to take a turn overnight for the watch."

Oh. She thought she'd said this aloud but realized she had not when he prompted some response. "Caitrin?"

"May I go with you?"

A long pause preceded his answer. "You're much safer here."

Caitrin shook her head. "I am safer with you." She was yet dazed, and fear was never so far away, but she knew this to be true. At the very least, she *believed* that she was safer in his company.

Another pause. And then, "Aye. Come on."

She hopped to her feet before he might have changed his mind.

There was nothing to bring, no preparations to make that they left Little Westcairn immediately, Caitrin moving quickly to keep up with his long, sure strides.

"You were busy today," he said by way of conversation as they moved through the forest.

"Yes," she said, "and yes, it did feel good to do something." She guessed he might be thinking something similar.

His short chuckle, wafting back to her as he walked, advised she might be right.

"We had a priest at Westcairn in my youth who droned endlessly about *satisfaction in your toil.*"

Caitrin allowed a brief grin. "It must have resonated, as you rarely sit still."

"There is much to be done."

They walked on, exiting the denser forest and then climbing a gradual incline, which lifted them up and out onto a shelf of rock that overlooked a narrow glen and showed a castle in the distance. Torches, so far away they were but dots upon the night landscape, lit up the fortress. Caitrin could make out little more than that bare light and then the outline of the castle, two towers specifically, which cut into the night sky above it.

"Is that Westcairn?" She asked as they stared out over the valley and across.

"Aye."

She turned her face toward Ross but could see little of him as well. "Does it pain you much, to be so close?"

"The senseless deaths pain me," he answered mildly. "To be so close has me seething with rage and impatience."

"And you do not fear that you might die yourself trying to take it back?"

"What is there to fear? If I dinna take it back, there is little point to my life." He paused a moment then added with intent, "And that is no' said to have you considering what point there is to your life now."

She shook her head but supposed he might not be able to see that response. "I...do not mean to sound maudlin—it's not self-pity or any such, only... truth—but I'm not sure there ever was much point to my life."

"Every life has meaning," he alleged quietly.

She said nothing, supposing that any comment she might make would only seem, after all, melancholic.

"So, what do you do?" She asked instead. "Sit and watch, wakeful all through the night?"

"Aye," he said and turned around, stepping away from the ledge. "But you needn't be. Cozy up and find your slumber."

It was dark and likely he would wish to be quiet, to concentrate on his task. Caitrin had already noticed that it was a wee bit colder up here than tucked inside the forest. Thus, she found a spot on the ground, which was so much more solid and uncomfortable than the mattress he'd gifted her, and sat at first, not yet ready to give in to her sleepiness. After a moment and while a stiff breeze chilled her, Caitrin rearranged the plaid to cover her head.

"I ken you like your distance—from everything and everyone," Ross said, "but you might want to move closer. Warmer here near me."

Caitrin's response to this was a stiffening of her entire body. First, wrought by his accusation, that she was aloof. She knew it was true but didn't want him remarking on it. Next, at the very idea of huddling with him—what else could he mean?—to stay warm. Her reaction was short-lived, however; she recalled very well, and not for the first time at this moment, how warm had been the weight of him when he'd woken her the other night when he believed there might be some trouble.

Thankfully, pride was rarely greater than cold or fear or so many other things that were unpleasant.

Standing, she closed the distance between them, sitting immediately at his side. He was leaned against the trunk of a tree, his legs stretched out before him. Crossing her own legs beneath her, she recoiled slightly when her knee inadvertently bumped his thigh and then held herself very still.

And she waited.

"It is not any warmer here," she said after a bit, tightening the plaid around her, and unable to keep the disappointment from her voice.

Another chuckle—*my, but he was in a fine mood today*—and he said, "You need to be closer still. I'm no' a fire, putting heat out. You have to take it."

Caitrin inched closer, fearing a long night unable to sleep because shivering kept her awake. Boldly now, she let her bent knee lay against his leg. She jerked only a wee bit when his hand landed softly on her back. She stared straight ahead when he moved his hand, under the bottom of the tartan blanket, to rest solidly against the middle of her back.

"It's in the contact, lass," he said casually. "There've been times we were gone from Westcairn, outdoors in frigid conditions, parts of the army. We dinna care about nothing but warmth some nights, would lie one against another, rows and rows of us."

"But how awkward," she remarked, imagining this as a picture in her mind. True, she and Mary, upon their narrow bed at the Lornes' house, had often cuddled together for warmth. She hadn't ever imagined that men might do the same.

"Aye, but we were sure that freezing to death might be more unpleasant. It's warm now, aye? Where my hand sets."

It was, deliciously so. Caitrin nodded. She scooched a wee bit closer but left off asking him to move his hand in circles around her cold back.

Of his own accord, he did, sliding his hand up and down a bit. Caitrin closed her eyes. The cold was forgotten for a while, all her attention given to the hand on her back.

Chapter Seven

Ross did not think he would have any trouble staying awake while on watch.

Not while Caitrin slept so peacefully, her head in his lap.

It hadn't started out that way. But several hours ago, she'd begun to doze, her head bobbing a bit.

"Canna sleep sitting up, no' for long," he'd said then.

She'd given in to her fatigue, had curled up on her side, her face close to his thigh. He'd moved his hand from her back to her shoulder. She had fallen asleep fairly quickly but had soon begun to shiver in her sleep. It took little effort for him to reach both hands around her and gently haul her closer, lifting her head onto his lap. She'd fussed only briefly, sleepily, until he'd chided, "Hush, it'll be warmer."

He would have combed his fingers through her hair or mayhap pushed the hair away from her forehead, but he'd chosen instead to arrange the plaid more generously over the top of her head. And thus she slept, soundlessly, only a slice of her profile available to his scrutiny. He kept his hand on her back again and availed himself to a leisurely look. This here, was a much better picture of Caitrin, what little the darkness showed him. In daylight, and always since he'd met her, there was a constant pinched look about her, as if she knew a physical pain. Aye, and she might, for what the world had shown her in only a couple of days.

But now, she was at peace. No lines furrowed her brow or sliced down between her eyes. Her lips were parted, her breathing slow and easy.

After a while of watching, in which time he learned nothing new but solidified his ongoing impression that she was truly captivating for her beauty, Ross leaned his head back and set his gaze out to the north, where those dim torches bathed the façade of Westcairn in a soft golden light.

Several hours later, but still a while before the dawn, Caitrin began to wake. Before she might have startled with any embarrassment for her position or even a fright for not recalling where she was, Ross said quietly, "Sleep on, lass. Still an hour before the sun will wake."

To his surprise, she relaxed and did not jerk away from him.

But she did not return to sleep. She pushed the plaid away from her face a bit and then let her hand sit on his thigh in front of her face.

"Why did the English seize Westcairn?" She asked after a few minutes, her voice a wee bit groggy.

He'd given that much thought, had already discussed with John and others about the why of it. "I imagine first, 'twas only opportunistic," he answered. "They may have only stumbled upon it. Westcairn provides no seaport to use it as a forward base for arms and men. Outside of the Highlands, it would no' be known to the English. It had to be simply happenstance: they discovered it and discerned the truth, that it was left depleted of the bulk of the army gone to fight. 'Tis the nature of the fighting beast, to take advantage of what they found."

"But what would their plans be?"

He shrugged a bit, having no sure idea of this answer, but said, "We were lately down to Caerlaverock, which the English seized for the second time in as many years. When they hold it, it's easier to subjugate the Scots all around it. That might be their hope here."

"And what if you cannot take it back?"

"That's no' an option, lass." He breathed sharply through his nose at the very idea, but explained further, "They can no' subjugate if they dinna ever come out from behind the wall. We'll be on them when they do. Won't get all of them at that time, but enough to then mount a siege against those that remain inside." Clearing his throat, he thought it prudent to add, "Caitrin, should it no' go our way, you keep with whoever remains. And you get on over to Blackwood keep and Gabriel Jamison. The others have this instruction as well."

Caitrin turned her head on his leg and looked up at him, regarding him with an anxious gaze. "Please do not die."

Ross smirked. "I dinna intend to."

It wasn't very long after that Martin approached them ready to take on the daylight shift in this location. By that time, Caitrin had given up on sleep and was sitting quietly at Ross's side. Ross exchanged a few words with the soldier before he escorted Caitrin away from the shelf of rock where they'd spent the night.

"If I had coin, I would give all of it for a bath," Caitrin said as Ross led her into the greater part of the forest.

Having taken note of her unkempt appearance over the last few days, Ross was heartened by this statement. She hadn't given up then. "We might be able to find you a bath," he said, skirting around the impossibly wide trunk of an ancient yew tree. "It'll no' be warm but it will surely wake all your senses."

"Tonight then?" She asked.

"Aye, I'll make that happen for you."

"You will sleep now?" She asked then. "Since you did not all night."

"I need but an hour or two," he said.

'You should rest inside the tent," she offered, "as I assume if not for me, it might have been your own."

"Dinna mind if I take you up on that, lass."

They passed the last of the dense trees and stepped into the relatively sparser woodland of Little Westcairn. The camp was already alive with activity. A steady breeze had woken with the sun so that three smaller fires burned now, with people gathered around each of them, some cooking and some warming themselves.

Ross turned to face Caitrin when they'd reached her tent at the edge of the camp. He would find his sleep now so that he might get about his day before too many hours got away from him.

"I should see what Arailt requires of me today," she said, having spotted that man near one of the fires.

Ross nodded and neither of them moved, not him to enter the tent, nor her to seek out Arailt as she'd just said.

Finally, she said, "Thank you for...letting me go with you."

The pinched look had returned, which was a shame, but he thought it was not as severe as it had been in days past. In the shadows of the forest, the green of her eyes was less bright and more vibrant, being near to emerald in color. She blinked once and then nodded at him and even offered what he supposed was meant to be a wee smile of appreciation before she turned and made her way toward Arailt.

One day at a time, he thought. She would be fine.

HE WOKE SUDDENLY NOT two hours later, his mind churning with a plan that had come to him while he'd slept. Turning onto his back, he considered the canvas walls of the tent and a bit of sunlight—what little was allowed to shine all the way to the forest floor—dancing with the outline of leaves on those walls. He wasted not another moment but left the tent and meant to find John or any other officer about and immediately put into play his newly conceived idea to rout more of the English from Westcairn.

As much as Ross was excited for his plot, he couldn't help but be waylaid by the sight of Caitrin, hard at work with young Daniel. In another year or two, Daniel would begin his training with the army, and a few years after that, he would join them on any march into war. But for now, the scrawny lad sat and worked with Caitrin, dehairing the red deer hides that had been hunted yesterday evening. Likely, Arailt had put them to this task.

Ross almost chuckled for how animated her face was now. As indifferent and bland as she'd been since he'd met her, today was an entirely different story. She wrinkled her nose and held her face to the side, her lips pressed with some distaste for the chore. The hand that held the hide in place gave away much of her discomfort, as her pinkie and second last finger were lifted away from the skin, as if she didn't want to touch any more of it than was strictly necessary.

He ought to stop and give her some grief, for being so skittish about the chore. He wondered if she would smile if he did so, if he teased her. Game to have the question answered, he approached her where she sat on the ground with the hide draped over a split log. The log had been stripped of its bark and was about three feet long, the top of it nestled between her knees while she shaved away the hair with a knife that presumably was not too sharp to dig into the hide itself.

"I'm no' sure scrunching your face up like that makes it any more pleasant," Ross said when his shadow had fallen over her and she lifted her face to him.

Caitrin lifted the hand that held the knife and used her forearm to wipe her brow. "I'm not sure there is anything in the world that would make this more pleasant."

Daniel, about the same chore in the same position, lifted his brown eyes to Ross and snickered a bit, equally as distressed as Caitrin it seemed.

"But a fine service you give," Ross said. "We need the arrows, more than what we have now."

Caitrin nodded and set her hand back down on the hide. Daniel might have rolled his eyes, Ross could not be sure.

"Arailt asked that we scour the immediate woods, hopeful we might come upon more dead critters whose hides he can boil for the glue."

"Aye, and feathers," said Daniel. "We're to collect any feathers we see."

"Won't be easy to find those, only waiting on you," Ross supposed. "I'll send Gideon and some lads out hunting geese, but it will no' be easy without the hawks and falcons, which are housed at Westcairn. And I'll have the entire army busy for the next few hours, so it'll have to wait until this evening."

"We might get lucky, come upon a carcass," Caitrin supposed.

Ross grinned. "More plucking, lass. Careful what you wish for."

She smiled at this.

Finally, a smile. One that was distracting for all its glory and then so very appealing as it showed her defenses were lowered, melted away.

He had no other reason to be here, but then didn't want to leave. He wanted to see another smile, wouldn't mind at all if he was somehow the cause of it. But he did have his own work to do.

"Stay close today, Caitrin," he instructed, "and dinna go off alone."

She nodded, her hands unmoving yet. He turned and left and thought she might be watching him walk away. He almost grinned again, thinking of all the times he'd watched her, and she must have known it. Was this what it felt like? That places on your back burned where surely that attentive gaze was set?

His plan, the idea that had woken him, was simple and when presented to his officers, they agreed it held much appeal.

"We only need to start a large fire, far away from Little Westcairn, but within sight of the keep. Use green wood to produce a good smoke, and then wait. They'll send out a unit to investigate—I ken we would if that were us on the wall—and we'll take them down. We might get lucky, and they'll send another group to check on the first. And we'll take them out as well."

John always wanted greater particulars, was a genius at seeing the whole picture. "Aye, naught but a dozen men round that fire for them to find, but with several more in the immediate area," he said. "We'll need spotters to watch for the number they send in response."

"And I want an entire unit positioned between where we set the trap and Little Westcairn," Ross said.

Samuel advised, "Set up an arc-ed perimeter, two dozen, north to south between this," he angled his head to the camp directly behind him, "and that, where we set up."

"I'd like to see archers arranged along that ridge above the glen," Ross added. "They'd have a clear view to the keep, catch any trying to flee back that way. How many arrows have we?" He asked, knowing that answer would not please him, but unwilling to wait for what more might be produced as soon as tomorrow, or the day after if they struggled to find proper feathers. They could make do with naked arrows in close range, but not for what he had planned today or going forward.

"Forty-three, last count," said Coll, one of the archers.

"Use them wisely," he cautioned.

They spent another half an hour, etching markings in a cleared-off space of the forest floor and then assigning all the ninety-three soldiers to four different units that would assume the designated positions.

With one last measuring glance at John, who gave a nod, believing it a sound plan, they broke off and departed Little Westcairn on horseback, intent on moving today's events far away from the campsite.

"May the gods and the odds forever be in your favor," Samuel said, as he often did, as they rode off.

NOTHING WENT AS EXPECTED, which meant that little could progress as planned. First, the number of English dispatched from the castle when the smoke that had burned for an hour was finally noticed was far greater than they might have expected. This gave Ross pause, though not for the coming battle but for what numbers in total must be contained behind the wall, if they dared to send out so many right now. Next, the fifty to sixty mounted men they did send out broke off into two groups, obviously with some intent to come upon the fire-makers from two sides.

All was not lost though, and these things were good to know. It was no green officer in charge of the regiment at Westcairn, then; whoever led these men and controlled the keep was gifted with a fair mind for strategy, and not so simple that he would walk straight into any trap.

As they'd specifically placed the luring fire outside the reach of English archers on the wall, at least they hadn't that to contend with. From his present position above the glen, where he'd kept watch last night, Ross counted only a dozen bows strung over shoulders in that marching line of Englishmen. When the gates closed behind those soldiers, Ross left the glen and raced his destrier to his next position with the men hiding in the trees just outside those pretending only to laze around the fire. He gave notice to each unit he passed, of the numbers coming at them and that they'd split in two.

To his chagrin, the English did not—as he and his men supposed—only approach the fire makers, intent on harassing them to depart. They came rushing in at full speed, swords drawn, and two Kildare soldiers were impaled by English steel before they'd even unsheathed their own weapons.

Cursing savagely, Ross gave the call to charge and then all hell broke loose.

A POWERFULLY BUILT golden eagle left its eyrie atop a rocky cliff and soared over its territory, south of the Kildare keep, over the hills and glens and forest it had claimed as its own two decades ago. If any person were gifted with her view, they'd have witnessed the clash of swords and bodies around that fire with the dense plumes of gray smoke. West of that, a quarter mile or so, a unit of English soldiers charged at the line of Kildare men, spread out in the shape of a sickle with twenty to thirty feet between one man and the next. The English bowmen picked off three Kildare men, who dropped immediately from their saddles, creating a gaping and perilous hole in their defensive formation. Others in that line were engaged, unable to give chase to the dozen Englishmen who slipped through the break and headed toward Little Westcairn. And while the Kildare laird led his men to rout the enemy who'd come to see about a fire, and another part of his army put up a resolute resistance to keep the majority of their line intact, the residents of Little Westcairn inside the forest were taken by surprise by a menacing horde thrashing into their quiet little camp.

Outside the camp, but close yet, thought to be safe, Agnes Nesch and her children were collecting whatever chestnuts and hazelnuts the squirrels and chipmunks might have missed. Agnes was bent and plucking two hidden chestnuts from beneath the leaves, admonishing her oldest daughter who held her smallest bairn to move into the shade, when she heard the godawful noise of a bloodcurdling scream. Her mother's instinct was swift and powerful, her heart constricting. In the next few seconds, she herded her brood to take cover behind an outcropping of rock and brush. Claiming the babe from her daughter, she untied the laces of her bodice and immediately put him to her breast so that he made no cry.

Thirteen Englishmen escaped the trap set near the fire. Fleeing for their lives, they did not turn to make their retreat in the direction of the keep but went southwest. It was the only avenue available to those who wanted out rather than staying to engage when they were clearly outnumbered at this location. At the edge of the Rosyth forest, they turned east along the river, fearful of encountering any more heathen Scots if they dared to go west. Eventually, they would have to cut through the forest if they wished to return to the keep they'd stolen while it was still daylight. But for now, they would remain in the open so that they could not be ambushed again.

SOUTH OF LITTLE WESTCAIRN, in the direction given by Arailt—"away from what trouble the laird and his army will beget in the northwest," the man had said—Caitrin and Daniel searched for hides and feathers, the young lad vocal in his disappointment for what little of the latter they'd found thus far and the very need of the former. Oliver did not accompany them as he had previously, as he was needed elsewhere, hence Arailt's additional caution to not stray too far.

"I dinna ken why he wants so many skins," Daniel said. "The red deer hide we cleaned is big, should make enough glue."

"I know nothing of glue-making," Caitrin said. She understood the process, that the hide and tissue were boiled and reduced to a sticky, gooey mess, but she wasn't sure how much was needed to produce enough glue for the fletching of feathers on the arrow shafts. "I'm only concerned that we might be asked to dehair anything we find."

They'd exited the forest at the south end and walked now in the heather moorland, where Arailt assured her they would have better luck finding feathers. The view was spectacular, the sloping landscape covered in various shades of purple over so many rolling hills of heather and cotton grass and mosses.

Daniel threw a sideways grin at her. "Mayhap all we'll find today is feathers."

Caitrin smiled as well. "I think you might be right." She glanced back from whence they'd come, making sure they did not stray too far. Her gaze was drawn to the cloudy smoke in the distance, to the north and west, which they had noticed here and there over the last hour.

Daniel had earlier enlightened her. "They're going to draw them out, some of the English."

To kill them, she knew, having heard some of the discussions that had taken place this morning.

More destruction, more lives gone. She cared not one whit for the lives of those Englishmen, but couldn't imagine there was ever a fight, large or small, in which every one of the Kildare men would or could escape wholly unscathed.

Daniel cried out, startling Caitrin until she jerked around to see that his exclamation had been one of joy and that he held up each of his scrawny arms, showing that he'd found two stray feathers. They looked to be from a black grouse and Caitrin didn't have the heart to tell the lad that Arailt would likely discount them as ineffectual or wholly unusable.

"Is there a stream or loch nearby?" She asked instead. "We might have better luck finding goose feathers. Arailt said those are preferred."

Daniel was not dejected by her vague dismissal of his find. Instead, his eyes lit up and he answered, "The river is just up ahead, the big one where we fish the better trout. There's always geese and ducks around there."

"Where is that?"

His answer was naught but a wave of his hand as he took off further down the heath strewn hill. Watching him run, she then noticed the loch and the river that fed it, in the landscape beyond his silhouette, where two mountain ranges seemed to dip low into the earth to make a groove for the river.

She enjoyed Daniel's company. The lad was uncomplicated, not sullied by fear or weighted down with his own misfortune—though he was an orphan as well, she'd learned yesterday. His parents were not unknown as they'd been denizens of the once great Westcairn, but they were unremembered by the boy as he'd been but a babe when they were lost. She did not pressure the lad to relate the circumstances and then was not encumbered with any desire to share her own tale, to commiserate with him. But she enjoyed him nonetheless, as he demanded little of her and did not stare at her with any emotion she wasn't sure what to do with.

She lifted her skirt and gave chase, not wanting him to get too far ahead. Running was pleasant when one was not being chased, Caitrin thought. There was a joy in how carefree it was, scampering along while her mind was nearly unencumbered.

When she heard the faint drumming of hoofbeats in the distance, she stopped and turned, her expression untroubled, expecting to see Ross and his men mayhap. The sound grew louder, closer, becoming a rhythmic stomping upon the packed earth.

Caitrin's lips parted when a dozen or more English soldiers crested the top of the hill from the west, angling downward and toward her. She did not move right away, watching the top of that hill a bit longer, waiting for Ross or some of his men to reveal themselves, giving chase to this enemy.

No other riders came into view and while her heart dropped like a weighted stone into her stomach, she turned and found Daniel, further down the slope, as frozen as she'd been, staring at the coming riders.

"Run!" She cried, finally able to do that herself. Her previous gambol down the hill was yet again a race for her life. "Run, Daniel!" She hollered louder and finally the boy moved, continuing in the same direction as she, well ahead of her, toward the river.

At this point, she didn't know that disbelief was part of this experience. Nothing shocked her anymore. The world was mean and angry, and it might just always be like this from now on. She wondered why she bothered to run, when death might prove easier. But run she did, keeping her gaze on Daniel's progress ahead of her, making better time, getting further away than she.

"Keep running! Don't look back!" She called when she knew they were gaining on her.

Damn them all to hell anyway.

Chapter Eight

They galloped at a breakneck speed across the glen between them and the forest, as fast as the sun and clouds moved over the landscape. None of them reduced their speed, even as they burst into the tall birch and pines. Ross's heart raced with dread over what tragedy he may have sent ahead of them—the English into Little Westcairn. Admittedly, his foremost thought was for Caitrin. He could only hope she'd stayed close as he'd advised, and that what men he'd left to defend their temporary site could at least hold them off until Ross and his unit arrived.

The only ones found inside Little Westcairn were those injured or dead. The carnage, as had been the camp itself, was widespread. The tent Caitrin had used looked to have been trampled by a swiftly moving animal, the stakes and rope yanked from the ground, lying useless upon the flattened canvas. Caitrin was nowhere to be found.

Finding Arailt on his back, blood spurting from his temple and neck, Ross leapt off his steed before it had come to a halt.

Arailt cursed and pushed impatiently at Ross's hands when he tried to sit him up. "I'm all right, leave it. The lass and Daniel are out on the moorland." He glanced at others gathered round him. "Agnes and her children are that way," he pointed in another direction.

Straightening, Ross called out commands, sending half the men with John toward Agnes and her family while he and Samuel led the party toward the moors.

They reached the rim of the forest in under two minutes and drew up at the top of the hill to survey the wide open vista, all the way down to the river.

"There!" Ross shouted and pointed, to the swath of a flattened grass, running on an angle diagonal toward the water.

How many times had he run or ridden over this moorland? Hundreds? More maybe, but never before with this rigid fierceness about him, that was half-rage and half-regret. She deserved better. And now this. Would he ever do right by her?

They raced on, following the trail left behind until they reached the boggy banks of the river, where the tracks were easier to follow. At some point, the trail moved away from the river, heading up the incline again to where it leveled out into a flat ridge that would only climb higher, above the forest even.

They meant to go up through the mountains to return to Westcairn, Ross realized.

Samuel drew up so sharply as to bring everyone to a halt just before they might have cleared the last hillock before the flatlands, a ground swell no taller than a man. Before he'd gained the top of the knoll, but when he was elevated enough to see beyond it, he stopped, holding up his hand and dancing his steed swiftly to the left and back down. All the other horses and riders followed suit.

"Just ahead," Samuel said, his voice steady but not too loud. "Dozen or more. She's there."

Ross inclined his head to Gideon and three more on his right. "Get to the trees on the opposite side of the meadow. Wait for us."

And with that, those that remained with Ross, another fifteen or so, moved further left and into the cover of the woodland, walking parallel now with those English who thought they were returning to Westcairn.

He spotted Caitrin's hair first, the bright golden locks shiny under the midday sun. In the midst of a dozen English soldiers.

She'd been stripped of the faded blue léine, covered now only in her sleeveless linen kirtle—the one Ross had torn already to make a bandage for her—which clung to her legs and revealed several cuts and scrapes about her bare arms. Her hands were tied together in front of her, the length of that rope extended to a mounted man, who tugged her along. Ross could not be sure but thought that she wore only one shoe. They taunted her, the Englishmen, this known only by the ribald laughter and the leering on several pale English faces.

"They should no' die easily," Samuel said, riding quietly alongside Ross.

"But die they will," he vowed. "Idgy, Martin, Alain—come," Ross said and then instructed, "Move on ahead, charge from the front. We need to come at them from all sides so that they dinna ken where to look."

The three men kicked their steeds into a fast trot to move along. They knew well enough as the forward team to make noise when they struck so that the other positions knew then to move as well.

Samuel said to Ross, "Dinna charge blindly. Wait for them to get into position if you want her to live."

Ross nodded. He understood they would use her against them if they were given the opportunity.

"Wait," Samuel cautioned again, sternly now, knowing well Ross's rage.

"Aye," Ross said through clenched teeth.

Through the trees, Ross's gaze never left Caitrin. He bared his teeth when he saw the man holding the rope was playing a little game, letting the rope go slack and then giving it a good yank to see if he could knock her off her feet. Twice she was jerked forward but managed to stay on her feet. The third time, the man wrenched the rope with greater force and this time, Caitrin was pulled so far forward that she fell on her front, her face smacking against her arms, her chest meeting the ground hard.

"Hold," Samuel's deep voice warned Ross.

He did, though it pained him greatly. He flexed his hand on his sword, wanting Idgy's call to be now.

It took as much as three to four minutes more than Ross had anticipated, but finally, just as Caitrin got to her feet amid the cackling and howling Englishmen, he heard the savage Kildare cry ringing out from the north end of the glen. Ross did not wait to see those men actually appear on the field but kneed his destrier relentlessly until the beast flew out of the woods and raced toward Caitrin.

And finally something played out as imagined and arranged. The English did not know where to defend, turning their steeds in circles as they faced an assault from three different directions, and by a party twice their size. Their circle shrank but the Scotsmen came so quickly that not one thought quickly enough to make use of their own captive to save themselves.

He thought it only dumb luck and not exactly a gift from the gods that the one who held the rope faced his direction and thus saw Ross rushing at him at a tremendous speed and with a deep-throated war cry. It would be the last thing he saw or knew in this life. Ross took note that Caitrin was yet inside a circle made by the English, but as much as twenty feet away from any mounted man. The man's arm trembled slightly as he lifted his sword, too stunned to turn and flee even. His wide eyes gave away both his fright and his realization that death had come for him. Before his war horse reached the head of the foe's steed, Ross drew on the reins and settled his destrier to a two-beat canter, raising his sword and swinging at the same time the enemy did. The minute their swords crossed and clanged, Ross kneed his horse to move swiftly, turning him sharply that he was now directly behind the Englishman, on his left, facing the same direction. His destrier knew to keep on his flank. There was no defense now, the Englishman's sword in his right hand, so that Ross and his horse met with the rump of the enemy's. Ross was able to strike his sword into the man's back, in that bare spot of the arm hole in the chain mail. He was toppled off his horse with the force of the blow.

The rest of the scene was chaos, as greater sword fights took place between Ross's men and the rest of the English. Trusting his men and their prowess, Ross vaulted from his destrier and dropped to his knees at Caitrin's side, using the bloody tip of his blade to slice away the rope that had tethered her to the now-dead Englishman. No sooner had he done this than a body landed almost on top of him. He rose to his full height and turned to stab at this one who been shoved from his horse, striking him in the cheek with his blade, the only part of him not covered in the protective mail.

As sometimes happened, the fighting ceased all at once, though the Kildare men continued to circle around the dead Englishmen. Ross surveyed the carnage, immediately taking stock of the condition of his men. It looked as if only Idgy and Gideon suffered wounds, but neither man had been unseated and still wore their brutal war miens that Ross was assured they were not life-threatening.

A noise turned him around again, the unmistakable sound of a sword striking against the metal of chain mail, *thwack, thwack, thwack.*

"*Jesu,*" someone breathed gruffly.

"Bluidy hell!" Ross cursed, and charged at Caitrin, who'd recovered the dropped sword of some dead man and was now standing above the one who'd yanked at the rope, using two hands to thrust the sword at his chest again and again and again. It barely pierced his armor, her weak strikes, and she sobbed with every thrust.

Ross rushed her from behind, wrapping both arms around her, sliding his hands along her bare arms until he touched the hilt. Her arms went limp in mid-strike, and he easily assumed the weapon from her and tossed it away. A second later, while he turned her away from the dead man and into his arms, her entire body wilted. She sagged against him, her forehead fallen against his chest. He stood still for a moment, holding her, until he thought she might fall to the ground, and then he scooped her up in his arms and turned to find his steed, which Samuel hurried to bring forward for him.

Not any man, Ross included, wore a plaid into battle so that he was sorry he had nothing to wrap her in. She was light and small in his embrace and while Samuel held the destrier still,

Ross mounted and settled her in front of him. She was limp and possibly incoherent, her cheek now leaned against his leather breastplate. Her legs dangled over his right thigh, and he saw that, indeed, she wore only one shoe.

They trotted back to Little Westcairn, needing to assess and realize the totality of today's efforts, and what, if anything, still progressed. His countenance grim, Ross hoped to God it was done for now. He couldn't send his men out to wage war and not lead them; he never had before. But then, he knew there was no way he could leave her now.

LITTLE WESTCAIRN WAS no more.

It was believed that as many as half a dozen Englishmen might have survived the day's battles, might have returned to Westcairn and have given notice of the location, so that everything was packed up and carted deeper into in the forest, almost another mile further from the Kildare keep. This seemed an unlikely and unnerving blow to some, as if they were moving in the wrong direction.

Still, there was some consolation to be had, that the Kildare army had managed to reduce the English numbers with so large a chunk dispatched today. As the hundred-plus Kildare coterie trudged quietly through the woods, there was some discussion that over the last week, they might have by now eliminated as many as thirty to forty of the enemy, thus making a storming or a siege of Westcairn more favorable at this time.

She'd found Daniel at old Little Westcairn, dripping wet still from the plunge he'd taken in the river to escape, and stumbled to get to him, to embrace him. She didn't care that she was garbed so inappropriately but hugged the boy fiercely. His arms were tight around her as well and they stayed like that for many seconds, until Caitrin opened her eyes and noticed the bodies of two of Westcairn's own, including old Oswald, who'd helped Arailt with fashioning the arrows. Her shoulders shook then with fresh sobs, but she was forced to release Daniel when Ross called to her. They needed to leave.

Seated with Ross atop his big black horse, Caitrin stared straight ahead but saw nothing. She was once again wrapped in a huge Kildare plaid, to conceal her state of undress, as they'd not taken the time to find her a léine to don but had instead seen to moving the camp quickly.

There was more discussion about the day's events, with John once more highlighting the success, that they'd slain so many English. "It's still a victory," John said with quiet emphasis.

"Except that they ken we're here," Samuel reminded them.

"The element of surprise would only ever work in our favor for a few minutes at best," Ross stated.

His voice was firm, but it lacked the ring of confidence she was accustomed to hearing. He shifted his arm, cradling Caitrin more securely in his embrace upon his big black steed. Gently, he tucked the edge of yet another borrowed plaid more firmly between his chest and her shoulder, covering her arm which was exposed when the plaid had slipped away. "We might have rushed the gates—and might still if we can get lucky—but that'll only put so many men inside."

"Always comes down to the numbers," John said, concurring. "We can make do, likely prevail, with less, but no' with one hundred less, and with us on the wrong side of the gate."

Caitrin listened with only half an ear, processing little, caring about even less.

Admittedly, she was pathetic, but right now she just did not care. These people walking and riding alongside them had suffered just as much as she but acknowledging this did not imbue her with any more interest in what they did or what they said or even where they went. She sat sluggishly in Ross's arms and stared straight ahead. And when they decided upon a location for their next camp, Caitrin sat huddled in the plaid on the hard ground while Ross erected the canvas tent once more. Again, any tents or little claims to land that were eked out by individuals or groups were arranged with a bit of distance between them. When it was done, he seemed only to wait, to see what she might do. Without a word, she crawled into the tent and closed her eyes, trying to bring something to mind—anything—that was beautiful and peaceful, tried to focus on something that had ever brought her joy.

The image of Ross came to her, but she discarded it. He was not joy, he was only her protector at the moment, nothing more. She slept after a while and when she woke it was dark.

Rolling onto her back, she listened to the sounds around her but heard little more than forest noises: a wispy crunching of leaves under the foot of some small creature; the nocturnal warbler's evening song; the drawn-out hoot of a tawny owl, calling for a mate.

And then it was quiet for a while. She couldn't say for how long, only that she just noticed it now. This unnerved her, that the natural denizens of the forest quieted all at once. So then came the chest-tightening unease, the same that had gripped her more in the last week than she'd known in all her life. And she might have cried for how pitiful she was, too afraid to be alone, too afraid to know or find out if she actually were, but that she hadn't any tears left or the energy to expend on them.

"Ross?" Her voice was naught but a croak, with barely any volume. Suddenly the haven of her tiny tent was too small, and too dark, and she didn't like that she couldn't see anything, what went on just outside. Jerking up to a sitting position, she stared at the front flap for a moment before bravely whipping it back.

"Caitrin?"

Relief was instant, came as soon as she recognized his voice. But then her shoulders slumped once more. She was so tired of being afraid.

Clearing her throat, she said in shaky voice, "All the noise stopped, the critters and...I thought someone was coming. It's too dark in here. I feel as if I can't breathe, as if the walls are closing in on me. I'm afraid to close my eyes and afraid to keep them open and—"

"There it is again, the birdsong. All is well." He was closer now, on his haunches near the open flap. "Tell me what you want."

Her voice broke yet more. "I don't know."

Silence reigned for several long seconds until he spoke again. "Move over."

She did, without hesitation, and Ross crawled inside the tent. Mayhap this is what she wanted then, that the impropriety of it didn't alarm her. He laid his sword on the right side of the mattress, which took up almost all the ground space inside the tent. He stretched out on his back and laid his arm across the other side, inviting, "C'mon. You'll sleep well this night, I promise."

It was unseemly, the very idea, and yet a part of her challenged, *what does it matter?* And so she laid down on his arm, which he immediately folded to bring her into his chest.

Oh, and this was heaven, warm and safe and perfect.

And yet, "I don't want to only feel safe when I'm with you."

"Aye, but the world is conspiring against you in that regard just now. One day at a time, lass."

"Tell me to get over it. Tell me to be stronger."

"You will, when you're ready."

"But I would, sooner, if instructed to do so."

"You canna force it, would only be false."

She relaxed then, surprised that she was still awake at all when she was bone-weary and heart-sore. Oh, but she was wonderfully warm, the length of her greedily accepting all the heat from his long frame. As a matter of comfort, she held her arms folded against her chest, her hands balled into fists. But then, in an effort to relax, she uncurled the fingers of her left hand and carefully laid them out against the side of his chest, near where her face was tucked into his shoulder.

She woke at some point when it was still dark. She knew no fear but did need a moment to understand where she was, to recall that Ross was with her inside the tent. Wrapped in both the heavy wool Kildare plaid and then Ross's arms, she was surprised to find that she was uncomfortably warm. She pushed a bit away from his shoulder, hoping to give herself breathing space.

He murmured something, sounding only half asleep.

And when she settled herself on her side, facing him, with only inches between them, he did the same.

His blue eyes were glittery dark orbs in the shadows, the only thing that moved until his hand did. He reached out and ran his finger over her brow and temple, moving a lock of hair away from her face, tucking it behind her ear. His hand skimmed downward, moving between them, finding her hand near her chest. He folded his fingers around hers and let them sit between them before closing his eyes again.

Caitrin sighed drowsily and closed her eyes as well. She fell asleep once more, holding Ross's hand this time.

AGNES NESCH WAS SOMETHING else. Caitrin had several times over the last few days watched the woman come and go, and labor with this or that, and wrangle her many bairns—to eat, to wash, to get about some chore. She struggled, Caitrin thought, keeping her voice to a hushed or hissed whisper, whatever the occasion needed, when she might have preferred a greater volume. Caitrin assumed that about her, that she was under normal circumstances—when not hiding in the forest—a gregarious person who was often loud. Sometimes her always-red cheeks would puff out, her lips clamped, to keep herself quiet. It pained her and to some degree, amused Caitrin. She was loud in other regards as well, that she was a constant presence around the center of the camp, if there were such a thing, involved in some way with almost everything that went on. Nosy, some might say, but well-intentioned mostly, Caitrin surmised before today. Here and there, she'd given a few inquisitive looks in Caitrin's direction. Previously Caitrin had thought it wouldn't have taken much, naught but a slight returned smile when she'd met Agnes's gaze that would have brought the woman to her side, filled with questions and then, whatever answers Caitrin might have sought.

Presently, Agnes Nesch carried one misbegotten and rumpled leather shoe, chasing around a softly giggling child of four or five, whose bum flashed every so often when his tunic floated about him, showing he wore nothing else. His mother might only be happy to attach a second shoe to that bare foot, but the bairn seemed only content to confound his mother.

Caitrin's view of these goings-on was blocked when Ross came to stand in front of her, where she sat on a thick fallen tree trunk near the tent. She'd waited this morning, as he'd advised, saying he would see what might be done about outfitting her, as her lone léine—not even hers, but borrowed from Eskaline—was lost to her now.

Tipping her head back on her neck, she met his gaze first, before she considered what he delivered to her. As ever, his eyes were a startling blue, not any more striking inside the vibrant colors of the forest, but different than how they might appear in the glistening sunshine of an open field.

Strangely, it had not been awkward to wake next to him inside the tent lighted by a golden morning sun, their hands still entwined. Maybe for a moment, until he'd said, "A good night's sleep, aye?"

Yes, it had been.

"Went back to the village, lass," he said now, "this was all I could find." A hint of a grimace tainted his features.

Reaching a hand out from inside the plaid blanket, she accepted his offer, shrugging a bit, "It will be fine." She didn't dare let her mind wander to whom this might have belonged, knowing that if he'd recovered it, the owner was likely dead. She most certainly did not entertain the dreadful possibility that the previous owner might have been wearing it when Ross confiscated it.

"Thank you." Briefly, she investigated the single, worn shoe that sat atop the pile of clothing. Curious, she sent a quizzical glance up to Ross.

"That was all to be found," he said. "Thankfully, it was the left shoe, which you need."

She mulled over his use of thankfully, wondering if that actually applied to anything anymore.

"Aye and I promised you a bath," he said next, "but that will have to wait until this evening. I dinna think you want to be soaking in the loch during the day."

He was very thoughtful. "I would not want to do that. This evening will be fine."

"And I've brought you this," he said, pulling a short-handled knife from his leather belt. The blade was short as well. Someone's eating knife, then. Ross flipped it in his hand, offering the handle to her. "It's for protection, Caitrin, though I suppose it might be useful for other things as well."

"I...I do not know how to use it for that purpose."

"Slash and strike are all you need to ken. Aim for the neck, stab at a hand reaching for you, go wild with it. As long as you dinna drop it, it's a decent weapon."

With a stiff nod, she folded the small dagger inside the plaid.

"I canna be around the camp today," he informed her with some regret. "I've got—"

"I'll be fine," she surprised him by saying. Clearing her throat, having only formed the idea in the last little bit, she announced, "I was thinking I would...introduce myself to Agnes, see what help I might be to her. She appears to be weighted down with work...and other things."

He didn't smile, but it looked as if he wanted to. His mouth moved, anyway, and she brought her gaze there. But then she knew he was watching her, and she forced her attention to his blue eyes again. Ross's stares never seemed so bold as they did thoughtful; he was only ever measuring her, she always thought. Mayhap the mystery behind his gaze was what beckoned her now, now that she truly considered what he might see when he stared, what he might think. Whatever it was, there was just now some irresistible pull toward him, that she could not take her gaze from him. After a week of horror and upheaval, she was frankly shocked that she felt anything at all. But the sensation—what that steady gaze of his did to her—intrigued her more than any other thing ever had.

"It's a good plan, lass."

Releasing her breath, the spell broken, Caitrin nodded. "Yes."

And yet he hesitated, stood in front of her still, that Caitrin stood, clutching both the plaid and the garments and the lone shoe to her, and said again, "I'll be fine, Ross."

Before she might have moved to change into this new léine and kirtle, she spied Daniel at the edge of the camp, engaged in a mock sword fight with another lad about his age, both wielding long and straight twigs, thrusting and parrying. Each boy laughed and goaded and let loose triumphant cries when occasioned.

She gave all her regard to Daniel, looking for any evidence of the ordeal he'd suffered only yesterday, and sighed when she found none.

CAITRIN DONNED THE frock Ross had found for her, appreciative that he'd also discovered and provided a fresh, long-sleeved kirtle of soft linen. The outer léine was of a heavier wool, not as soft as the shift, but of a pleasing burgundy color. It was again too large for her, but it was clean and warm, and she could find no fault with it. The shoe was not so fine as the gown, relatively speaking, and it was very large on her foot, but she was able to fit it better by tying the laces tight. She braided her hair and drew a deep breath, marching across the lone spot of sun in this new site, over to where Agnes sat near a trio of small tents.

Agnes carried a robust figure and Caitrin had noticed that she was as quick to smile as she was to frown. Her laugh was more an unrestrained cackle and any scolding of her bairns was usually delivered in a tone that suggested even she was weary of hollering at them. She regularly wore an apron tied around her neck with more strings secured around her ample middle, and her hair was thick and choppy and the exact color of a worn leather saddle though not nearly as smooth.

"Good morrow," Caitrin said when she stood in front of the woman, who was perched on a standing stump of a tree and plucked all the gray feathers from a capercaillie sitting on the apron in her lap.

"Aye and I was wondering how long it'd take for ye to find your way over," said Agnes. While the words themselves suggested some annoyance for the days that had passed until now, the look about her was not harsh. "Are ye needing something then?"

"No. I thought I might introduce myself and see what you might need," Caitrin told her, much the same as she'd said to Ross this morning.

And now the woman grinned, showing a mouthful of crooked and crowded teeth. "Verra good. And yer the lass, Caitrin, I hear. And I am Agnes and what are ye wanting to help with?"

"I'm not sure, whatever you might require, wherever I might be useful."

"Aye, and I like that," Agnes said with a chortle, "and is there no' plenty to get at. But first, sit a spell with me while I finish with this beast. We'll catch up a wee bit."

As there was no other stump or seat, Caitrin sat on the ground. She picked up one of the scattered feathers, wondering if it might be suitable for the fletching on the arrows.

As if reading her mind, Agnes said, "Nae, they're too weak. Arailt said they'll no' provide any stability in flight, certainly no' for distance."

"That is a shame then, as we had little luck finding any others."

"Aye, and after the fright of yesterday, I'd no' be thinking you'll be allowed to step foot outside camp again."

"Allowed?" Was she to be a prisoner? Not that she had any ambition or would be so brave to navigate the surrounding area by herself, but she should be able to, if she chose.

Agnes cackled at this. "Allowed. Persuaded. Whatever ye want to label it. The laird'll no' be so lenient again. I saw that look, when he carried ye back. Crazed with the rage, and him so even-keeled all the time." Agnes's brows were naturally arched, with plenty of space between her lid and the brow itself. She lifted them higher now, into the middle of her forehead and grinned at Caitrin. "Ye dinna want to cause him fits, aye? Raise anything else, lass, but no' his protective ire!" With this, Agnes's whole body shook with the rumble of her attendant, hearty chuckle.

Caitrin wasn't sure what to understand from this but had already decided she did not want to be the topic in any conversation. "But what about you, Agnes? You have several children, but...was your husband lost when the keep was seized?"

She snorted. It was more comical than disdainful, but then her response was just the opposite. "That one, he done himself in more than a year ago, 'fore Willie was birthed. Too drunk, too stupid to get out of his own way. Chasing sheep along the cliffs—soused, by my imagining. So, over he goes, with seven woolly beasts, and I dinna have the time—nor the heart—to mourn him. Get on just fine by myself."

Oh, my.

"Nae, I'm no' so cold-hearted as what yer face is saying yer thinking. I only ken fairly soon into the marriage that he was no' ever going to be any use to me—though he did give me some nice bairns. So then I canna mourn what I've no' lost, aye?"

Feeling as if some response—approval, mayhap—was expected of her, Caitrin judged kindly, "The practical sort."

"Aye, and I'll spare the emotion to those deserving of it and no' regret what can't be undone."

Agnes stared pointedly at Caitrin as she said this, her fingers only blindly plucking at the feathers for a few seconds that Caitrin understood she might be giving a lecture, that she was to draw some enlightenment from her words.

Caitrin couldn't help but like her, how her moods and expressions changed so easily, how quick she was to laugh.

She spent the day with Agnes, eventually meeting all of her five children. Marion, Rachel, and Mildred were the oldest, twelve, eleven, and seven years-old, respectively. The youngest were Isaac, the imp who liked to have his mother chase him, and then the babe, Willie. The lasses were sweet, well-behaved but a little mischievous when it pleased them, Caitrin decided, as quick to laugh as their mam. When her children were near, Agnes did a lot of barking, though the lasses needed little guidance or even reminders to get about their chores.

"Dinna leave the bucket there."

"Nae, dinna let him chew on that."

"Aye now, wipe his face."

"Get on then, take this off to Hamish now, he'll stew it slow in the pot."

They took it all in stride, accustomed to their mam, how she chattered continuously.

Chapter Nine

Of course he understood he should feel no guilt for having abandoned Caitrin yet again today. He felt no such thing about any other Kildare person. In fact, he was not abandoning her but seeing to the safety of her. And others.

He was still angry at himself for the disaster that was yesterday. All of it. He knew better than to underestimate an enemy, knew better than to assume things he just could not know. It would not happen again. And he would not dwell on it and be made incompetent by second-guessing himself.

Aye, they would remain on the offensive, stripping away at that English little by little until they were in a position to wage a larger war against the thieves of Westcairn. Despite the tragedy of yesterday—Caitrin's near abduction and losing seven men in all the chaos—he did not discount the greater losses of the English. They counted thirty-seven bodies around all the battle sites. True, they came at a price, but those were numbers that were hard to ignore, and to a degree, not celebrate.

With sturdy ropes and a provoking intent, they dragged all the bodies of the English to a place inside the glen before Westcairn, making no effort to not be seen. Just the opposite. It could not be unseen or unrealized that they'd stripped the dead English of anything of value, including their weapons, chain mail, and helms; in some cases, even their fine leather boots had been pilfered. When the last of the corpses had been tossed into the pile, Ross made a show of lighting a torch on a long pike and holding it up for all those on the wall of Westcairn to see. John and Idgy and Gideon did the same. They held them aloft for several seconds before Ross struck his flame between two bodies, into the slices of pine bark they'd added to the pyre, riddled with the flammable pine resin. The huge bonfire was aflame in seconds.

He might have preferred to let these bodies rot where they'd been felled, but for the problems that might arise from such neglect, enticing wild animals or even lowly but diseased critters. Ross kept his gaze on the wall but discerned little reaction to the burning of their fallen comrades. One man there lifted his sword and shook it with rage, but that was all.

When they were assured that the fire was spread evenly and would continue to burn for some time, consuming all but bone in the end, Ross turned his steed toward the forest. Next they needed to bury their own. This was done privately, deep inside the forest, attended only by Ross and his soldiers. The regular folks of Westcairn need not be burdened with this.

They would keep that constant vigil on the gates of Westcairn from the ridge above the glen that separated the keep from the forest. Ross didn't imagine the gate would open and show a large force exiting the keep, sent out to find them. Those English knew they were out here now and might have some idea of the Kildare numbers. But if they came, they'd use the smaller, not easily accessible gate at the rear of the curtain wall, hoping to surprise them. Thus, Ross set up a revolving watch from another point, which had a clear view of the only road to that postern gate.

Returning to the newest location of Little Westcairn at what would normally be the dinner hour, Ross was pleased to see Fiona crossing the clearing carrying a basket of flatbreads.

Gideon's wife did not miss his happy expression and smiled at him. "Ida and I made an earthen oven, laird. Once the stones are heated, barely smokes at all. We'll have bread from here on out."

"And praise be," called one of Ross's soldiers, riding in with him.

"Well done, Fiona," Ross commended. He was pleased for this boon. Their situation was not dire here in the woods, but it was unsustainable if they subsisted only on game and ale. At the very least, morale would sink. Bread was life, after all, his mother had always claimed.

He sought out Caitrin, as was his habit in the last few days. Despite the plan she'd shared with him this morning, he rather expected to find her distant once again, mayhap in or around her own tent, not yet willing or able to fraternize with the others. He was then pleasantly surprised to see her entrenched with Aggie's brood, sitting on the ground in front of Aggie's tent, and—low and behold—holding the babe, Willie, in her lap. Aggie's daughter, Marion, sat close to her, scoring chestnuts with a small knife, her mouth moving at the speed of her mother's, bending Caitrin's ear.

Ross dismounted at the other side of the camp, and though there was much that needed his attention yet—more plans to make to regain Westcairn and discussions of the like with his officers—he found himself striding across the distance between himself and Caitrin.

There was some charm to the discomfort of her posture and expression. Clearly, she'd not spent any great amount of time with any wee bairns, and he guessed she'd rather have kept it that way. She held her hands under the babe's arms, holding him steady and seated, but appeared to react to each movement of his, almost suggesting a fear that some harm might come to him while he only sat, facing her, his chubby hands playing with the long end of her braid.

She lifted her gaze when he'd closed half the distance.

They were safer here, so deep inside the forest, but this spot in particular was not crowded with one tree so close to the next. Thus, the camp itself saw more dappled sunlight, and presently Caitrin sat where the sun streamed through the leafy canopy, highlighting the flush to her cheeks and the green of her eyes. Her lips were a perfect shade of pink, rosy and healthy, not that pale, bloodless shade he'd seen too often upon her face. Right now, watching him stride toward her, the beginning of a smile tipped the corners of her mouth. Sadly, as most others he'd been teased with, the smile never evolved fully.

Still, this was the most enchanting she'd ever been. Her gaze was bright and unclouded and her expression—while yet guarded—was fairly bemused, either with her ease today or because of Marion's endless prattle, he could not say, and dared not hope that it had anything to do with his coming. But he was captivated, nonetheless. She should be so every day, all her life, be just this unencumbered, simply this lovely. Magnificent actually, for the serenity about her now, for how bedeviling was that almost-smile.

He inclined his head to Agnes, acknowledging her industry with an old kirtle, which she was cutting into long rectangles with a sharp knife. Nappies, he had to assume.

"You've made a friend," he teased Caitrin, not at all discounting his satisfaction when he was sure he detected some relief to see him.

"I have made several," she said. "Marion here is telling me all about the one hundred things you can do or make with chestnuts." She was only more likable then, for how her gaze was so pointed and yet—dare he believe?—nearly merry. She wasn't making fun of Marion, was only letting Ross know she was unaccustomed to anyone who talked so incessantly.

Ross's smile grew, the first effortless one in many days.

"But we'll only roast these, Mam said," added Marion, ignorant of the look exchanged.

"Might I steal Caitrin for a while?" He asked specifically of Marion, but also threw his gaze over to Agnes, whom—he was not surprised to note—watched their brief exchange with a shrewd-eyed look.

"But you'll bring her back?" Marion wanted to be assured.

"I promise," Ross committed.

When he looked to Agnes now, she wore her own smile, this one well-pleased. She stood and collected her bairn and Ross lent his hand to Caitrin to bring her to her feet.

"This way," he instructed, leading her back to where he'd left his steed. "I promised you a bath," he told her.

At his side, she turned her face on her shoulder. "And I had every intention of holding you to that, but it is still light now. I shouldn't like to...."

She let that trail off as they reached his horse, where Roland kept him waiting.

Ross said to her, "It'll be dark by the time we get there," and with her nod, lifted her into the saddle, using the stirrup to raise himself to sit behind her. It felt natural now, at this point, to wrap his arm snugly around her slim waist, but this was the first time she applied her own there, covering his forearm and hand with her own.

They rode at an unhurried gait through the forest, emerging at the far east side, well outside the boundaries of Westcairn, just as the sun was dipping low over the mountain peaks in the west.

Because the silence seemed unnatural when it was only the two of them in that quiet forest for so long, he'd asked her what her day had been like.

"Well, as previously stated, I have been made aware of every blessed thing you might want to do with a chestnut," she began. "As I am sure you are aware, Ross, Agnes and her children are quite amusing."

Jesu, but something so simple as the sound of his name from her lips should not stir him so. At least he did not think it should. "Entertaining, aye. But often akin to the healer's remedies, best to be consumed in small doses."

She did not laugh at this, but her tone was lighthearted when she commented, "Best not let Agnes hear you say as much. She'll spend all day upbraiding all of them but then so easily will take their part if vilified. She took Idgy to task when he asked her to quiet the wailing babe."

"Aye, we all ken that about Aggie. She's a fierce mother wolf to her cubs."

She'd said she'd been amused today, had shown interest in engaging with people, had said to him she'd meant to hold him to his promise of a bath—as close to teasing as she might ever come—and yet he still hadn't heard a laugh, had known no smile that was genuine and full. Why did he continue to believe that this reserved, polite persona was not her true person, that she was—had been and should be again—a lass of a lively character?

Could he make her so again? Was it his responsibility?

In that land outside of Westcairn, which had not ever been claimed by any mormaer in ancient times or by any current chief or laird—it was too rocky and hilly to be of much use for any purpose, either farming or sheep-raising—Ross navigated carefully down the steep slope until they reached the loch nestled where the base of three hills converged.

"I dinna ken the water has a name," he told her as he dismounted and lowered her to the ground as well. "it's sometimes called *amar beag*." The little bath. "It's no' any warmer—or colder—than the loch closer to us, but there'll be no prying eyes here."

While he could not decipher the look she gave him then—a lifted brow and widened eyes—Ross explained, "The soldiers make regular use of the loch up there. You'd have no peace."

Recalling the extra provisions he brought for her, Ross dug into his saddle bags and withdrew a soft cotton towel and what scraps remained of his own soap, which had served him well and was the last of his precious supply, purchased many months ago when he'd gone through Glasgow.

"It's sandalwood or clove or such—marketed to the soldiers riding through the city center," he said to her when he showed her the soap. "But I dinna ken you'd mind."

"Not at all. Thank you."

Turning, he pointed further up the slope they'd just come down. "I'll be up there, far enough to give you privacy, close enough should...you have need of me."

With yet another murmured bit of appreciation, she glanced around, likely wondering where she might know even greater privacy to strip down for her bath.

Once the sun had disappeared, it did darken swiftly, that each of them were only muted gray shadows. When he moved up the hill, he'd see even less, that she'd be naught but a dark shape in the night.

Obligingly, Ross indicated the tall brush at the loch's shore, to her left. "That might work, that spot there. Call if you need me," he said then over his shoulder, already climbing up the slope.

"Ross?"

He stopped and turned. She hadn't moved yet. "Aye?"

"Please do not go so far," she said. "It's dark enough."

He knew it was fear that forced the request, but he thought her brave to have voiced it.

"I'll be close, Caitrin."

He sat midway up the incline, his knees bent, and his arms hung over them. Below, the loch was a shimmery inky carpet. The last of the sun's light was gone, faded with the night, and the moon was already standing sentinel over the murky landscape, laying a strip of golden light upon the loch. His breath caught when Caitrin appeared below, emerging from behind the dwarf birch at the water's edge. She entered the water with that sliver of light upon the water's surface directly in front of her so that for one moment, her naked body was silhouetted in that glow. She was barely curved, being so lean, but shapely nonetheless, graceful and lithe as she stepped carefully into the lake. Too late he thought to remove his gaze, surveying the surrounding terrain in darkness instead. But, unable to resist, his attention returned to her, just as she lifted her arms and walked out further, sinking her thighs and her curved hips and bottom, letting out a vocal shiver for the coldness of the water. She shifted to the left and Ross was teased briefly by the uplifted curve of her breast before decency removed his gaze again.

"It's colder than imagined," she said softly, her voice carrying easily over the quiet night.

This swung his gaze back to her. She was now covered up to her chest. He tried to answer but found he needed to clear his throat first. "Ay—ahem—aye, but still feels good, I would guess."

She gave some affirmative response and then vanished completely, ducking her head to wet her hair. Her silhouette then showed her busy with the bath itself, using the soap he'd lent her to lather her hair and presumably her body when her arms and hands disappeared beneath the surface.

His body responded, picturing all the places her hands and fingers might touch, but it came not with that pleasant expectation of his cock rising—though his cock did wake. He only knew some shame that he did react, as their circumstance—hers specifically—did not lend itself to amorous responses or intentions.

"The longer I stay in, the less cold it feels," she said after a few minutes.

"Only a few more weeks though, lass," he cautioned. "The heavier frosts will come and any summer warmth remaining will be chased away."

"Aye, I imagine."

He leapt to his feet when a new sound caught his attention. In an instant, his sword was in his hand while he faced the direction of the noise, above him on the hill. Nothing and no one burst out at him that he relaxed, deciding 'twas only some critter prowling at night.

"Ross?"

"'Tis fine," he assured her, but remained watchful.

This, however, must have put her on edge that she dunked her head again to rinse away the soap from her hair, and when this was done, she began to walk out of the water, with greater speed than she'd used to enter.

Needing to be alert to their surroundings and thus, her safety, Ross only stole a few quick glances at her now, a wee bit surprised that she did not duck back behind that dwarf birch to dry and dress but did so efficiently just there at the bottom of the hill. Aye, and mayhap it was a good thing she did not stand in that sliver of light upon the loch's surface now, but was in complete shadows, the water beyond her glassy and black that there was little for him to see.

A minute later, she announced she was ready and began walking upward toward Ross.

He sheathed his sword and unhitched his destrier, surprised when she mounted herself, as it required her lifting her foot high to reach the stirrup since his steed was so tall. She seated herself astride, and Ross followed suit, planting himself just behind her, squeezed onto the saddle with her. As was his habit, he held the reins with one hand and circled her middle with his other.

"I've a query for you," he said, when they'd gained the level ridge above the loch. "You may choose to answer, or you may no', 'tis fine. But I'm curious: yesterday was yet another horrific day for you...." he stopped, debating the wisdom of pursuing this. His constant, sometimes ardent curiosity about her prevailed. "But today, you are... in a better frame of mind than previously."

She did not acknowledge that yes, she was. But she concurred nonetheless with her next request. "But please do not ask me how or why. I cannot explain it. Mayhap I only realized that I know nothing but that I will die," she said stoically. "As will any and all of us. Yet I cannot... keep living as if that is my only expectation."

If she'd looked at him then, she'd have witnessed his reaction to this, a solemn pride in her, for whatever internal dialogue and fortitude had brought her here.

"I was not always so cautious," she went on. "I miss that girl, the wild and carefree one. I cannot fathom how or when she went away. She actually left long before our trip to Calasraid."

Quietly joyful, mayhap even merry, he might imagine of her; wild and carefree, he could not.

He chuckled a bit, didn't mind that she heard it. "I'll need examples, lass. I've seen no evidence of this—justified of late, to be sure, but you understand it has me floundering here, trying to reconcile my quiet little Caitrin with some wild creature."

He shouldn't have said *my*, but he supposed it was true, he thought of her as such. He couldn't say how or from when, but there it was. He'd been drawn to her from the start, the initial reasons obvious, for who could not have been captivated by the ethereal Caitrin he'd first come upon? Even as she'd been so haunted then, and sometimes since, he thought few who'd met her could have been indifferent to that fragile figure with the haunting green eyes. It had never been pity, he understood, not for him. Mayhap it should have been, but always he'd only been enthralled by the hollowness of her gaze, the suspension of her reality while she'd lived in that grief, and that sense that it was up to him to do something about it even as he knew it must come from her.

She was as evasive and as elusive as ever, only shrugged and said, "Maybe one day I'll see her again. And then you will, too."

The isolated camp of new Little Westcairn was quiet upon their return. They'd passed two sentries posted, both alert, answering Ross's call of identification swiftly and with some relief. Caitrin dismounted with only his hand for help and Ross tended his steed while she walked across the bare clearing to her tent.

When he approached the tent, meaning to make his bed just outside, he saw that the flap was thrown open, not closed for the night.

"It'll be warmer with it closed," he said quietly, when he stood directly outside. The darkness and the triangle opening showed only her skirts and leather-clad feet and the edge of the mattress.

"I was waiting for you," came her slowly-given reply.

Ross's brow lifted but he did not move immediately. He wasn't keen to assume anything, that she might be inviting him within for a second time, but then he couldn't quite squash the hope raised that this might be the case, even as he wasn't sure it was a good idea.

"It is selfish, I understand," she whispered, "but I did sleep better when you were next to me."

His own reasons were greedy, despite knowing some satisfaction over her admission, and he only hesitated long enough to know if he would, internally, be persuaded against such an action. He was not and in the next moment made his way inside the shelter with her. As before, the space which might normally seem plentiful when only she filled it, was shrunk with his added length and mass. He stretched out on the soft mattress but did not presume so much that she might want or need the same circumstance as last night, the comfort of his arm around her. He laid on his side, using his arm as a pillow, facing her, allowing her to advise what exactly she wanted of him.

Caitrin was on her side as well, her arms folded at her front. It was darker than the night in here that he saw only that her eyes blinked, but not what expression she wore.

Ross wasn't sure that at any time last night he explicitly thought of kissing Caitrin, but he knew that he did now. It seemed misplaced, the desire, and he tried to ignore it. But then she confounded him by lifting her hand to lay her fingers lightly against his chest, chiseling away at any intent to keep his hands to himself.

Her bath aside—and that tantalizing view she had inadvertently shown him—he couldn't remember the last time he'd been roused by anything at all. Not for years, he guessed.

Unaccountably, he did something he'd never done before in all his twenty-nine years: he forecasted his intention, his voice low. "I dinna ken if it's circumstantial or if it's grounded in only base needs but I need to kiss you, Caitrin." No sooner were those words given that he regretted them. He couldn't know for sure, but he had kissed enough women to understand she might prefer more eloquent—less primal and impersonal—reasons for wanting a kiss. More importantly, he'd left out the grander motive, that he was, and had been since he'd met her, drawn to her in the way that people were fascinated by something previously unknown, something rare, something that evoked a primitive desire, even a feral need.

Thankfully, Caitrin heard only the crux of it, did not take issue with his sloppily-given motives.

"I do not want you to kiss me." Her fingers slid away from what contact they'd made against his tunic.

Having acknowledged the truth of his want inside himself, he wasn't about to give up so easily. "If I believed that, I might have an easier time acceding to your wishes."

"Why do you not believe what I've said?" Her voice was that of a lover, breathy and low, growing huskier by the minute.

He kept his tone as soft as hers, so that no other could hear. "Because you keep staring at my lips as if you do want a kiss." He could barely see her eyes but knew they were not wide and lifted to his eyes, but that her lids were lowered as she only stared at his mouth. At his accusation, she raised her gaze to his.

"I—I do not. I... have never thought about a kiss. I wouldn't know..."

"All the more reason—curiosity, then." *Jesu*, but the prelude to a kiss had never stirred him more than this. His heart pounded inside his chest. He hadn't moved his hands yet, but it was only sheer force of will that kept them still, until she consented.

"I am not curious," she stated and then contradicted those very words by adding, "I am... a wretch for even wondering—"

"Curiosity is no' a crime, lass—no matter what, no matter when."

"But so many are—"

"Aye, they're gone, so many over the last week. And over the last month, I've lost another score of men, and before that, even more, all gone. But I'm right here, Caitrin, and so are you."

He sighed then at the same time she shook her head side to side, slowly, as if she weren't fully resolved in her decision. So be it. He would not force her. The time would come though, he somehow knew. Settling onto his back more comfortably, he slid his arm under her and curled it toward his body, bringing Caitrin nearly upon his chest. "Close your eyes, lass. It will keep."

Ross shut his eyes, just tired enough that he thought sleep might come anyway, despite the risen hope for a kiss, which had roused him above exhaustion for that small space of time. But Caitrin did not relax in his arms, was stiff and awake, he knew. The staccato beat of her elevated heart rate knocked against his side. After a minute, her fingers began to drum against his chest and he grinned when he said, "You will no' sleep if you can no' relax. And I will no sleep if you keep thumping your fingers on me."

Her fingers went still immediately. "Sorry."

Staring at the canopy above his head, he thought her eyes might yet be open.

"What turns in your mind now?" He asked.

Her head moved on his chest, but it was several seconds before her voice came to him in the darkness.

"I think all the blame should rest with you," she whispered, "but now I am thinking about...kissing."

She would have no idea that he smiled in response to this. Likewise, she wouldn't know that his impulse was to uproot himself from his cozy position and roll her onto her back in one smooth motion so that he might devour her with a kiss. He remained still and breathed levelly, as best he could, and said, "Go to sleep, Caitrin." He even thought it sounded as if he meant it.

Another entire minute passed.

"I don't think I can," she said then. "Not now. You have me...intrigued and wondering."

She was indeed a brave lass, even if she did not come right out and say, *Aye, I want to know a kiss.*

And now Ross did shift, which effectively put her on the mattress and not his arm, on her back. He lifted himself on his elbow and stared down at her. He couldn't help himself then, that he showed her a roguish grin, which she might see if her eyes had adjusted a wee bit to the darkness. "If only to appease your curiosity, lass." Undoubtedly, the tone of this statement revealed his grin as well.

He had no hope that she might respond positively to his quip, let alone so spectacularly; he'd thought only to lighten the seriousness of his plea, as that would make any rejection easier to bear if that should be the case. But she amazed him by expelling a nervous laugh, the first of any joy—such as it was—that he'd heard from her. And even though it was quiet and soft, it was a glorious noise.

So then he felt he had no choice but to kiss her.

As he lowered his head toward her, she opened her mouth to say something else. Whatever this would have been was smothered by his kiss. He would remember this for some time, the very first taste and feel of her lips, soft and supple and warm, if not initially responsive. That was his job, then, to coax her response. The blood that raged in his veins skidded to a halt as he moved his mouth back and forth across hers, waiting for her to engage. After the second pass, he used his tongue, wetting her lips, tracing the seam. Her breaths became pants and when she opened her mouth to release a little gasp, Ross seized on this, sliding his tongue between her moist lips. Despite his body urging him to devour her, to take more or all, he held himself in check, lingering over the kiss, savoring every sensation.

But when she touched his chest with her hand as she opened her mouth more and tentatively joined her tongue with his, Ross felt the control slip and the kiss became demanding. He'd recognized his want prior to kissing her but wasn't prepared for the vast hunger that gripped him, that made him grind his mouth and pull her toward him with a hand at her hip. *Jesu*, but she was sweet. And soft, and so eager to know what a kiss was about. He'd have to have been made of stone to not respond, to not revel in it, to want more.

There could be no more than a kiss, not here, not now. He let it go on until he could stand no more, until stopping would no longer be an option if he persisted.

Possibly only she could hear the low grumble of the groan that heralded the end of their kiss. He didn't want to stop, not ever, but really had no choice unless he intended to ravage her right here, within a dozen yards of where Samuel and John and a few others had made their beds. Breathing a bit forcefully himself, he let his forehead drop to hers and brought his hand up to cradle the side of her face, using his thumb to trace the smooth skin under her eye.

He whispered to her, "I hope, lass, that dinna satisfy all your curiosity. It only whetted mine and I'll be wanting more."

He hadn't noticed that she was holding her breath until she released it in a strangled whoosh, the warm air stirring against his mouth. He thought her fingers moved against his chest, mayhap toyed nervously with the fabric of his tunic.

"I do not know what to make of it," she replied. "It has left me...befuddled."

He grinned but did not know if she could see it. Leaning forward, he put his face against her hair, near her ear, inhaling the clean scent of her soft, still-damp locks. "Aye, then, we did it right, Caitrin," he whispered.

Somehow, he was surprised that she said nothing to this, though he felt her bare nod against him. Lazy now, even as his pulse was yet pounding, Ross backed away, putting several inches between them, pleased to be able to study her shadowy profile in the darkness.

Aye, he would definitely want another kiss from her.

Chapter Ten

The next morning, Caitrin told herself that this was only one of many firsts she would know in the days and weeks to come, just as she'd realized so many firsts over the last week. Everything would be new to her, including what she fretted about now, how to face Ross this morning after he'd kissed her so enjoyably last night.

She'd not gone into the event entirely unknowing, but what little she did know had come to her secondhand, via Mary, who'd known kisses from more than one lad back home. Curiously, Mary had always spoken about what she'd made the boy feel—*he was wild for me*, and, *I did not give him everything he craved, but left him wanting more*, chief among her assertions. But never had Mary conveyed, in any way, what a kiss was, how it consumed you, and weakened you and thrilled you at the same time. Honestly, Caitrin believed if she had known the power of a kiss, she'd have chased Ross Kildare down days ago to know it with him. There was—had been—some pull toward him that she neither understood nor had explored yet. But she was aware of its existence, that Ross was different to her, that what she felt in his presence or under his regard, or at the touch of his hand, was not anything like what she might know from anyone else, Samuel or Tavis or John or any other, that it seemed to have a life of its own.

And though she hadn't known a kiss before last night, she somehow understood that it was only a natural progression of whatever it was that consumed her whenever Ross was near.

Aye, and she might have suffered guilt for the poor timing of it—her own curiosity—and for the fact that she didn't stop it before it started, that she had mostly made it happen. But a part of her truly believed and convinced all the rest of her that life was just too short—as evidenced by the events of the last several days—and that it was simply too unpredictable to wait forever for such a thing as proper timing in a world gone mad.

Caitrin didn't know what Ross felt about the kiss, and frankly, last night she might have said she didn't care. She only knew what she'd experienced, what she'd felt—none of which she could properly put into words, even within her mind. His kiss was both gentle and fierce and while the mechanics of it were all new to her, she realized that she'd been less concerned about doing it right, and more affected by what she was feeling, how it was so decadent and delicious, but then so wicked, the latter harkening back to the poor timing of it, that she should experience something so moving and titillating when she should yet be grieving the loss of Mary and so many others.

When she woke in the morning, Ross was already gone from the tent. Truthfully, she was thankful for this, that she suffered no immediate embarrassment for how wanton she'd behaved. She saw to her morning ablutions and braided her now dry hair and wrapped the Kildare plaid around her shoulders to ward off the chill, something she realized she rarely knew or was aware of when she was with Ross.

Her reprieve was short-lived, as Ross appeared soon enough, walking and talking with his brother and Samuel. They approached Arailt, who'd recovered quickly from his wound and was again about the chore of making fine, straight shafts for arrows with a hand-held plane.

Caitrin might have approached Arailt herself—as she did not see Agnes and her children anywhere—asking what use she might be toward the arrow-making but decided to wait until he was no longer engaged with his laird and the others. Thus she spent a few minutes with the mattress, shaking and fluffing some freshness into the straw that had been flattened last night.

When she backed out of the tent and stood up, Ross's officers had disappeared, Arailt was bent over his work again, and Ross himself was striding toward her.

He did not stop before her and say good morning but took her hand as he passed, thus pulling her along with him as he marched deeper into the forest. He walked quite a ways, far outside the view of any who might be watching, she would later think, turning around a pine tree as wide as his shoulders and then pivoting, and pinning her against it.

Caitrin caught only the gleam of his smoldering gaze before his mouth crashed onto hers. All her responses happened at once—her breath caught, her chest heaved with a burst of excitement, and she closed her eyes, more an intuitive reaction than a conscious deed. She'd only learned last night what he might expect of her from a kiss but was keen to put her limited knowledge into play, knowing what pleasure she would receive. She opened her mouth to him, gave him her tongue, tasted him, set her hands upon his hard chest, and thought she might weep for all of it: his pursuit of this kiss, that he'd sought out this with her; how sweet and hungry it was; the way her insides clamored and cried for more.

She felt his hands at her sides, his fingers dug possessively into the top of her hips.

But oh, how ridiculous was she, that she wanted to cry and to laugh at the same time? She shuddered and sagged against the tree while Ross ravaged her with his kiss and leaned his hard body against hers.

When he finally pulled his lips from hers, he kept them close, breathing out the first words given to her today. "I've thought of little else all morning but having your lips against mine."

While these words stirred her as fantastically as did his touch, she couldn't honestly say the same. She'd not thought of another kiss, had only dwelled so happily upon the previous one. But she nodded, her forehead scraping against his, not understanding what any of it meant, but that she, too, was thrilled to have more of it.

"Caitrin," he said then, remaining close, laying his palm against her cheek, "dinna overthink it, dinna scold yourself, just let it be. Aye, the world is twisted right now, so much is lost, but this...this is something to dream on, something to keep us going."

She nodded more fervently now, eager to cling to his reasoning, to dispel the guilt that naturally came with knowing any joy. His lips touched hers again and she closed her eyes. This kiss was only a long and sweet caress before he separated from her. His hands upon her hips were the last thing to leave her.

Caitrin opened her eyes again, breathless. Inexplicably, she felt a smile coming even as his expression was so severe for its intensity, even as she was sure his teeth were clamped, and while one of his hands was fisted.

The smile was stalled by these things. "Why are you angry?"

Ross unclenched his fist, though his blue gaze remained as fiery. "I'm no' angry, lass. I want more. But now...it has to wait."

She wasn't completely unschooled in these matters, had some vague understanding of what *it* might mean. She was hazy for sure on the particulars, but imagined if it felt as good, was as knee-knocking as Ross Kildare's kiss, she would want to know more as well.

Seeming to regain his composure, having greater success than she to put aside thoughts of that kiss or another, Ross gave a curt sigh and told her what his plans were for the day.

"We're no' done with those English," he said, "but are thinking to bring a little warfare to their door—which is our door. I'll leave a larger unit within the camp, but lass, dinna go away from it. Stay near Samuel or Arailt all the day, aye?"

"I will." But now she would worry for him, taking the fight directly to the enemy. "Is this a good idea?"

He snickered with some contriteness, the sound humorless. "By God's grace, the plans will only improve."

Caitrin gasped at what this implied and at how self-absorbed she'd been. She touched two fingers to her lips, where Ross had only seconds ago. "How selfish of me. Ross, I am sorry for your loss—losses." And for the pain and the regret that he must be enduring. "I should not have—"

He rushed her, closed the distance between them in two quick strides, shaking his head as he did. "We canna live like that," he said, holding up a finger between them to enunciate his point. "We just can no'. It will only wreak havoc on the insides and render us useless for the coming fight. Caitrin, we do the best we can, by whatever means we can, our hearts always in the right. That is all we can do, the best that we ken how."

She'd been right about him since the start. He was older than his years, was a good leader to his men and his people. How fortunate—or incredible—was he to have such stalwart reserves and steadiness of mind to guide him!

Thoughtfully, as it occurred to her—from whence came such presence of mind—she said softly, "Your parents must have been remarkable people." Or mayhap he'd trained with—

Ross's bark of laughter was as unexpected as it was breathtaking. He tipped his head back, letting out a rich and full-bodied chuckle, which in turn elicited an answering—if confused—smile from Caitrin. Mesmerized, she watched him as he tried to rein it in. When he laughed, he was ten years younger but fully ten times more handsome, his blue eyes sparkling, his mouth shaped so gorgeously around his open smile.

How wonderful.

Finally, he explained his sudden merriment. "Lass, I'd like to claim some ownership for my sensible and wise habits. Great folks they were, but I'm no' without my own resources." There was a light of mischief in his gaze now that was impossible to ignore.

She knew she was being teased a wee bit and relaxed, holding onto her smile. And she did something that days ago, that even yesterday she would have thought impossible: she teased him back. "I would wager it mostly has to do with your upbringing and those fine parents."

She was in love with the crinkling at the corners of his eyes, in love with the way something danced in her belly with fluttery wings. And she knew he was going to kiss her again when his light-hearted gaze fell onto her lips and his expression changed, went so swiftly from ease to something else, something that looked like hunger.

Smoothly, he bent his head and took her lips in a kiss of velvet warmth, one that sent her pulse racing.

What a glorious feeling.

And when next he looked at her, delight bubbled in her, shining in her eyes.

"Why would you cry now?" He asked gently.

Embarrassed, she could only admit, "I'd forgotten how warm and beautiful joy is, how rare."

This gave him pause, in that he studied her so intently, his gaze moving all around her face, until he said with some confidence, "There will be joy, Caitrin. I *will* make that happen."

ANY DAY MIGHT WELL see his end. Today or tomorrow might be that day, with what plans they had to antagonize those English in his home. But damn, if he didn't feel like he'd go down smiling, the taste of Caitrin's kiss still on his lips.

Still, he was neither an unseasoned warrior nor a green lad savoring his first and only kiss, that he was able to compartmentalize, focusing on the task ahead. There was much to be done yet and he was more eager than ever to get about the work of recovering Westcairn.

All this morning, the sounds of striking and hammering axes rung out across the land while one unit of his army worked to prepare the long shilterns. They would not be outfitted with the usual iron cross as their lances were, but would be solid, six to eight foot long pikes, with speared heads on either end, carved out with knives or hatchets to deadly points.

At this time, all of his army was mounted, or could be mounted if needed, as they'd taken almost every horse of every Englishman they'd dispatched over the last week. Feeding and keeping almost one hundred warhorses was an exhausting job in and of itself and Ross had been forced to move four men away from different units preparing for battle only to assist Roland with the task. Westcairn's stablemaster was presumed dead, likely caught inside Westcairn when the siege came.

As they were further away from Westcairn and since the morning had been foggy and a misty rain fell in the early afternoon, several fires burned within the camp, their usage required and their safety almost guaranteed. Hamish manned one of them, as he had of late, cooking suppers large enough to feed the masses. The red deer had always been blessedly plentiful around Westcairn; fishing was good in any of the lochs nearby; and Agnes's girls did a fine job of providing nuts and mushrooms and wild onions for flavor. With Fiona's breads, they ate well, with plenty of food to spare. John had had the foresight, when first they'd arrived at Westcairn a week ago to send off three men, with six of the English steeds they'd amassed at that point, back to Perth. There they'd sold the horses and had purchased oatmeal, barley, salt, four barrels of ale, and—at John's request—garlic and pepper, since they had no access to what was kept at Westcairn.

Having spent the morning giving instructions to only small units for things he'd like to accomplish, he now gathered the bulk of his army, minus those on watch presently, for a briefing inside the new Little Westcairn. It was not commonplace for him to explain himself in detail to his men or any others. Going into battle, he discussed strategy with his officers, and they relayed intent and plans to their men. But this was different. They were building things and making preparations in and around the forest and the people of Westcairn should know what they were about, and what was expected of them.

On the rare occasions he or his father before him had called meetings inside the keep, they'd have used either the great hall itself, which could hold standing bodies of over one hundred, or the courtyard of the keep, where he or his father might have stood high on the gatehouse wall which overlooked both the outside and the bailey. Here, at the campsite, Ross remained mounted upon his tall destrier so that he could be seen, while everyone gathered around him.

Those people inside the camp, who'd halted with some curiosity when they saw the bulk of the army gathering into a tight space, now turned their attention to their laird. Agnes stopped her jawing with Fiona and even her children went silent. Caitrin, seated next to Arailt, about the business of making arrows, stared not only at Ross but passed her gaze over all the men coming. When too many soldiers found spots in front of her, blocking her view, she stood, her blonde hair easily found toward the rear of the gathered group.

Under Ross's firm hand, his destrier remained still and waited until there was no more movement, until all were here and waiting. Ross moved his gaze slowly over his people, from his brother John's stoic mien to that of Samuel, his thick brows low over his eyes. Idgy scratched behind his ear, but his gaze was steadfast upon Ross. Agnes frowned a bit, holding her babe. Hamish, Fiona, and others only waited with some expectation.

Ross found Caitrin's gaze as she shifted her position, moving between two Kildare soldiers. He held her gaze as he began, mesmerized as ever by how green were her eyes.

"It's no' been easy of late. And we've no' really begun to address it. We have a long haul ahead of us, like as no' an ugly fight on the horizon, but ye ken—you ken me—that I'll no' rest until Westcairn is recovered. With that said, we ken we need to draw them out yet more. But they'll come hard now that they ken we have some strength in numbers. They'll be better equipped—armor and shields and more weapons than we can make in a month." He paused, remembering his father's habit of doing the same, reading the faces, the reception of what was said thus far. All were alert, anticipating yet more. "Our best chance at ultimate success is to deplete their numbers still, and our best chance of that is by unconventional means. Man for man, I have no fear we'd prevail—but for their greater numbers and their advantages of being well-armored. The English place no value on the foot soldier, choosing to hide behind their mailclad knights. The very thing that favors their odds—their horses and arms and heavy mail—will prove their undoing. We will be swift and mobile, setting traps and striking swiftly. But it will take all of us to build this plan and put it to use." Pausing again, he scanned the crowd, seeing some nods, hearing the murmured assent. "We will work in groups, in different sections of the forest, with several objectives. The next few days should see us constructive, busy with the plans that we've produced thus far." He looked at Agnes and said, "John will arrange travel for any who wish to journey to Blackwood and the Jamisons for safekeeping, to be recalled when it's done. With the bairns, Aggie, I ken you—" He stopped when she began to shake her head emphatically.

"I'll no' run, no' from my own home. You'll get us there, laird. I ken you will."

This was not foreign to him, the unwavering confidence they placed in him. Aye, it was a burden at times—he did not have all the answers, he erred as much as any man—but it was gratifying all the same, filling him with pride, that they assigned their hopes to him.

With a nod, he continued. "Aye, I fight for what's mine—Westcairn. But it's no' only mine. It belongs to all of us. In the end, we will prevail. Until then, dinna think for one minute we dinna or will no' mourn those lost. We cherish them, and value their sacrifice. When we return to Westcairn, we will celebrate them."

A chorus of *aye, aye* greeted this, and Ross then gave over the address to his brother, who laid out more details and announced who would lead each party. They'd already discussed where certain people should be placed and had earlier assumed that Agnes would not choose to leave, that few if any would take them up on their offer to find shelter and security at Blackwood. And though there would be no person journeying to Blackwood for protection, Ross and John had decided that a messenger should go there, that notice should be given to the Jamison—who would likely see it traveled further—that the English had come to the Highlands.

This evening, for the first time since Ross and the army had come, they would enjoy a communal meal. The murky rain continued, luckily not heavy enough to dampen the fire over which roasted the second red deer today. The first, which had cooked all morning, was laid upon a crude table pilfered from a vacant village home last week. Idgy carved up that venison while

Hamish cooked the other. Another fire, this one wide and low, cradled several thick flat stones, laid onto coals, where a few dozen fish were cooked.

Before he ate, Ross walked the perimeter of the camp, checking in with each man on duty, while John rode out to the ridge to receive a report from those sentries on any movements from the keep. Satisfied that all was quiet and might remain so for the night, Ross looked forward to sitting down to a meal, enjoying the fine company of his family.

He might well get used to it, that his eyes sought out Caitrin whenever he was near or thought he might be so lucky to happen upon her. He already understood that he liked best to know of her whereabouts before she did his. He could watch her then, unnoticed, while she was unguarded.

Just now such an occasion presented itself as he returned to camp. She was sitting in profile, talking with Daniel while both of them wound the silk thread around the fletching of arrows and glue. It seemed she was more talkative today, lifting her gaze and moving her lips with some frequency. Daniel grinned at something she said, and she shrugged in return, the gesture natural, easy.

Samuel stepped up to the pair, laying down another bundle of shafts at her feet. He spoke with her about something, which gave her pause. Her hands stilled as she tipped her face up to the big man. She shook her head at something he said and when Samuel then addressed Daniel, Caitrin smiled prettily at whatever he said, her gaze moving between the man and the boy. She was comfortable, not withdrawn, and then so damn bonny in her ill-fitted gown and her mismatched shoes.

Agnes's girls then ran by, playful, tossing handfuls of flower petals over Caitrin as if they were naught but cherubs, frolicking upon a meadow of wildflowers, as if no great hardship had befallen them. Agnes called from a distance, scolding her girls to, "stop with the nonsense," but neither her daughters nor Caitrin were affected by her brusque manner.

Caitrin's response was spellbinding. She'd seen the girls running toward her, was not startled, but smiled beatifically when she saw what they were about, when the silky petals floated down over her. Her laughter was perfect, suited her immensely, soft and light. It might not be her best, was not yet undiluted, but it was sweet and drew more than only his attention.

It is well. As it should be, he thought.

"That's nice to hear finally." John had come to his side. "I ken she'll need a stick to fight 'em off now, if any of the lads think the laughter signifies she's done with her grief."

Ross shook his head and never took his eyes off Caitrin. "Nae," he said quietly. "She is mine."

His brother chuckled softly. "Aye and then *ye* might see a fight or two about that."

No, he would not.

He'd been born to assume the position he now held, laird of Westcairn and chief to all its people. In his youth, he'd been educated precisely and purposefully, so that one day he would be a fair and steady leader. He'd been expected to be—and mostly succeeded at being— courageous and honest, and a man of integrity. The one trait that had always come easily to him, spawned by his own innate confidence and his father's unwavering pride in him, was his decisiveness. Rarely did he second-guess himself, his wishes, or his decisions. This one was right, he knew.

When there came no response to his announcement, Ross finally wrenched his gaze from Caitrin and sought out his brother's reaction.

Hands on his hips, his pose similar to Ross's, John grinned. "Dinna ken that'll come as a surprise to many."

Ross gave this no great thought, undisturbed by what people believed or saw or thought they understood. He grinned at his brother and went to wash up before supper. This day was done, the sun was dipping low, and yet lightness and energy were breathed into him with what he'd just revealed to John. He found himself equally anxious to take back Westcairn as he was to make Caitrin his.

Chapter Eleven

Caitrin might believe that the evening passed was one of the most enjoyable she'd ever known in all her life. True, she'd known much sorrow of late, and true, she was more displaced than even these folks with whom she shared such a fine meal, but the atmosphere of this camp and these people awed her.

The misty rain that had hung heavy in the air all day finally quit. The two low burning fires chased away any remaining dampness if one sat close enough. The carpet of pine needles was wet yet, but none seemed to care, gathering in smaller groups and circles inside the golden glow of the small flames and the orange and red coals.

Caitrin sat cross-legged next to Ross, using the flatbreads Fiona had made as her trencher. The fish was cooked perfectly, light and flaking away easily with her knife. She wasn't like Mary, who could so easily make conversation without any prompting, but she enjoyed listening to all that went on around her. Agnes and Fiona had some discussion about whether or not they could make a pottage tomorrow, if they might be so fortunate to find some root vegetables, either by luck inside the forest, or, Fiona batted her lashes at her husband, Gideon, "If I can talk a big, strong man to raid what remains of Westcairn's acres."

"Och, I ken you could, lass," Agnes said with a laugh.

Samuel and Arailt sat to her right, beyond Ross. Caitrin had learned that these two were more serious than most, that much of their conversation was business-like, always about the arrows, including best-practices, mistakes they'd made in the slow production, and how best to increase the output on the morrow.

When she was done with her supper, Agnes took Willie into her lap and snuggled him close and lovingly. She swayed a bit, rocking the drowsy bairn, and began to hum a pretty tune. Caitrin grinned when two of her daughters, sitting close to their mam, with Marion leaning her head against Agnes's arm, began to hum along with her, the tune well-known, it seemed.

At her side, Ross was, and had been for most of the meal, engaged in conversation with John. She didn't eavesdrop, though she also did not assume that any of it was to be secret, but knew they too spoke of the days ahead and what they should expect to face. She stole glances at him, thinking that Ross had a completely different look about him in the orange and yellow shadows. By day, he was a blond-haired, blue-eyed god, striking in appearance at first because of his unusual habit of keeping his hair shorn and his face free of whiskers. She knew it wasn't true at all, but thought it was almost as if he knew how handsome he was and did not want to conceal any part of it. The blue and green threads of his plaid, so often draped over his shoulder, the pleats always perfect as if this was one thing he must control when everything else was in such disarray, only heightened the color of his eyes. He was remarkable in his beauty, a fair glorious knight to whom surely many a maid had given a kiss or her heart, or more.

At night, now, he was more striking for how the fire flung shadows at him, accentuating the chiseled cheekbones and jawline and putting some menace onto those broad shoulders, so that he appeared a hulking and mysterious form. He spoke in low tones to his brother, his deep and quiet baritone enveloping Caitrin in a warm and pleasant haze, not unlike the voice he used with her inside the tent at night.

She thought of the brief speech he'd given late this afternoon. He'd been magnificent. Not because he'd spoken so movingly, though he had, or because he was so remarkable and towering upon his splendid steed, but because he spoke honestly and simply to them, had laid out his plans, had not ignored the dead, had given them hope that things would be better, would return to what these people would know as normal.

With Agnes and her girls humming and Ross talking with John, whose voice was equally as pleasing though not as deep, Caitrin felt about as comfortable as she ever had. Her eyelids began to feel heavy, though. Drawing her own plaid closed at her front, she let her shoulders drop and didn't fight it when she began to doze.

"Sorry, lass," she heard next and felt a hand give her a little shake.

Ross was on his feet, his hand at her shoulder, but then moved in front of her, offering her a lift. "I've got watch on the ridge tonight. We should leave soon, before you fall asleep completely."

Her response was sleepy but instant, slipping her hand outside the plaid to lay it in his. As she stood, Agnes bid her a good night.

"And to you," Caitrin responded, grinning at the picture Agnes and her children made, all cuddled together while she continued to rock Willie and all the others sat around her, each of them touching their mam in some fashion.

She caught Agnes's pleased smile and then John's steady stare as she turned to follow Ross away from the fire. Ross's brother's expression showed no disapproval that she was to accompany Ross, which begged the question inside: would it matter if she came up against condemnation from any Kildare for what some might perceive as special consideration from their laird?

To this, she surprised herself by answering, *I have too many other things to worry about.*

They would ride out to the ridge since they were so much further from it than when they had made their home at the original Little Westcairn. Once seated, Ross guided the animal quietly through the forest, away from the cozy fire and good company. And while she was sleepy, Caitrin was not immune to a stirring in her belly, being so close to him, her back meeting with his hard chest, his hand now familiarly around her waist. Her body quivered with a bit of thrill, wondering if Ross would kiss her again.

"Now I ken we'll be alone all through the night, lass," he said near her ear in the next second, "but there can be no kissing. I need to be alert, as you ken. Your job then will be to keep your hands off me."

As sluggish as she was yet, her reaction to this was swift. She understood immediately that he was teasing her, but the mischief in his tone, because of its intimacy, did nothing to calm her suddenly pounding pulse. And yet, the burst of laughter that came was unexpected, that some of it escaped before she was able to cover it by clamping her hand over her mouth. She'd laughed for the first time in weeks only this afternoon—and it had felt good but still somehow inappropriate—but this one she could not contain, so caught off guard by what he'd said and implied with such boyish charm.

When she had recovered herself, Caitrin lowered her hand and turned her face toward him. The top of her head scraped his chin. "I shall endeavor to control myself."

He kept on. "A mighty feat, I'm sure."

"But one that might become easier, if you continue to speak so."

His chuckle rumbled along her spine and warmed her tremendously. She thought he might have let it loose, as he'd done before, but for the night and their want to he unheard, undetected, in the forest.

"Aye, and I'll be quiet then, lass," he whispered at her ear. "I dinna want you embracing the idea too strongly, certainly no' after this night is done."

His arm tightened around her middle and she pictured him smiling and her own remained for a wee little bit.

She didn't know this person, this woman who'd just exchanged teasing banter with a man, but she liked her and hoped she might stay a while. She brought with her a plethora of sweet and giddy emotions.

"SEE?" SAMUEL SAID, holding out his handiwork to show Fiona and Caitrin and Ida. "It's naught but weaving, vines and twigs, to make a cover for the hole."

"Aye, I got it," Fiona said. "But how big do ye need it to be?"

"Big enough to conceal the trough we're digging," Samuel answered, pointing to the group of soldiers with them, armed with shovels and pickaxes, excavating an area of the forest floor.

They only just started but had marked out the length and width of the hole they planned to dig, which looked as if it would stretch all the way across the path when done and be about as wide as Caitrin was tall.

Ida's brown eyes widened, and she gasped. "Och, but ye're going to crash them into the hole when they come by."

"If all goes well, aye, that's the plan," said Samuel, with a grin for what the lass had figured out.

Fiona snatched the beginnings of the woven piece from Samuel. "We've got it, then. We ken what we're about." She met Caitrin's and then Ida's gaze. "C'mon. Let's have at it."

Samuel nodded, pleased they understood their objective and moved away, grabbing up his own shovel to begin digging with six other men.

They were not near the camp, were quite a distance away, closer to Westcairn and upon what looked to be a regular route through the woodland. The winding path was free of any trees or brush and the ground was nearly void of pine needles and leaves as well. Ross wasn't here, but twenty other Kildare soldiers were, and Caitrin didn't suffer any fear that she wasn't safe. She'd ridden the palfrey here, sharing the saddle with Ida, after Samuel had asked that she accompany them. He'd told her only they had some work to do.

She and Fiona and Ida first collected what raw materials they would need, thinner twigs and limbs and whatever vine-y plants they could find. They needed to break and saw away at some shrubs and then strip them clean to collect enough. It was nearly thirty minutes later when they sat down, just off the path, to begin the task.

All three women sat crossed legged, the growing piece wedged on all their laps while they worked different sections. Fiona had begun to call it fencing. Caitrin thought it did rather resemble the wattle Dorcas had used to enclose her kitchen garden.

Fiona was nearly as gregarious as Agnes, though with much less volume, and plenty of giggling. Ida, whom Caitrin had only met today, was chatty but less giggly, and mayhap a year or two younger than Caitrin. Caitrin envied their easy relationship, that they must have known each other all their lives and spoke so familiarly about people Caitrin had not met or didn't know. But she enjoyed their company and considered them and the chore a pleasant distraction. She was happy to be of use, included even, in both the task and the conversation. When she and Ross had returned to camp this morning, she had rather wondered what she might do after Ross had slipped inside the tent to catch a few hours of sleep, and after Arailt had informed her they were out of silk thread and would have to rely on the glue they'd used to hold the feathers.

"Gideon said ye lost all yer family, lass," Fiona said when she'd finished speaking of someone named Finn—a soldier, Caitrin assumed, and one that Agnes might be sweet on, if she understood the context of that discussion. Fiona worked on, her fingers efficient upon the sticks and shoots, even as she lifted her gaze to Caitrin.

"I did. That's where they found me, just...after." She understood that to become friendly—to make friends—she would have to speak of this at times, but she did not relish it.

"Aye, and I dinna ken what yer circumstance was," Fiona said, "but you ken you're lucky to have been picked up by the laird?"

She had certainly considered this, more than once. "Aye, I do believe that."

Fiona giggled. "And Aggie says the laird has a keen eye for ye—"

"He does?" Ida squeaked, her fingers paused on the mat of fencing. "Och, and I'm always the last to ken."

Thus, her disgruntlement was attached to this, her lack of perception or knowledge, and not particularly because her laird might have a *keen eye* for Caitrin.

It was as pleasing and as common as any silly conversation she might have had with Mary. Grinning, Caitrin wondered, "And what does that mean, a keen eye? He watches over everyone and everything. I barely know him, but I've already observed that much."

With another giggle, Fiona imparted, "Aye, but he dinna watch at Idgy or Tavis with that brooding, eat-you-alive stare."

Ida shivered. "Ooh, gives me the gooseflesh, thinking on those blue eyes staring at me like that. I'll be watching now, make no doubt. I want to see it." She burst into giggles then and warned them through a smirk, "But dinna be telling my Uilleam I've said as much."

It was ridiculous and frivolous, the entire discussion, and then not entirely accurate. True, Ross's gaze was sometimes piercing in its intensity, but *eat-you-alive*? How fanciful! But she didn't mind the talk, only gave a shrug with an accompanying grin, enjoying very much how she felt right now, like they *were* friends, and they were interested in her.

"She's gonna be coy now, Ida," teased Fiona. "Aye, and that's fine. I've got eyes to keep watch—"

"Hush!" Samuel hissed from the trail several yards away, cutting off Fiona's jibing.

Everyone stopped moving. Caitrin looked at Samuel, wondering what had alarmed him. In the next second, her heart began that now-familiar beating, so fast and hard she was sure she could hear it.

"Riders coming," one of the soldiers announced his assessment just as Caitrin felt it, the rumble beneath her.

Not many, she decided; the reverberation was not so strong.

"To the woods!" Samuel gave the order in a deep hiss.

"We're no' ready," Ida whined, frozen a bit.

Fiona whisper-called to Samuel, "We can stall them while you take positions. Otherwise they'll only ride around the hole—it's no' covered yet." She jumped to her feet and grabbed a shovel from her husband, pushing at his chest to send him out of sight. "Go on. Come running when they stop."

While Gideon only appeared stupefied, Samuel considered this, a pained look about his face, while his gaze locked with Caitrin.

"We canna let them get away," someone said, "No' if they see the hole and ken what we're about."

"But no' Caitrin," Samuel finally agreed, waving his hand at her, indicating he wanted her to go with him. "He'll kill me if I put her in danger."

"I can do it," she heard herself say, lifting her chin, pretending her voice hadn't squeaked and her knees didn't knock. It wasn't fair, that she should be exempt from danger while Fiona and Ida were not.

Through clenched teeth, moving backwards into the woods as the riders came closer, Samuel growled ferociously, "Come. Now."

Shaking her head, Caitrin stood and walked to where Fiona had, near the hole. She picked up a discarded shovel and panted through her nose, and exchanged a terrified look with Ida, who stood next to her, holding a pickaxe.

"Saints alive, Caitrin. I'm going to—"

Samuel's threat was cut short by the advent of the riders, coming too close for him to not get out of sight, to not be heard. He disappeared into the trees.

And when the riders came around the closest bend and into sight, they saw only three lasses, standing over a shallow hole in the ground. Caitrin realized immediately some relief that there were only a half dozen English riding toward them, knowing that so many more Kildares surrounded them, just out of sight.

They reined in sharply, being so close to the bend in the trail that they came upon them rather suddenly. Caitrin turned her face to the side, as a bit of ground was spewed into the air.

She hadn't considered her exact position when she'd taken this spot. She'd only formed a loose circle with Fiona and Ida. But now, turned to face this enemy, Caitrin stood at the forefront, that after the nearest Englishman passed his scathing gaze over the three of them, he settled it upon Caitrin.

"These lands are now confiscated by Edward, King of England, Lord of Ireland, Duke of Aquitaine," the man said, leering down at her, "and overlord of the kingdom of Scotland. What is your business here?"

Swallowing the terror in her throat, Caitrin sent a nervous, pleading glance to Fiona, having no idea what to say.

But all Fiona's initial bravery seemed to vanish that she only stared mutely at the man, her mouth open.

"We're burying our father," Caitrin said, lifting the shovel as if it had not been noted along with the hole in the ground.

"In the middle of the road?" Challenged one of the mounted men, while his horse danced a bit with agitation.

"It was our da's own grandfather who first carved this path," Caitrin invented. "'Tis where he wished to be."

"I believe you might be lying to me," said the forward man, his black eyes narrowed sharply upon Caitrin.

After what seemed like an enormously long pause, she breathed, "I might be," having caught sight of the Kildares rushing forward one brief second before a war cry was roared and the Kildares erupted all at once from their positions.

Getting out of the way was the only thing Caitrin thought to do. She grabbed at Ida's hand and pushed roughly at Fiona, moving them off the path, away from the fight. A wretched, high-pitched scream sounded behind them as steel met flesh. A thump was heard and then another. A vicious growl preceded a clang of swords. A horse whinnied angrily, a man howled with pain.

Caitrin heard it all but kept moving, shoving Fiona ahead of her, past where their half-finished trap door laid, and further. "Keep going," she urged.

"Gideon!" Fiona protested.

"Won't be helped by us stopping."

Caitrin corralled the two women behind a tree not wide enough to conceal them, but which Ida drooped against, and Caitrin and Fiona turned to take stock of what was happening upon the trail.

Fiona dropped a vocal cry, but it was one of relief. They hadn't run for more than twenty or thirty seconds, but in that time, the Kildares had made quick work of those Englishmen, that six horses were now riderless and all the Kildares stood around, panting, surveying the necessary carnage themselves.

A bolting horse headed toward them. Instinctively, Caitrin stepped in its path, holding up one hand to stop the beast from fleeing. Though the horse reared up to halt his frantic charge, he was not very close to Caitrin that she didn't need to scoot out of the way. "Shh," she said, walking forward. She cooed again, softer now, and reached to collect the forfeited reins.

And just when she thought her heartrate might have slowed to normal, there came the sound of more riders coming. She patted the horse's neck and turned, holding out her hand to Fiona and Ida. They could flee, if need be, the three of them on this horse. Fiona and Ida crashed into her, and someone's fingers curled into her upper arm while all three looked back to where the Kildares waited, several swords drawn back with two hands, assuming a striking pose. Fiona shifted and darted to the left, trying to see her husband through the trees.

Caitrin could only see a few of the men or parts of them, so many obscured by the limbs and the leaves, but she saw swords lowered and the flash of blue and green—more Kildare plaids—as the riders arrived on scene. Next, she heard Ross's voice. "Where is she?"

Giving yet another abrupt sigh of relief, Caitrin began to walk the horse and Ida forward. Fiona was already running through the woods to Gideon. There was an absurd amount of chatter, several soldiers at the same time giving an account to their laird, of what had just happened.

"Goddamn it, Samuel!" Ross roared then, quieting all of them at once.

"There was no time! And she dinna listen!" Samuel shot back, his roar deeper but without the fury of Ross's.

Caitrin hurried her pace, lest Samuel be subjected to more of his laird's fury. "We're here!" She called out, ahead of her stepping out onto the road.

Ross turned at the sound of her voice. Caitrin did not see what his reaction was to her coming, her own gaze riveted on these dead bodies. Her shoulders slumped. She had neither love nor use for any English person, but death in general saddened her. Here, felled upon foreign soil, was someone's son or husband or brother.

She stopped near where Gideon had just released Fiona from his embrace and found her hand yanked from Ida's as Ross took hold of her, his critical blue eyes scouring her face and gown and hands.

"Do not take Samuel to task for what I chose to do," she said, her voice surprisingly level. Admittedly, if his anger were directed at her, she might have wilted a bit. But she found herself stronger in defense of another.

"Och, laird!" Cried Ida, her relieved excitement still palpable. "Ye should've seen her—*I might be*, she says to the dark-eyed devil."

It was then that Caitrin determined that Ida wasn't much for reading people, that the lass made no distinction between the ferocious scowl about him now and any other less formidable look he might give.

Fiona caught the look. "Hush," she snapped at Ida, who then stopped smiling and moved her gaze from Ross to Fiona, and then to Caitrin, before she looked at Ross again and gulped down a nervous swallow.

Ross said to Caitrin, his voice slow and dangerous, "If you ever—ever—do something so foolish, so bluidy dangerous again, I promise you—"

"Why should I be excused from any of it?" She challenged him, standing tall in the face of his unaccountable fury. "I have no more value than any other person."

He opened his mouth, a retort nearly spat at her, before he clamped his lips, struggling mightily it seemed to not snarl at her.

Fiona stepped in, having to peel Ross's hand away from Caitrin's. "Come. We've still work to do while they...clean this up." And she turned, grabbing Ida's hand as well, leading them back to where they'd dropped their project.

Caitrin's back burned where she was quite sure Ross's gaze scorched a hole.

Without any verbal declaration of intention, each woman then sat with their backs to the remains of the slaughter on the narrow path and silently continued where they'd left off with the twigs and vine.

They did not speak for quite some time, listening to the sounds of what went on behind them. They heard the men discuss and then discard the idea of simply tossing the bodies into the pit they were digging. This was followed by noises that could only be bodies being dragged away. And the digging continued, the trench reaching a satisfactory depth at about the same time Caitrin and Fiona and Ida finished with their production, more than an hour later.

They stood all at once, dragging the long rectangle piece of woven tree parts toward the hole. Two soldiers hopped forward and took charge of the thing, positioning it carefully over the opening. It was too large, but at least they would have no fear that it might fall into the hole itself. Next, they collected leaves and grass and other debris and scattered it all about the wattle fencing that secreted the four-foot deep hole. They took some time to sprinkle more of the debris all around the path in this location so that the cover of the wattle did not stand out so much.

When this was done, Samuel announced they would repeat the making of a similar trap in another area tomorrow and the party began to mount up, ready to return to Little Westcairn.

Caitrin finally met Ross's gaze again, the first time since Fiona had wrested her away from him earlier. He seethed still, she saw, but could not say why. He handed off the shovel he'd used last to one of his soldiers and said to Caitrin, "You can ride back with me."

"I rode the palfrey here," she told him, he on one side of the hole, she on the other.

In response to this, Ross ground out, "And someone else will see the mare returned."

Just then, she saw that Ida sat behind Samuel on his steed as they walked on by. Resigned, she followed Ross to where he'd left his horse at the far side of the path.

He stood at the side of the horse, holding it still, waiting, his jaw clenched and twitching.

Before she might have gotten on the horse, and while the last of their party moved on back to Little Westcairn, Caitrin appealed to him, "Do not be angry. There was no time—"

He erupted again, instantly and furiously, his face reddened with his stewing anger. "You run, Caitrin," he hollered at her. "You always run! Leave the fight to those trained to do it."

She wasn't dense and did understand that his wrath was borne of concern, but still she thought it overdone. "But Fiona was staying. And Ida. As I said, it wouldn't have been fair. I have no more value than either one—"

He interrupted her, his sharp gaze clawing at her like talons. "Goddamn it, Caitrin. To me, you do."

While the ferocity of his passion about this was shocking, what he revealed with that dramatically delivered statement was mind-numbing, so much so that Caitrin was rendered speechless.

With a flare of his nostrils, he barked, "Get up there."

Jerked into motion, Caitrin did, putting her left foot into the stirrup and swinging her right leg over the horse's back. She flinched a bit when he perched behind her, his actions so stiff and aggressive. Even the hand that snaked around her waist as he wheeled the destrier around to follow the others was unyielding, as if he would not ever let her go.

The guilt she felt then was not for what she had done. She was proud of herself for having shown even that wee bit of courage. She only felt shame for being dismissive about what she now understood was his worry.

As she had many times before, she turned her face to the side, so that she saw his broad shoulder and he might hear what she would say. "Ross, I apologize—"

"Dinna do that to me again, lass," he clipped, though his rage was diluted to some degree. His rigid arm flexed and then softened around her. "Dinna make me fear for you."

Chapter Twelve

With one arm beneath his head and the other lazing about his midsection, Ross stared at the canvas suspended over him. He didn't particularly care for sleeping inside a tent, felt too constrained, too vulnerable, as if he would more easily be caught unawares. When he'd first come inside the tent several days ago, it had been for her benefit. He'd told himself they were well-protected, that the perimeter guard should be able to give them any warning needed if something amiss should arise.

And he'd slept fairly well all these nights. Until last night.

He might have slept better—she was right here beside him—but that the events of yesterday afternoon had leapt to life and squawked inside his head all night.

There had been countless times in his life when the sounds of battle had been known to him. The clanging of steel, the grunts of fighting men, the cries of the dying ones, were not noises that could be mistaken. When he'd ridden out to where Arailt had said Samuel and his party were, Caitrin included, his pace had been unhurried, even as he'd been anxious to see what progress they'd made on what Idgy called the *murder holes*. It didn't matter where you were—in a forest, upon a wide open meadow, along the shoreline of the sea—two swords clashing in battle created a sound unlike any other, which carried easily over and above every other sound.

In any other circumstance, his blood would have pumped with fuel for the fight. Yesterday, upon hearing that first war cry —he'd have known Samuel's deafening roar anywhere—and then that first clang of steel on steel, Ross's heart had dropped like lead into his stomach. So rarely did he know fear that he didn't recognize it immediately, only raced forward, toward the fight. It was only in hindsight, coming upon the finished scrum, that he recognized it as fear and knew exactly what it was about. Who it was about.

To hear then what she had done, how she had risked herself, nearly tore him apart. At that moment, either fear or rage might have split him in two, being equally powerful.

Aye, and she'd apologized, but she didn't get it, didn't understand why he'd been so angry. Fiona and even Ida were different from her and not only because his feelings for Caitrin were far greater, but because those lasses were Highland bred, their whole lives surrounded by warriors and war. They were a hardscrabble lot, impervious to the cold, inured to hardships and misfortune, desensitized to blood and gore and dehairing hides and hell, even to weaving mats to cover murder holes.

Caitrin was gently reared. Not of the nobility, but softer than a Highland lass. She spoke a more genteel voice, was graceful in movement, might even know how to read and write, was just...softer than the hardy women of Westcairn.

Aye, but wasn't her heart made of iron?

A humorless grin creased his features with some niggling recollection, an inconsistency of information from his mother and father, many moons ago.

"The heart is mush," his father had scolded him once, when the child Ross had hesitated and then refused to kill the squirrel in sight of his bow. "Malleable and unreliable," his father had lectured. "Not to be trusted. Follow your gut and your instinct and your brain, lad, and dinna be ruled by the heart."

His mother must have been made aware of his deficiency that day for she sought him out the next and said quietly to him, "The heart is the ruler, Ross, and dinna ever believe otherwise. It guides a clever and just man, makes all the right decisions, and will always cast out fear for what needs to be done. Dinna fear to be ruled by the heart. The heart is iron, my son."

Caitrin began to stir at his side and Ross turned his head on his arm to watch her wake. Her lashes fluttered only once before she opened her eyes. She was facing the peak inside the tent but immediately, first thing upon waking, turned to seek out his face. Her expression was quizzical, wondering at his mood this morning no doubt. He'd not kissed her last night, had thought himself too worked up yet, even then so many hours after the fact, had feared he'd not have been able to stop, or worse, that he might have frightened her with the angry energy coiled inside him.

Presently, he made some effort to relax his features.

She rolled her lips inward, either holding back words or trying to school her own expression to calmness.

Turning onto his side, Ross lifted himself onto his elbow and moved the hair off the left side of her face. "Might I let you out of this tent today? Or have you plans to cause my heart to stop again?"

A hint of a smile teased her full lips. "You know, Ross, more than any, that I would not ever invite danger."

He raised his brows at her, expecting there was more.

Caitrin scratched her nose with her knuckle before saying, "I am not sorry for my actions. I am only sorry that they frightened you—if that was what put you in such a rage." Only the creases forming outside her eyes gave any indication of improved humor. "If *you* were fearful, just imagine how I felt."

Softly, with little rancor, he charged, "That is no' funny."

She brought the plaid up between them, lifting it over her mouth, to cover her expanding grin, no doubt.

"It is no' funny, lass."

"It is not. Not in the least."

"Then why are you smiling?"

"Honestly, I do not know. What reason have I to smile? What is there to smile about?"

"And yet here you are. Smiling," he said, drawing the blanket down away from her face, a smile of his own threatening. She said nothing, worked again to contain her grin. "Why are you smiling, Caitrin?"

She lifted her eyes to his, the green vivid and bright this morning. Her gaze was steady upon him, did not dart around his features. She opened her mouth but then closed it and smiled softly at him, mayhap with a bit of regret.

"Aye then, keep your secrets, lass," he allowed, supposing he might have some idea of what had wrought the smile. He felt it, mayhap what she did, a simple pleasure in her company, a want of more. A hope that happiness was within reach. "Let's go," he said then. "Plenty of work to be done."

SHE'D BEEN SMILING because she was happy, and she was happiest when she was with Ross.

It was only that simple and just that complicated. Simple, aye, because apparently it needed little more than his warm gaze resting upon her, simple because of the teasing glint in his eye when he'd challenged her that her quip about her own fears of yesterday was not funny. Simple, for how so many parts of her body felt and reacted to his gaze, that her heart pitter-pattered, and her cheeks flushed, while there was a tingling in the pit of her stomach, none of these unpleasant. He radiated a vitality that was impossible to either ignore or overlook.

But aye, complicated as well. First, how had this happened so quickly? Two weeks ago, she did not know that he existed. How had he gone from unknown to the giver of joy? She could only imagine that it was somehow tied to his role in her life, that of savior and now protector. But was it only that? Could gratitude alone make her so enamored of a person? And so quickly?

And then, mostly it was complicated because of her own tenuous position—within the bosom of this clan and within life itself. She was once only an orphan and now had been diminished to a displaced orphan, with neither family nor home. For all their kindness, she felt like an outsider here with these people, something she'd never known, even in all her years with the Lornes. But she'd had Mary then, she reasoned, which likely had mitigated any niggling feeling of not belonging.

When she rose and emerged from the tent, the camp was already teeming with activity. She took care of her morning ablutions and broke her fast with Fiona and Ida's flatbreads, making herself comfortable with Aggie and her children, pleased with the invitation Marion had extended.

When she was done, she approached Samuel and asked what might be her chore today. The big man held up both hands as if he wanted nothing to do with that decision. "Ask him," he said. "I'll no' be whipped by him again when ye dinna listen."

Caitrin gasped and her stomach flipped now with some regret. "I'm sorry, Samuel. I did not mean to cause you grief." She did not go so far as to promise it would not happen again, believing that if a similar circumstance arose, she'd make the same decision.

Samuel gave her a curt nod but appeared not so aggrieved as she first suspected. "People who dinna listen get dead, lass," he said, his tone lacking its initial bite. "And then the people whom they do no' listen to get a blistering as well. Dinna do that again."

"I am sorry," she said once more.

Thus, when the time for work had come, she was sent along with the group under Ross's direction and did not suppose that was not by design. With Fiona and Ida once more, they spent the morning doing exactly as they had yesterday, constructing a woven top to cover another hole dug. This one was on an actual road and dangerously close to Westcairn keep, though around a bend where trees prevented any at Westcairn from seeing them or the work.

Because of their proximity to the enemy, and despite the watchful soldiers whose only job was to make sure no one left the keep and headed their way while they labored, they worked mostly in silence, unnerved by the possibility of danger that hung over them.

Although at one point, Ida whispered, "I'm no' sure how much good this will do. I was thinking on it last night—a man can climb out of the hole fairly easily."

Fiona understood its intent far better and explained, "It's no' made to hold them, only to unseat them and disrupt their charge should there be one. Picture twenty mounted men riding, three or four abreast. The first ones stumble into the hole and three or four are down, useless then. If they're moving fast, the second row of riders will no' have time to stop. We can immobilize as many as six to eight English without lifting a finger and without being directly involved—no danger to us."

"But then, they'll just climb out and continue on," Ida argued.

Caitrin supposed, "And then it will be as the laird says: without their horses, the English are certainly disadvantaged, no match for the Kildares."

"Oh," Ida said, but Caitrin could see that she had yet to grasp the entire concept.

"Gideon says that the element of surprise is half the battle," Fiona went on. "He also says always their objective is to throw the enemy off theirs. Something so simple as the disruption this hole in the ground will cause could upend their confidence, have them skittish, which only benefits us."

They finished this gated cover much quicker than yesterday's. Likewise the hole was dug with greater efficiency that the women only had to wait a quarter hour before Ross decided it was deep enough and the wattle fence was laid over top.

Next they moved to another section of the forest and began a completely different project. Caitrin was rather pleased with herself that she was beginning to understand their whereabouts, knew that just now they were directly south of Westcairn and mayhap a half mile southwest of Little Westcairn.

Before Ross explained what they were about here, Idgy and Tavis—who seemed to regularly travel about as a pair—arrived with a cart full of the spears they'd made days before. And then

John came, bringing with him enough rope to wrap the entire curtain wall of Westcairn, it seemed.

"We've got two projects here," Ross said to this labor force. He turned his gaze onto Fiona, Ida, and Caitrin. "We'll need two more wattle fences, as tall as me but only as wide as this." He held his hands to indicate a width of about three feet. Next, he instructed the men that they should collect as many large stones as they could find. "John will work all the ropes about the trees."

Caitrin exchanged a glance with Fiona and Ida, shrugging at this last bit, having no idea what rocks and ropes might be used for, and quickly got about the job, once more collecting branches, limbs, and twine to make the fencing. They ducked into the woods on the east side of this trail and began searching. Caitrin wrestled for some time with a nice, thick vine, heavier than what they'd used thus far, but one that she imagined would be more useful as they wouldn't need so much of it; a single weave might hold the fencing intact. She gave some vague and short-lived attention to John, hammering chunks of wood into a tree and climbing higher with each step he created. She was sure when it was done, she would know what he was about.

It was a rare, gorgeous day for the middle of October. The sky was cloudless, and the sun was bright, and the inside of the woodland felt like a fine summer day. Dropping the vine she'd wrestled away from all it was attached to, into the growing pile she and Fiona and Ida were making, Caitrin noticed that several of the digging men had doffed their tunics, being bare-chested inside the widening pit. She gave them only a cursory glance and went back for more usable brush.

There was enough quiet activity in this area that she was not startled by someone coming close to her as she bent to fetch a perfectly straight skinny limb, until a hand snaked around her waist from behind. She gulped down a scream as she was drawn up against a hard wall of a chest and Ross's voice sounded at her ear.

"You dinna kiss me today."

The scream dissolved into sighed relief, which then quickly escalated into a thrill at his words.

Standing still, with her back pressed against his chest, she challenged, "Or you have not kissed me."

"Whatever the case, it should be easy enough to rectify."

A quick glance around showed no one close, no one watching. Caitrin turned in his arms, her pulse responding as it did when he was near, when a kiss seemed happily inevitable.

"What makes you desire a kiss," she thought to ask, "when there is so much to be done?"

He was once again that charming and playful rogue, his crooked grin only making him more handsome, so much more irresistible. "I dinna ken what this reply might say about me, lass. But you breathe or speak or so much as chew and I've been wondering if I could read an invitation in any of those gestures. God help me when you smile."

"There is little to smile about of late," she thought to remind him. This was given in what sounded to her like a wispy, faraway voice, as she was lost in the sight that greeted her. Ross, too, had discarded his tunic. Her lips parted at she glanced down at him. Before she noticed anything else, she realized that he must regularly work without his tunic, as his chest was not untouched by the sun, but was nearly as golden as his sun-loved face and arms and hands. But it was his sculpted bronzed chest that held her attention now, being covered in a mat of light brown hair that could not conceal how broad and strong and shockingly enticing it appeared to her. She fisted her hand before she might have lifted it to touch him, moving her gaze downward, where his breeches held, low on his lean hips.

"Kisses, Caitrin," he said while she ogled him. "We can smile about a kiss."

This statement jerked her gaze back to his. And without letting one more second escape, Ross kissed her. She did not go rigid, but she did go still. She was amazed, not for the first time, that his lips were soft. Despite his beauty—so far greater than her own, she knew without a doubt—there was nothing soft about him. She was currently pressed against further proof of this, as he'd pulled her against his strong upper body. It seemed natural to bring her hands up between them, not to push him away but to feel him, the flesh that had beckoned and held her gaze. Truth be told, though, she was rather invested in experiencing the feel of him that she wasn't cognizant enough of so much else, and thus gave little effort to the kiss.

Until she realized that he'd stopped kissing her.

He was too close to be able to discern if he might be grinning, since his forehead was dropped against her now. But he might well be, as his eyes were crinkled in the corners, all the pale skin that never saw the sun when he squinted disappearing into the tiny folds of the crease. "If you would be so kind as to close your eyes, lass," he teased, "I'll feel so much less like I'm being judged on my performance."

These words went in and out of her brain. She could make no sense of them. How marvelous was his boyish and light mood. How curious. Did a kiss do that? Could a kiss have that much sway, that much power? She'd only found thus far that his kiss left her muddled and dazed.

"I will close my eyes," she said, entrenched in that dreamy stupor right now.

The creases at the corners of his eyes expanded while a smile definitely tugged at his lips. "And I will kiss you."

She nodded and blinked, waiting. When his mouth touched hers again and he closed his eyes, Caitrin did the same, let her lids fall softly closed.

Previously, she'd given no thought to closing her eyes, though she supposed she must have. Impulse likely wrought that action; she wasn't convinced of the necessity of closing eyes when being kissed. Because it had been mentioned, she now gave it greater thought. And she understood immediately why eyes should be shut. Everything was felt then and not seen.

His mouth slid over hers, corner to corner, in a slow and exhilarating exploration of the shape and feel of her lips. The single arm around her tightened as he deepened the kiss, his lips stroking hers warmly, persuasively. He made a brief foray into her mouth with his tongue, delving lightly, sensuously, waiting her reaction. Caitrin returned the intimate kiss, sliding her hands up his chest and over his broad shoulders. Leaning into him, she gave him her tongue and the kiss quickly became demanding and she a willing and eager participant.

To her surprise, her commitment to the kiss made him abruptly end the kiss and their contact, his hand pushing them apart.

Knowing she was pink-cheeked from the fires lit within her or from the awkwardness for how the kiss ceased unexpectedly, she wondered breathlessly, "Why did you stop?"

"Because," he began and then chuckled, softly, sheepishly, "I canna believe I'd forgotten about your passion, lass, how quickly it stirs me. But we—*I*—canna be provoked to distraction here."

She was obliged to suggest the obvious, "You shouldn't have kissed me, then."

"Like as no," he agreed, "but it dinna often feel like I have any choice."

Caitrin stared at him, beginning to understand so many things about kisses. At the same time, a thought had come to her, one she needed to share with him, that he needed to know.

"I stayed on that road yesterday on purpose, Ross."

He'd bent to scoop up the brush she'd dropped when he first touched her but straightened now and gave her his suddenly stormy regard, his brows drawn low over blue eyes that only a moment ago were alight with the stirrings of passion. "What do you mean, *on purpose*?"

She met his gaze steadily and confessed what she'd only pieced together after the fact. "I will not be a witless and terrified victim ever again. I will stand and fight." His scowl only darkened in response to this, but Caitrin stood firm, adding, "I will not run. Not ever again." She never again wished to be reduced to that fleeing, helpless girl, who believed that running was the only option available to her. Aye, likely it was not the wisest choice, but at least it would be her choice, a life—and possibly a death—lived on her terms, and not at the whim of another.

Ross's cheek throbbed and twitched for several seconds, while he gritted his teeth and decided how to address this. Finally he said, "You ken there is a difference between bravery and foolishness."

Caitrin lifted her chin. "I do. But this is about having a choice, a say in the matter."

"Do I get no say?"

A world of sorrow tinted her features when she shook her head at him. "You do not, Ross." She was utterly convinced that he, more than any other person in her world, would understand. "And you know that, that it would be wrong to live a life by someone else's choices, only ever reacting."

His expression did not ease, even as he nodded. "I understand it, Caitrin. I really do. But I dinna like it, no' one bit."

Of course he understood. Ross Kildare had likely never in his life turned his back on a fight. He faced everything head on, she knew.

"I will be a better—complete—person to live this way."

Holding the brush he'd collected out to his side, he used his free arm to wrap around her waist and draw her close. His blue eyes never wavered from hers. He kissed her briefly and said, with quiet emphasis, "It'll be my job then, to be sure you are never again put into such a circumstance where you have that choice to make, fight or flight."

How amazingly confident he was, how this warmed her, that he thought he might control all the world around him to see her always safe. Laying her hand against the smooth skin of his cheek, she returned his quick peck, the first kiss she had ever given him. "Thank you, Ross."

She did not give gratitude for his acquiescence, and she did not suspect he was actually and wholly capable of keeping her free from danger all her life. She was only grateful that he thought her worthy of such a vow.

With his arm still around her, he yanked her toward him once more. The kiss that followed nearly undid her, being so possessive and imbued with so much fierceness that she succumbed easily, gave herself up to his vast hunger. As before, she moaned her displeasure when he stopped.

To this, he released her and gave her a heart-jumping wink before taking the brush back to the larger pile. Caitrin watched him leave, treated to a view of his back, those hard contours nearly as attractive and impressive as the front. Softly, she touched her lips where he had and was surprised by what decision came to her.

I will allow myself to love him.

This brash and titillating thought came to her unbidden, but she recognized it for what it was, only a temporary plan, as she could not shake the nagging little fear inside her that nothing could endure, that not one thing—good or bad—would last. Aye, she would live free, and make her own choices, but she did not yet believe she would live long enough to thrive.

Still, *I might love him while I live.*

"That's about as addle-cocked as I've ever ken him."

Stunned from her reverie, Caitrin jerked around to see Ross's brother, John, standing upon a low branch of a tall and narrow oak tree whose leaves were mostly fallen.

Sweet St. Andrew!— but how long had he been there, watching, listening?

Having no idea how to respond to that, or what to make of the roguish smirk he wore while he leaned his shoulder lazily against the trunk of the tree, well fifteen feet above her, Caitrin stalled by repeating, "Addle-cocked?"

She walked beneath the tree and tipped her face up to John.

He stared down at her, lifting a brow as he clarified, "Aye, addle-cocked, as in taken, smitten, besotted—call it what you will."

She could not contain a laugh, which was rather snorted out. *Besotted*? Ross Kildare? She thought not.

John swung round the tree, latching onto the rungs he'd attached himself, saying as he descended, "It's no' a bad thing, lass, only unheard of. He's all about the fighting, routing the English." When his thighs were eye level with Caitrin, he hopped down the remaining distance, landing firmly on the ground. Wiping his hands on each other, he turned to Caitrin and added, "And he's no' only been about routing the enemy since we've come home this time. Been at that all his adult life, I guess." While his grin had disappeared, his tone was yet light. "I dinna ken if ever a lass caught his eye. Until you."

She did not feel the need to defend the kiss he'd surely witnessed or his assumption of Ross's *besottedness*, but she did say, "But it's...surely misplaced at this time."

"At this time?" His brows drew low over his eyes. "Aye, lass and will you tell a babe when to come or the snow not to fly or bring on the rain for crops only with hope? Timing only needs your consideration for things you can control—planned battles, such as what we're about, and when to plant, and when to put the ram to the ewe. Timing dinna respect things you have no choice on."

Ducking her head, giving her regard to a few twigs at her feet that might come in handy, she bent and snatched those up and felt his gaze on her yet. It felt strange to have this conversation with anyone, let alone Ross's brother. But then he did not sound or seem annoyed by his brother's interest in Caitrin. She straightened and met his gaze once more, telling him what she'd thought only moments ago, the never-far-away hopelessness creeping in, "Like as not, it will have no time to amount to anything."

This altered his expression drastically. John's face scrunched up with no small amount of disbelief. He blinked, showing some bafflement and his tone, when he spoke next, evidenced his incredulity. "You dinna ken yet to have faith in him?"

Caitrin gasped silently and stared at John. Aye, she put faith in Ross that he could keep her safe, but somewhere in the back of her mind, there was that despair, believing it was only temporary; people were dying every day, it was only a matter of time until it was her turn.

Clearing her throat, Caitrin pointed up into the tree where several ropes were strung all about, from one tree to the next. "What is all that?"

Delivered from his probing stare, John's humor was restored. He followed her gaze and told her proudly, "A little chaos for the English, lass. Last thing we'll do 'fore we leave is plant the rope that trips it. Once someone does, a barrage of rocks, attached to all these different ropes, will swing down from every direction. They'll scramble or be unseated and then someone will run up against the other trap, those spears that'll spring from the ground."

Good Lord, how wicked! "Who thinks of these things?"

John shrugged at her wide-eyed gaze. "My brothers and I were a wee bit wild growing up. We had a lot of ideas, most of which we were happy to implement in and around Westcairn. 'Tis no' our first trap laid, we used to set them for each other."

"Probably caused your mother fits," she guessed, grinning at the very idea.

"Aye, at times," he allowed. "And da' as well, as he was once felled—knocked out for more than an hour—by a rigged system just like this."

Caitrin clapped her hand over her mouth, her eyes wide once more.

John nodded, confirming it as truth. "Aye, he walloped us good, but he did give praise, commended the operation."

Caitrin concluded with a larger smile, "So you and your brothers were holy terrors?"

Another shrug, another grin. "Aye, a fair assessment."

After ten minutes of conversing with John Kildare, she knew little about him but had gathered already that he was as different from his brother in looks as he was in manner and temperament. He was very earnest, but then clearly the more mischievous. He was handsome as well, but he had not the command nor the physical presence of his brother. This, then, made her wonder if Ross, obviously being the firstborn son to have ascended to laird, was born with all that commanding authority or if he'd grown into and worked at it, knowing what would be required of him to lead men.

Chapter Thirteen

Ross turned away from Arailt, his inspection of the clever stone-tipped arrows interrupted when a rider came racing hellbent into the clearing.

It was Idgy and he didn't bother to leave his horse at the edge of the camp but rode straight for Ross, drawing to an abrupt halt directly in front of him.

His frantic entry said clearly that something was amiss. Idgy did not make him wait to find out what it was.

"There's a bluidy army coming," he said, panting heavily. "Coming up the Braemar-Crathie road—sixty to eighty English."

Ross cursed roundly, his mind instantly swarming with ideas to counter this. He squinted fiercely at Idgy. "Bringing men or supplies?"

"Naught but two carts, no larger weaponry," Idgy answered. "Warm, fighting bodies, is my guess."

At this point, Samuel and John had come close to hear this news. Ross addressed them. "We need to put it into play now, with this coming army."

John nodded. "Aye, if we intercept them south of Forter's loch, that'll send them scattering into all the traps we've set."

Aye, it would. But, "Son of a bitch, we're no' ready." And all that they've worked over the last few days was meant for the enemy they already knew, not another coming. But that didn't matter now. He ordered, "Divide the troops, just as we planned. Four units, 'round each of the traps. We canna let any of them reach the keep." He turned to Arailt. "Three archers with each unit, make sure their quivers are full." While he had faith that Arailt had tested the capacity of these unconventional arrows, his archers had yet to work with them. Next, he said to Samuel, "You and yours are the draw. Engage them down there by the loch, but you've got to give them no choice but the forest as their escape and you follow. Hard. Right behind them."

With a nod, Samuel left, giving a sharp call to gather his unit.

John said to Ross, "Caitrin and the others are finishing up at that last location, with Hamish and Gideon."

He knew that. He always knew where Caitrin was. "Aye, I'll head there." He assigned John and Idgy to the other two locations and advised Arailt and Simidh they were in charge of the camp's defense. He would assume nothing, not after the English had already once happened upon Little Westcairn, but he had no serious concern that would be the case now, as they'd moved Little Westcairn so much deeper—away from the keep—into the forest.

When Ross had donned his padded leather breastplate and tucked his long fighting dagger into his belt, and the rest of his unit was mounted and outfitted with full quivers, Ross gave the call to move. Not more than five minutes after Idgy had come barreling into Little Westcairn, the nearly twenty men took off in a hard gallop through the trees to the site of the most recently constructed trap. Ross hoped to God it was finished.

While the party they came upon was not besieged by any English—he knew it was too soon for that—Ross suffered a momentary pang of fear when he rode into that site and saw Fiona and Ida and Hamish and others, but no Caitrin. Holding the reins in a white-knuckled grip, he spun his gaze all around.

Fiona soothed him instantly, having spied his frantic search, pointing above her head. "She's there, laird. Setting the rocks on the limbs."

Ross tipped his head back on his neck, walking his horse forward to see into the thick limbs. While so many broadleaved trees nearby had shed their leaves already, this tall beech tree was relatively heavy with leaves yet. Caitrin stood in the crook where a stout branch extended from the trunk, one arm wrapped around the trunk, the other hand holding both the rope she was busy with and a thinner branch just above her head.

God in Heaven. He seethed but kept it tamped down. Ross didn't want to know how she'd climbed up so high, being nearly twenty-five feet or more above his head—and while wearing a léine whose skirts no doubt hampered her ability to climb easily. The canopy was dense but like so many trees in this ancient forest, it had lost its lower limbs over time. Now was not the time to upbraid her and everyone else about how unseemly this was, that Caitrin should be the one to ascend the tree to set the bloody stones in place.

"I'm almost done," she called down to him. There was a slight hesitation to her voice, as if she expected him to take her to task for what she was about. Wisps of her hair hung all around her face, dropped while she glanced down at him.

At his side, Martin remarked casually, "Best leave 'er there. Safer than the ground."

Ross's scowl eased a bit when he considered this, that dense canopy he'd noticed only a moment ago, and Caitrin's dull burgundy gown, which was fairly imperceptible, hidden by the colorful golden orange foliage. He discarded it almost at once, as she would be trapped if she were discovered. Not that he expected to afford the English time to be looking to create trouble. He intended only that they were dispatched immediately or running for their lives.

Dismounting, waiting at the base of the tree, Ross discussed with Hamish and Gideon what was happening, how at any moment Samuel's unit might be terrorizing the large English force, sending them scattering into the forest. He gave Hamish instructions to escort Fiona and Caitrin back to Little Westcairn and then moved around to the back of the tree, to where Caitrin was descending, using the stair rungs someone had punched into the trunk. Her skirt caught up on one of the jagged steps and she fussed with that for a moment. When she was within reach, Ross grabbed her by the waist and lowered her effortlessly to the ground.

"They are coming now?" She asked then.

Ross sensed her disquiet, though she tried to conceal it by holding herself erect, straightening her spine. Her gaze sat unblinking on him.

Finding her hand, he lifted it and gave it a reassuring squeeze. "Aye, so get on with Hamish. Stay near Arailt inside Little Westcairn." He shifted his attention to Gideon then. "Is this all set?"

"It is. If they dinna trip the lead rope, John arranged it so it can be hacked there," Gideon said, pointing to the end of one of the lengths of rope, which had been wound around a stout peg hammered into a tree. "Slice that one. It'll set the whole thing into motion." Gideon cast his gaze around the mounted warriors who'd come with Ross. "Be aware of the swinging rocks. Will no' do us any good if they only meet with any of us."

Ross clarified their intent. "They're meant to upset them as they race through here, so that they are already perplexed before we rush out at them."

Gideon shrugged. "Aye, and that's the plan."

"Go then," Ross ordered Caitrin and Fiona and Ida, who had no place here now. He watched a few seconds later as they left, Hamish capably managing with only one hand an English steed they'd confiscated in the last week while Caitrin and Fiona shared the saddle on the palfrey, the reins held in Caitrin's white-knuckled hands.

While Fiona, hanging onto Caitrin's waist, met Gideon's eye, Caitrin sent one last look at Ross. He nodded tightly at her but made no promise to her that all would be well.

LITTLE WESTCAIRN SHOULD have been quiet. After the last encounter with a larger party of English, which had only blindly stumbled upon their camp, it had been decided that those who did not fight directly would remain idle at camp, quiet, without any fire burning. They would be ready to bolt or ready to fight, if either need arose.

When Caitrin and Fiona rode up into the camp, they found instead a wailing Agnes, her hands covering the bottom half of her face while Arailt tried to calm her. Caitrin did not leave the palfrey with the lad, Roland, but walked the horse to where Agnes was crying to Arailt.

Agnes, who appeared not even to realize her coming until she was inside her periphery, looked up to Caitrin, her expression one of silent agony. She dropped her hands and opened her mouth. And while she looked about to say something, she convulsed with anguish and was unable to get out any words.

"The lass, Marion, is missing," Arailt said. "Agnes has been searching for the last hour."

Caitrin's heart dropped into her belly. "Give me a dagger," she said to Arailt.

He scoffed at this. "Nae, lass. Oliver and Simidh are searching. She'll be returned in—"

"It's been an hour," Caitrin challenged. She thought of her own fear, hiding from those devils when Mary and Peigi and the Lornes had been killed, how she'd been convinced at that time that fright might be fatal. She couldn't imagine Marion's terror, even if she were only lost, and not surprised by any English. "Give me a dagger," she said, with more conviction this time.

"Me as well," Fiona said behind her, her fingers tightening around Caitrin's middle.

Arailt grumbled a curse and pulled his own dagger from his belt, stepping forward to lift it up to Caitrin. He turned and walked away then, mumbling something about the laird dining on his innards at meal time.

Agnes rushed the horse and the women on it. She clutched at fistfuls of both their skirts. "Please find her. Ye ken they're all I have, the bairns. I would no'—"

"We will not return without Marion," Caitrin promised. "Where was she last?"

"She only went to the brook, lass," Agnes wept, the words barely discernable, "to wash her face and hands. It's no' far." She pointed to the trees beyond where Caitrin's tent was set up, toward the winding little brook Caitrin herself used every morning to wash her face and hands.

Arailt returned, holding up another dagger, which Fiona claimed as her own now. He gave Caitrin a frosty-eyed glare and admonished, "Stay to the south and east only. I mean it, lass. Dinna be treading where the English are coming."

"We're going to find Marion," she said as she wheeled the horse around, "where ever that takes us." This last part was given with greater conviction, but with less volume so that Arailt didn't fuss so much.

"Och, the poor thing," Fiona said at Caitrin's back.

"We'll find her," Caitrin vowed.

They found the softly roiling brook and followed that, encountering Oliver and Simidh within a half mile.

"Marion?" Caitrin asked needlessly. The child was not with them.

Oliver expressed a wee bit of his own agony when he said, "We canna stay on the search. Laird says we're to stay in Little Westcairn."

He and Simidh were part of the camp's small defense.

"Go on then," Fiona said from behind Caitrin. "We'll keep on."

Oliver's mouth opened, and he shared a tortured look with both women. "Does the laird ken this? Och, he's no' going to—"

Caitrin kneed the palfrey into motion once more. "We'll be back before he knows we're gone."

"And with Marion!" Fiona called over her shoulder as they left the two gaped-jawed men. Only seconds later, she asked of Caitrin, "But what do we do if we come upon the English?"

"Outrun them? Circle around back to where Ross is?" Was all she could think, as she had no real plan for such a circumstance, only a hope that their luck should not prove so dastardly. "If I were lost and afraid and heard a horse coming, I would hide," she said next to Fiona. "I think she'll need to hear our voices."

"Aye," Fiona agreed, but her assent was laced with uncertainty.

Calling out for the child would only invite others to discern their whereabouts in the forest.

"Marion!" Caitrin called, believing there was no other choice. "Marion! Come out!"

And then the damage—if there should be any—was done, that Fiona added her voice to the search as they rode on.

THERE WERE TIMES WHEN there was no choice but to leave things to chance. A fighting man preferred not to live that way, though, not if he could help it. As it was, the traps they'd laid had been set to snare the English inside the keep, after they'd drawn them out. So, they would not be used for whom they were intended, but Ross was thankful that they were available for this occasion just the same.

They had been constructed with the knowledge that they would cause more confusion than actual destruction of large numbers. If they worked as intended, however, the chaos would allow the Kildares to inflict plenty of damage. Ross's army presently might be greater in number than this regimen headed to Westcairn, but they knew they could not afford to lose any of their own against this additional and unexpected threat, as they needed every man available and able to fight when it came time to lay their own siege on the Kildare keep.

With this in mind, Samuel's party's initial assault on the coming army was not made to engage them in close combat but carried out in an attempt to scatter the English troops into the forest. Surrounding them on three sides, the archers first put those stone-tipped arrows to the test, firing from the ridge above and the trees on either side of them. This had the desired and simple effect of catching them off guard. The English were further dismayed by the roar of battle cries shouted from the trees, surely voice by a rebel troop of greater numbers than their own, the roar both deafening and bloodcurdling. A chaotic dancing of horses and men ensued, while they searched in every direction for the unseen enemy and when the second barrage of arrows flew, they did as hoped and dispersed desperately back the way they had come. Their retreat lasted but seconds, met then by the third wall of Samuel's unit and yet another onslaught of flying missiles, which then sent them, as planned, into the forest, away from the open road where they were only exposed and easy targets.

The trails about the forest, which the Kildares had known and used for centuries, had been cleared of debris over the last few days. The leaves and twigs and pine cones had been scraped away with rakes so that the path was effortlessly found, and a fleeing man might be happy to come upon it to make swift his escape.

One group followed what the Kildares referred to as the *cairn trail*, as it cut through the forest, as straight as the crow flies, toward the ancient stone formation, a once tall landmark of stacked stones that the English would never see as it was miles away. Upon the trail, racing away from what they were sure must have been hundreds of savage Scotsmen, the man who led that reckless retreat and his steed suddenly stumbled as the ground beneath them gave way. They went down hard and three more, immediately upon his flank, crashed on top of him, unable to draw up so quickly to prevent the catastrophe from expanding. In a matter of seconds the large hole in the earth had swallowed up horses and men, the former crushing two of the latter. And while the next few men were given extra seconds to react and then avoid a similar fate, they were met with the Kildares' stone arrows, and only seconds later, four more men were unseated, their flight disrupted. And then the trees all around seemed to open up and spew forth a multitude of roaring Scots and the fight was on. It lasted but a few minutes, the English who remained being no match for the shock and awe of the Kildares' campaign.

In another part of the forest, down another trail conveniently made visible, the front line of fleeing Englishmen was met by a barricade of sharp spears contained between two panels of woven fencing and lifted up from the ground when the rope was tripped, and the pulley was activated. There was not a Scot who witnessed this who did not mourn the injury to these good steeds. They did not waste time on regret, though, but watched as into this chaos heavy rocks began to swing, launched from every direction, making contact with a number of startled Englishmen. Those who survived these two elements of war were then greeted by a third component, the warriors who burst from the trees to deprive them of either escape or life.

Not so far from that scene, yet another one played out. More English charged through the woods and straight into the snares set for them. This ambush went the way of the others, bewilderment and shock putting the English in a sorry state so that they were readily overwhelmed, by gaps in the earth and stones that flew out of trees and then Kildares and their mighty swords.

They spent the better part of an hour chasing down any who had managed to escape, those numbers fewer than a handful and then reduced to zero when the Kildares were done with them.

And victory tasted sweet, and they were neither quiet nor sober in celebrating their triumph. It could be heard all throughout the forest, the invigorated state of mind of battle lasting long after the fight was done and returning to Little Westcairn with them.

There, the celebration was clipped neatly and efficiently by the news that Marion had gone missing and that Caitrin and Fiona, attempting to find her, were feared lost as well. Thus, there was no rest, as the army had barely settled into camp before they sprang into action once more.

In its entirety, the Kildare army was able to cover a lot of ground. Still, the favorable mood was quickly dampened with each passing hour when no sign of any of the missing females was found. They were able to follow the palfrey's tracks for a while but lost this ability when the prints moved away from the grassy banks of the creek and up higher, onto ground that was either too rocky or carpeted with dry pine needles that rarely gave up information about who might have passed over it.

They continued searching though, into the night and the falling darkness until several more hours went by, and John Kildare insisted no more could be done on this moonless night. They would try again tomorrow.

ROSS WAS ON THE MOVE again before the sun had made its presence known in the morning, his neck and jaw throbbing for the long night passed clenched as he barely slept. And while he didn't need Agnes to tell him yesterday to harbor no misplaced anger toward Caitrin, that she was brave and clever to have taken on the task herself, it had been necessary for John and Samuel to physically restrain him from going on last night with the search for all three of them.

He knew that about Caitrin, had sensed it almost from the beginning, that the shell of a woman he'd come upon and had known in those first days was only that, a shadow of the courageous girl who dwelled within. She was so much stronger and braver than what a person assumed by looking at her, possibly tougher than even she supposed herself.

She's out there. And she's fine, he told himself. And something, he knew not what, insisted that he would know if she were in danger. Or worse.

He scoured all the area along the creek as they had yesterday but went farther and faster now, knowing already where they were not, in the area already searched. At one point, he sat upon his steed on a great cliff overlooking the glen below and all the mountains and lochs and forests beyond, the view—and thus the possibilities—endless. But he stayed up on that high land. They were only lost, he told himself, not set upon or taken. Thus, believing they were only trying to find their way back to Little Westcairn, he knew Caitrin was indeed clever enough to not confront and attempt to traverse unnavigated territory such as this. And so he turned his horse around and continued his search along the narrow and winding brook.

"LIKE AS NO," FIONA said, "it's a good thing we dinna keep on last night. Would've come to harm, I ken, the way this ground dips and rises."

Caitrin agreed. "Aye, or this fine girl might have stumbled, lost her footing, or worse." She patted the neck of the palfrey with great affection, for how sweet and patient she'd been.

"Ma's going to have my head," Marion predicted in a moan.

Fiona laughed. "Aye, she will, but that'll come after, when she's done hugging ye so tight you think ye'll expire for lack of air to breathe."

"I see that as a certainty," Caitrin contributed with a weary grin, walking alongside the pair on the horse. She was unaccustomed to riding so much as they did yesterday and though the mare might well have managed to carry all three of them, she was perfectly happy to go on foot, her bottom not yet recovered from all the hours spent in the saddle yesterday. They'd come upon a teary-eyed and terrified Marion only about an hour after they'd met with and passed Oliver and Simidh. The child had indeed only lost her way, initially chasing what she was sure was an elusive pine marten, until she lost sight of the cat-sized weasel and realized she'd lost her bearings as well. She thought she might have heard Oliver and Simidh looking for her, but as they'd not called her name, they were only riders to be avoided and she'd run further into the forest. She'd been scraped up and wore tear tracks down her ruddy cheeks but was otherwise unharmed when she finally came running to Caitrin and Fiona's calls. By that time, however, they'd gone further than any previous jaunts around the forest and landscape of Westcairn and were at a bit of a loss themselves about direction. The sky, which had been gray all day, offered no help, being so overcast that no direction could be discerned by the sun's position. They'd traveled then in what they only thought might be the right direction, but only until they began to second-guess that decision. And then darkness had come, and Fiona and Caitrin agreed that they were better off staying put until the sun rose, hopefully in a cloudless sky.

And now, while Marion agonized over her poor mother's possible fear and anger at her long absence, Caitrin was more anxious over Ross's reaction, what fury he would thrust upon her for her actions, what he might assume was beyond her capability. He would tell her she had no business riding around the forest with only Fiona for company, assuming a role best left to those who could manage it better. Oh, he'd be angry all right.

Part of her just didn't care. The night had been awful, and while neither Fiona nor Marion had struggled to sleep, the three of them huddled together for warmth and security, Caitrin had spent most of the long hours awake, listening to all the night sounds. Now, she was hungry and tired and cold and wanted only food and sleep and not Ross's condemnation.

Marion chattered on, likely in some attempt to keep her mind from being besieged with worry over her mother's sure upset and the expected reprisal, and they trudged on.

"This is right, aye Caitrin?" Fiona said after a few more minutes when nothing in the landscape looked familiar yet. "We're no' getting more lost?"

Caitrin froze momentarily, her gaze upon a shifting shape moving about the trees a hundred yards ahead. She grabbed at the halter of the palfrey so that the horse paused as well and looked at Fiona and Marion, pressing her forefinger to her lips to quiet them.

Just as she thought, *I will swat the mare on the rump to send Fiona and Marion away while I run in the opposite direction*, a loud call reverberated through the woods.

"Caitrin!"

Instantly, her shoulders sagged with relief. Ross had come.

Fiona laughed, her own relief evident. "Guess he's no' wondering where me and Marion are." But she only teased, was not upset that it was Caitrin's name he called.

"Here!" Caitrin called back then and thought wistfully of all the times Ross had ridden to find her or had come to save her.

"He sounds angry," Marion whispered, a bit of a wince to her expression.

"And that will be my trouble and not yours," Caitrin assured her, though her pulse raced a bit, having detected a desperate bent to his loud call.

He'd only been walking his horse, but now picked up speed, winding around trees and brush to reach them. Caitrin watched, sure she would never tire of how magnificent he was, so tall and majestic upon his huge destrier. His handsomeness was only part of the present appeal, his eyes so blue, his jaw so square, and his lips so full, their taste and texture already met. Otherwise, it was the overall picture he made, a fierce warrior so steady and sure, his posture rigid, his hand firm upon the reins, the very height and breadth of him a marvelous thing to behold.

His gaze only skimmed over Marion and Fiona as he neared, before settling with some unfathomable but dark-eyed expression upon Caitrin. She did not shudder or wilt under the force of his gaze but straightened her spine and asked, "Are we very far off track?"

Shaking his head, while his expression inexplicably eased, he answered, "Far from camp, but headed in the right direction." He gave his regard to Marion then. "You all right, lass?"

Marion nodded swiftly and that was enough, it seemed, that Ross moved the destrier toward Caitrin, lowering his hand to her. "Let's get on back then."

Once more upon the big horse with Ross, his arm cozily and comfortably settled around her, they rode for nearly fifteen minutes in silence. All the while Caitrin waited, hardly able to believe he had no strong or angry words for her, for what she had dared. Until she could stand it no more.

"You have nothing to say to me?" She asked, turning her face toward his chest. "I rather expected I would face a sound scolding for my actions. But you should know," she hurried on, before he did just that, "I'd do the same again, if a similar circumstance presented itself. Ross, I couldn't just let—why are you shaking your head?" She'd felt his chin scrape against her hair.

"Nae, lass," he said quietly, close to her ear. "You scared the hell out of me, but I ken that works both ways. You had your own worry and misgivings to contend with when you left that site yesterday, where you ken there would be a scrum. I saw that on your face. Aye, and you managed that and then went off to find Marion when others could not." His arm tightened possessively around her middle. "I ken it's a fine trait for a laird's wife, to put another's safety above her own."

Chapter Fourteen

Possibly, these were the most provocative words that had ever been uttered to her. So much so, that she was quite sure that she misheard, or more likely, that she misunderstood the essence of what he was saying.

A fine trait for a laird's wife.

Her bewilderment remained, her lips parted with wonder, when they were confronted with John and Tavis and others, coming toward them. They announced their presence much as Ross had, with loud calls, shouting the names of all three lasses.

It was Fiona who hollered their location to the other searchers while Ross and Caitrin sat silently upon his steed, she processing his cryptic statement while he might well be waiting some reply or response from her.

Gideon was not among these rescuers, meaning Fiona's reunion with her husband would have to wait. Caitrin tried to answer John's quizzical perusal, which clearly wondered if she were all right or if he should make anything out of her befuddled expression. Possibly, the smile she attempted for his benefit was yet perplexed; he was not placated, his risen brows dropping into a curious and concerned frown.

"All is well," Ross said to his brother, whose gaze then shifted there, behind Caitrin.

The larger group then continued onto Little Westcairn, the mood enlivened by the happy resolution of the lost girls. Tavis teased Marion, said her mother was going to tether her to her side for at least a week.

"A week, my arse," said another. "Yer done for, lass. Yer mam'll no' ever let you out of her sight again."

"She'll tell ye now, first thing," Mercer predicted, "ye took ten years from her life. Mark my words."

Even John contributed to the good-natured jibing. "Your days are set in stone now, lass. But it's no' a bad thing, aye?"

And all the while, Caitrin said not a word, contributed nothing to the charming levity of these fine people who cared so much for each other.

They arrived at Little Westcairn after another quarter of an hour. The tableau was as expected: Agnes wept with joy and relief and squeezed her daughter tight to her bosom. She expressed considerable praise and appreciation to both Caitrin and Fiona—"Ye lasses saved my life"—and the latter was reunited with Gideon, whose pale façade was quickly returned to a healthy color at the sight of his wife.

To encourage what the men had predicted only moments ago, Tavis suggested to Agnes, "Ye keep a keen eye on that lass, aye, Aggie?"

Agnes kissed the top of Marion's head once more and drew a round of satisfied laughter from all those near when she said, "Aye, and she'll no' go far. I ken she put me closer to the grave with that scare."

And Ross slid off the back of the destrier and gave all his steady regard to Caitrin, while a hint of a grin tugged at the corners of his mouth. "Awfully quiet there, lass," he remarked. "More so than normal."

As a natural course of action, something they'd done many times by now, they reached for each other at the same time. Ross raised his hands to her waist while Caitrin turned and reached for his shoulders. She was pulled from the steed and set on her feet, and she lifted her face to Ross.

The impending grin evolved a wee bit more. "You have me worried now, fearing you are not of a similar mind."

"A similar mind... to what?" Aye, it might be obvious, what he'd insinuated. But he'd only done that, hinted at something as unexpected as it was exhilarating. Still, she was in no position to assume or to ascribe anything else to his ambiguous words. No matter how much her heart fluttered with hope at what he might have been suggesting.

He sent a glance over the people gathered round Agnes and Marion, his smile pleased yet, and then gave his attention once more to Caitrin. "Let us walk a spell."

They did, the din of the quiet revelers growing lower and lower as they distanced themselves, moving deeper into the forest. Caitrin was weary and today felt particularly dirty, and she thought there might even be cobwebs in her hair from where she had not slept but had sat against a scaly-barked tree with Fiona and Marion on either side of her. She had not heard and had yet to ask what had transpired yesterday, with an army of English coming at them, though she deemed that the jovial moods of the Kildares this morning—Ross's stomach-fluttering grin of moments ago included—must surely signify that the confrontation and outcome had been tipped in favor of the Kildares.

And yet she walked along silently with Ross, her entire body and mind taken with his presence and what might come next—if they'd move away from camp as she suspected so that he might explain thoroughly what he'd thus far only implied with so much ambiguity. But then they only continued to walk, and Ross did not dive into any conversation to explain himself, that Caitrin became agitated by what she suspected but did not know, and why he was making her wait yet more to have things clarified.

As they came upon a clearing, she might have supposed he waited only for this, a pleasant setting to have a discussion with her. The clearing was extraordinary in that it was a wide swath of green grass inside the forest, where no trees stood. She could walk from one end to another in only seconds, 'twas not so large. But it was curious also because the very center of this spot of ground seemed to have at one time been carved away. The earth dipped lower there, revealing large and jagged rocks in that tiny glen, into which Ross leapt. He extended his hand, assisting Caitrin as she descended the slope to stand upon more soft grass, surrounded by a circle of boulders, around which the ground had been cleaved. There were two rocks specifically that were rather flat-topped, and Ross sat on one of these, indicating that Caitrin might do the same across from him.

She did and smiled at this, at this site and how lovely it was, for the sun being able to shine directly upon it, how warm that was, and for the impression it lent, as if they sat upon chairs in a cozy garden, with sunshine and greenery and chirping birds all around.

"'Tis very pretty," she told Ross, when she'd swung her gaze all around and returned it once more to him. And because he seemed only to be waiting for some opinion on so charming a spot.

"My brothers and I found this," he said. "Must be a score or more years ago by now. We waged war from this spot, preying upon an invented enemy—who by the way, sometimes rained down from the sky. Any hour not dedicated to our actual training or any other thing that required our attention or attendance, we came here."

She liked that. First, that he'd shared this with her, and then, as she pictured a much younger Ross—much blonder, mayhap less reserved, a wild and fearless lad fighting imagined dragons or what have you—her smile only grew.

She was comfortable with Ross, enjoyed time with him and those sweet kisses they'd not yet explored to her satisfaction, or any occasion that put them in a close circumstance that saw him touching her, abed inside that tent at night or front to back upon his steed. But she did not now know a certain comfort or ease, speaking with a man who liked to kiss her: being courted, she might guess it resembled. Everything with Ross was unchartered territory, all so new to her. Thus, she opted for directness, which abetted her want of answers.

"It sounded to me—and correct me if I am wrong—as if you were thinking to wed me." Possibly, this now was the bravest she had ever been in her life, to have put that out there, to have been unable to do so without that high-pitched nervousness resounding in her tone, which likely betrayed her own thoughts on the matter. No doubt her face was flushed beet red.

Bravery had its limits, though, that she'd made that statement while only staring at the corded veins of his sun-colored neck. However, her gaze was drawn to his eyes almost immediately, the responding smile not unseen in her periphery.

Oh, and she was smitten indeed, so tantalized by the warmth and pleasure she read in his blue eyes.

"I am," he replied with an unnerving amount of simplicity, which begged a bit of confusion from Caitrin.

"But why?"

He was the most handsome she had ever known him at that moment, sitting so straight and proud, his shoulders broad, and his cropped hair and mesmerizing blue eyes brightened by the sun. His legs were not held together as were Caitrin's, but splayed wide on the seat, the pose so confident and...manly. Incredibly attractive for all it was worth.

"If my plans for those thieving English and Westcairn dinna go as intended, if aught goes awry, you will have a home, no matter where that is, with the Kildares. Truth be told, that was the first notion I had when I conceived the idea," he paused, giving her a meaningful look that held some reprimand yet, "since I could no' sleep last night, but instead spent so much time tortured by some fairly vivid thoughts, wondering where you might be and if you were scared or in danger or... worse." He breathed deeply, with that put out, and continued. "I ken it makes sense otherwise as well," he said. "I've been making free with you, kissing you, wanting more. I dinna have a wife. Likewise, you've no husband. We could be that, to each other."

At that moment, wondering if this, what he'd just said, was the entirety of his motivation, Caitrin had to consider her own—since yes, the idea appealed to her greatly. But the why of it escaped her, or mayhap she'd simply not explored it at all. On a daily basis, Ross was only the beautiful man who had lifted her above death and disaster, who had given her another chance at life, a life so far different than what she'd known, but one that was almost more fulfilling now—because of him? And he liked to kiss her, and she enjoyed those very much as well. But... had she considered more with him, or even what might constitute *more*?

Though she had not put any of this conjecture into words, Ross said then, "You worry for me, for my well-being. Is that only about the protection I provide, what would become of you if I were no' here, or is there more to it?"

"Well, I..." she paused and let that thought die. She did not misunderstand what he was asking, she was only unsure what to reveal, or how much to reveal. "There is more," she told him quietly. Certainly, when she considered what danger might befall him, it was grounded in something larger than her own selfishness.

"Aye, and I worry about you, ken it's *my* responsibility," he said, pointing to his chest, "to keep you safe, as I promised you weeks ago. But lass, my heart dinna drop to my knees when Agnes's daughter goes missing, or when the English are descending upon us, or God forgive me, when I lose a good man to the war." The look he gave her then was a wee bit tortured. "But when you go missing or danger threatens you or your lips touch mine or you smile at me, I...well, aye, so much happens inside. I dinna ken all of it. But I ken I dinna want you to go away, not anywhere far from me. I find myself eager to ken so much more with you." He gave a small shrug while his mouth pursed momentarily. "I ken I want you by my side, and no' just now, or for only a little while."

"But...you cannot be in love with me?" She rather blurted, some wonder attached to the question, even as what he said made it sound as if he might be. And thus, if that were so—and knowing she could easily say, *aye, I agree with all of it, I feel the same way*—then she might well be in love with him.

Was this possible?

Ross's wide shoulders lifted and fell again, slowly once more. There was a boyish charm to that gesture, not unknown to her, when he grinned along with it, looked almost awkward. If he'd kicked his foot around on the ground and gave that motion all his attention while his cheeks pinkened, it would have coincided perfectly with his posture now.

"I dinna ken love, naught outside the obligatory—though genuine—affection for my family. I dinna ken what it is, that makes me want to shelter you from every storm or see you gowned in silks and velvets, pearls and gold—whatever you desire. That keeps my gaze so steadfast and captivated upon you, so often when it should no' be."

She smiled. The reason behind the smile was twofold, that he'd uttered such gorgeous words to *her*, Caitrin Lorne of unknown origins and currently—in every practical sense—homeless and devoid of family as well. The smile was wrought then as well because she might have returned those exact words to him, verbatim, and it would have been true. She didn't know what to call it, how her pulse raced whenever he was near, how warm and fulfilled she'd felt every time he'd shared a smile with her, how the memory of his kiss only increased her want of more.

"Mayhap there is love," she said and when he only gave her silent regard, probing her with that measuring gaze of his, she added, "on this side as well." She was quite sure the flush that crept up her neck with such bold words was visible to him, but then she was so much less concerned with this than she might normally have been, than she might have been only a day ago or even an hour ago. She had no thought to diminish the truth, but she did think to lighten the suddenly and vibrantly charged air around them. "I cannot envision you clothed in silks and velvets, but if you desired such a thing, and if I had the power to make it so, I feel as if I would."

The next smile he showed her sent her pulse racing once more.

"Aye, then we will wed."

Caitrin nodded. "Very well."

And they sat then, without words, for several long minutes. Here and there, their gazes met, still appraising each other, what all of it meant, considering not only short term benefits, that she would forever be a Kildare and thus cared for, but contemplating long-term possibilities, a life together, children, a home—whether it be Westcairn or another—and naturally, more kissing, touching, and all that accompanied or was tied in with that. Of this last thing, she was sure their thoughts diverged, Caitrin lamenting her inadequate knowledge that offered so little to dwell upon while imagining that Ross might have more experience from which to draw.

This prompted her to reveal what he might already know. "I have never lain with a man before."

He did not show any surprise for how plainly she'd shared this information.

"And you never will again, none but me, Caitrin."

"You have...?"

"There have been... I have bedded women, aye."

"But you will no more, none but me?"

"None but you, all my life."

"Will I like it?" Mary had told her only men enjoy the coupling. Dorcas had once said offhandedly when Gordon Lorne was not near, that, *It is only our lot, to grin and bear it, and ye have yerself a happy home.*

"I will make sure that you do," Ross told her now.

She sensed another grin coming, waited for it, though it did not develop fully. But his eyes crinkled a bit, and she thought his jaw might now be clenched, as if he might be holding it back.

"You are laughing at me."

"I am no." And now he did smile. "I confess to a wee bit of surprise for your plain speaking—which I dinna mind one bit—though I believe I can almost see your mind humming with questions." He lifted his hand from his lap and twirled it around in one full revolution.

"I can ask those questions?"

"Aye. I will be your husband. There is nothing you can no' say to me or ask of me."

"'Tis said that it is painful."

His expression blank, he asked, "'Tis said by whom?"

Caitrin shrugged. "Mary had said as much. Dorcas said it never got any better, only worse over the years."

His reaction to this was only a slight lifting of his brow. "I'll suggest, lass, that you take out of your head any of their opinions or thoughts on the matter and discard them completely. Aye, there will be pain the first time. I dinna ken the how or why of it, but it does get better, and it is my job to make it so." He paused, waiting for some reaction from her, and when there was none but a nervous little nod, he asked, "What do you feel when I kiss you?"

Oh, gosh. Everything. So much. All of it wonderful. Oh, but how to put it into words.

"It's...it is pleasant—very pleasant—but stirs something inside me," she said, and tapped her fingers against her belly and stared at him. "Here."

"And that from a kiss," he said. "Everything that follows will only multiply that feeling. Expand it. It will stagger you, but so happily that you will beg for more."

"I believe you, but I cannot imagine it, what you mean exactly."

Sometimes, his grin had almost the same bedeviling effect as a kiss, that a tingle swelled within her.

"I will have to demonstrate, I fear," he said and did not look at all sorry for what he felt he must do. Ross rose from the charming seat inside the tiny cavern of the clearing and closed the space between them, pulling Caitrin to her feet as well.

Holding her hand still, he used the other to brush aside her hair, the action warmly familiar to her, the gesture almost loving for how softly and slowly he went about it. It seemed to contain some reverence, but did nothing to calm her pulse, which had leapt to life only seconds ago.

He lowered his head at the same time he tilted up her chin with a finger beneath it. Their lips met and any calm she might have pretended to know was shattered, gone on the wind for the immediate hunger of this kiss. Caitrin had neither the will nor the desire to resist, only wanted to taste him and know more of this. Ross glided his lips seductively across her soft ones, using his tongue to tease and taste her. Caitrin capitulated fully, her shoulders softening, her lips becoming pliant, inquisitive. She all but sagged against him, and it was she who furthered contact between them when she slid her hands up his chest and curled her fingers into the rough linen of his tunic.

When Ross's lips parted, unyielding, tasting her fully, a brief shiver rippled through her. She moved her lips to match his own apparent need to devour, opening her mouth as he had done, as seemed natural. She heard the muted groan deep in his chest moments before his tongue entered her mouth, slick and knowledgeable, tasting and probing, rendering her limbs utterly useless, her mind dysfunctional. Responding to him and his kiss was all she was capable of, pushing her tongue into him. Suddenly then, he was all hands, cupping the sides of her head, turning her face one way and then the other to better slant his mouth against her. Long fingers of velvet steel slid across her neck and over her shoulders, drawing their bodies nearer.

Caitrin withstood the near painful grasp of his hands on her shoulders, feeling this same urgency as she raised her hands further, away from his tunic and up along his neck and around, her fingers sliding into the short blond hair at his nape, as soft as everything else about him was hard. There was something almost carnal in how roughly and tightly he held her, how forcefully he kissed her.

His lips left hers though he did not relinquish his hold completely, only set his hot mouth upon the skin at her neck, and along her bare collarbone, pushing aside the wool fabric of her léine as he progressed. This gave Caitrin only a moment's pause, until the exhilarating sensation of his wet mouth on her bare flesh overtook everything else. She let her head fall back and closed her eyes once again, reveling in the feel of him, and the delightful things his touch did to her insides. The warmth of his embrace, the heat of his kiss was so male, so bracing, Caitrin shuddered once more while her belly flipped with delight. And when he jerked at the léine more and kissed another spot of bare flesh, she whimpered and clung to him as her skin prickled at his touch.

She suffered not even a moment's pang of unease when he lowered the léine yet more, exposing one breast, still covered by the thin cotton chemise. His hand, cupping her breast from below, pushed it upward, an offering to his mouth. He kneaded the small globe and drew his tongue tantalizingly over the peak. When his teeth tugged at her nipple through the fabric of her shift, Caitrin thought she died a little death. Her breathing spasmed, a noise escaped, sounding to her ears much like a purr. She moaned in his arms, never having felt anything so glorious as this, in her wildest dreams not suspecting such a thrill was possible.

Untutored she might be, but her body knew what it wanted. Caitrin leaned into his hand and his mouth and his hips and sighed his name as he teased her breast and its bud. *This is love*, she was able to think. *It must be, that he feels so good, and I know no fear.*

"I want to make you feel like this," she said. Her voice was not her own, but belonged to some mysterious creature, husky and seductive.

"Aye, and you do," he breathed against the fabric that covered her breast, which was wet now from his mouth and tongue.

Deluged with awe—for what was happening, for how unexpected it was—she said, "You touch only one breast, but both of them quiver in response. And I feel it lower, in my belly and then...lower still."

As a reply to this, Ross took hold of her hips and ground his own against her, hard against soft, rigid against trembling. And the quivering expanded and heated and made her moan. He brought his lips back to hers and devoured her in another kiss before he said, panting through his words, "Aye, and there's a fine reason to wed, lass. There's so much more I want to show you and do with you."

"I feel alive." She liked it very much. "I want to wed you, Ross."

He touched his forehead to hers. "Quickly now, so that we can finish this."

Chapter Fifteen

"Recall, if ye will, lass," Agnes said, "that when I made vows with the waster, I ken hope and what I believed was love."

Caitrin nodded, already having some idea of this, that Agnes's marriage had not been favorable, mayhap not anything close, but she didn't ever think it had begun that way.

Agnes held a linen wrapped bundle in her right hand, her left hand gently patting the top of it. It had been recovered from Agnes's croft by Gideon and Tavis, whom she'd sent on a mission. "They'll no' have found it, those rotten English," Agnes had told those two men earlier. "It's tucked under the cupboard in the corner. Ye ken the one, Gideon, ye've been there," she'd said, raising her brow at Fiona's husband. "Inside the narrow cupboard, lift the board on the floor. I'd hid some treasures there. Ye bring back only the soft one, swathed in linen, tied with blue threads. Can ye do that?"

They could. They had, making a quick excursion into the empty village and into the croft where Agnes had born and raised her bairns, where she hoped to know many more years. They'd returned in less than an hour.

"So aye," Agnes said now to Caitrin, "there is no bitterness attached to this, no hopelessness, and no' an ounce of regret or fear." She shrugged her thick shoulders at Caitrin and grinned her toothy grin. "That all came later."

Caitrin managed to curtail the sorry grin that wanted to come, waiting for more, as Agnes drew another breath, which normally proceeded so many of her long sentences.

"Aye and I'll be asking, did your mam explain all the wedding night business to ye?"

"I—I didn't have a mother, Agnes," Caitrin answered swiftly, before she'd processed what the woman was actually asking.

Agnes frowned, drawn off topic as well, her expression quizzical. "But then how'd ye end up so sweet and brave?"

This elicited a wee chuckle from Caitrin. But then she was shocked into a straight face by Agnes's abrupt about-face, how her cheeks flushed as Caitrin had never seen them do, how she stammered for the first time ever.

"I-I suppose it'll be on me then, to...fill ye in, what to expect on the wedding night," Agnes guessed, not bothering to hide her dread. "And all that." She waved her hand airily, likely distracted by the very idea of the task she thought now fell to her.

At their side, Fiona giggled and whispered, "Oh, good grief."

Thinking to save the poor woman further unease, Caitrin said to Agnes, "I am not...unaware of what will come, Agnes. I have no concerns, nothing that is torturing me." She recalled Ross asking her to discard anything another had told her about relations between a man and a woman and had to wonder if anything Agnes might have said might have only been more misinformation, colored dark and gloomy by who and what her mate had been.

But wasn't she sweet, dear Agnes? That she would take on the chore of informing Caitrin about something her expression indicated she had not enjoyed so much. Caitrin was not harmed by this, not tormented at all by any sudden unease. Ross had said she would like it, had said he would make sure she did. And truly, it was hard to imagine that anything that felt so good as his kiss could lead to something not equally as nice.

It will stagger you, he'd said. Caitrin smiled a secret little smile now, sure as she was that Ross would not disappoint her.

Rachel groaned at her mother's side, poking at the item in her hand. "Mam, get on with it."

Agnes, lost in her own reverie—of only God knew what—shook herself free with a short bark of laughter and lifted the package to Caitrin. "But ye'll wear this, and may it serve ye well, lass."

"You are very kind," Caitrin said, accepting the gift. Carefully, she untied the threads and unwrapped the linen to reveal a gown of dark green velvet. Caitrin's jaw gaped. As Agnes had given several clues in the last hour, Caitrin had expected it to be a fine gown, but she was not prepared for precisely how lovely it would be. Rachel and Marion tugged at the linen packaging, pulling it all away. Caitrin took hold of the shoulders of the gown and let the length fall to her feet.

Her amazement only grew. The velvet was sumptuous, the green as vibrant as the leaves in spring. 'Twas a simple a-frame silhouette with a narrow, hip-hugging waist and a fuller skirt. The bodice was peculiar, charmingly so, in that it crisscrossed, one side over the other, the edge of each side embroidered with cream and blue threads, detailing a vine of leaves and thistles.

Agnes looked wistfully upon her old gown. "Would've been prettier if mam'd had gold threads," she said touching her plump fingers to the embroidery with some reverence, "but I ken the threads are fine enough."

"Agnes, this is..." Caitrin began, stunned yet for the beauty of the piece, and then more so for the generosity of the woman, "this is the loveliest thing I have ever seen." She leapt forward and hugged the woman, the gown crushed between them. "Oh, thank you. Thank you. You are too kind."

"Aye and now we're family," Agnes said, a bit dismissively, showing some discomfort for Caitrin's effusive appreciation. "Or thereabouts, all one people under the Kildare banner. We'll take care of each other, all our days. Aye?"

"Aye," Caitrin agreed readily. And then, more heartily, her eyes shining with her gratitude, "Yes, indeed."

At their side, Rachel spoke up, looking from the long, narrow gown to her mam. "You wore this?"

Agnes laughed, "Aye, and dinna be cheeky. I was once thin and bonny, too."

"And ye still are," said Fiona, her smile broad. "But put it aside for now, lass," she said to Caitrin. "We've got much to do yet. They're boiling the water now, just for the bride. You'll have a nice warm bath today, Caitrin, set ye right 'fore ye wed."

Oh, but this was too much, and these women were too sweet.

Fiona laughed. "Och, and dinna be tearing yet. Time enough for crying later, when you realize what you've done."

And now all the adult women chuckled at this, and then Gideon appeared, setting a large wooden tub on the ground between Fiona and Ida.

"Thank ye, luv, and off ye go."

Caitrin gaped at the tub. What a marvelous boon for her wedding day.

"It'll leak out 'fore the bath is done," Fiona said with a shrug, "but we'll keep it full as long as we can."

Fiona and Ida, with the help of Agnes's girls, began to hang long sheets of cotton and a few plaids about the trees, hung with rope or slung over low boughs, which would serve as a privacy screen, with the tub sitting directly in the center.

Caitrin looked around at all the faces inside this secluded spot with her. Her heart swelled with more gratitude, that she'd been allowed to meet and know such fine people as this. And now she would truly be one of them.

NAKED AS THE DAY HE was born, Ross dove head first into the loch, clutching the scrap of soap, all the remained until he found or purchased more. There were rarely any perfect days for loch swimming. Even in the height of summer, the deep water in these Highlands lochs never warmed to any genuinely desirable temperature. On this day—his wedding day, as it were—it was misty and cool, the loch itself shrouded in a gray fog, the water chilling. Still, he tarried a bit, a wee bit distracted by what the day would bring.

He was not surprised that all the people of Westcairn—specifically those that mattered most, his brother foremost among them—showed so much joy when he'd given them the news, that he would handfast with Caitrin this afternoon.

Her blush at that time, when that necessarily quiet cheer had gone up, would forever be ingrained upon him, how shy and red-cheeked she'd been then, how bonny was her bashful smile that responded to the joy shown her.

He did not investigate the evolution of his thinking, how he arrived at that point, that he wanted to wed her. It was there, in his mind, and then put out to her, and it felt right. He'd not misspoken, knew it was no lie to have said to her that he wanted her at his side, for all his days, if the God he knew might be so generous to him.

He thought of his parents and their thirty year union and hoped he might be so fortunate to achieve something close to what they had, either in longevity or more importantly, in terms of pure happiness. His father was a sometimes gruff man, who was rarely wrong—all you had to do was ask him—and liked to shout a lot. Only his wife could soothe him. Ross's mother had been both silly and wonderful. As a child, he'd only thought she looked like a mam. He was of an age now that he understood she'd been lovely, in her youth for sure and then even in her later years, poised and quietly confident, a smile always at the ready. Upon reflection, he thought he must be much like his father, entranced and happily captivated by his bride, that he did as his father so often had, sought her out first, upon entering a room in which she sat or the hall for the evening meal. Ross did that, rode or walked into the camp and looked first for Caitrin. One day, he would walk the same steps his father had, into the great hall of Westcairn, and his eyes would search the room for her. Perchance they would trade glances, he and Caitrin, just as his parents had, sharing some private and pleased glow of awareness. Ross liked the idea of it, of growing old with Caitrin, trading hundreds of glances over many, many years.

He was barefoot upon the shore, wet and cold, his plaid wrapped around his waist, when his brother John found him.

"Little cool for pensive reflections upon the bank, garbed as you are," John tossed out at him.

"Aye, but I'm beginning to think that considering one's own wedding is an invigorating thing." Gamely, he thumped his fists onto his hips. He straightened his spine and thrust out his naked chest in an exaggerated pose.

"Warms your cold heart?" John asked drolly.

Ignoring the lazy jibe, Ross grinned. "Aye, it does. And I was thinking on da' and mam."

John narrowed his gaze. "About what?"

Ross shook his head, still working out his own reflections. "There must have been dozens of times I'd watched da' come into the hall and Mother would jerk her gaze to him. As you ken, he often came blustering into any room. For so long—until only the last few weeks—I honestly thought that mam looked at him to gauge his mood. Would he be sour and fretting over something? Was he in a jovial mood? Was he angry? It wasn't about that. She was...simply looking at him. And her gaze softened. Every single time. Again, I thought it was in some effort to calm him—you ken she was the only one who ever could." He shook his head and grinned a bit. "It was no' about that. She just liked to look at him. Mam loved da'."

John took a moment to ponder this. "Aye, they dealt well together." Glancing once more at Ross, he teased, "Bluidy hell, dinna say handfasting with a bonny lass makes you softhearted, maudlin even."

Ross was unphased. Nothing could dampen his mood today. Tomorrow, when they resumed their plans for Westcairn, was another matter entirely. But for today, he would live as a man about to wed, a man well-pleased with his choice. "Your turn will come. I'll give you grief just the same. So go on, I can take it."

John only smiled and stuck out his hand to his brother. "No grief, brother. I am happy for you." When Ross clamped his hand and they pumped at the same time, John said, "It's good for all, a wee bit of attention drawn from reality, planted onto a happy union."

"Thank you, brother." Thinking on something else, Ross added, "You ken she's to be taken care of, should anything happen to me. She's a Kildare, the laird's wife, must be—"

"*Jesu*, is that why you're marrying her? Christ, Ross, we'd have looked after her all the same, married or no."

"Nae, that's no' the reason, that's naught but a boon." One that put his mind at ease, would afford him a clear head in the days to come.

But first, the wedding. Ross grinned once more at John and began to dress.

He tipped his face up to the solid gray sky and lightly falling rain.

"It's a beautiful day for a handfasting, is it no'?"

WHILE ALL THE KILDARES of Westcairn gathered beneath the canopy of a towering yew tree, Ross went to that curtained area the ladies had created earlier. His heart thudded mildly in his chest, and he touched his hand lightly to one of the draped sheets of cotton.

"It is time, lass."

Three seconds preceded her answer of, "I am ready."

With that, Ross pulled back the curtain and Caitrin stepped out and stood next to him.

And many, many seconds passed before he was able to form words. She was beyond breathtaking, and he was rendered speechless for his shock. He'd expected that she might have braided her hair neatly, might have brushed clean the burgundy léine, made it presentable. That was all he'd thought her capable of in this circumstance. And he'd have been pleased with that, even less, he imagined.

But she surpassed even his wildest imaginings, gowned in soft velvet, the green of which only highlighted the perfect light of her gaze. The gown itself hugged her lean curves as he would do this very night, accentuating the flare of her hips and the swell of her breasts. The creamy skin of her cheeks was flushed a becoming pink while her lips were tilted with a sweet but nervous smile. Ross's lips parted in response, amazed and delightfully so, when he raked his gaze over her hair. It was as he'd never seen it before, loose and flowing, shiny and sleek, falling over her shoulders in soft waves over her breast and down to the middle of her back. Atop her head sat a crown of flora, green leaves and a few red clover buds and dried heather pieces for luck.

"You are unbelievable," he said softly to her, his tone giving away his gratified surprise. Her blush grew just as Ross thought that *unbelievable* did not convey—not in the least—what she was, how she appeared to him right now. "Caitrin, you are...stunning." And then he might have kicked himself, that he'd done little more than what he supposed she'd have done. Though he'd cleaned his boots and plaid thoroughly, he'd only brushed off the cleanest of his tunics and breeches, and felt just now, wholly inadequate to take this woman as his bride.

"You are magnificent, Ross," she said softly, and it was apparent that she rarely gave praise, as even this tinted her cheeks redder. She lifted her hand and touched her fingers to the Kildare brooch he'd rescued from his saddlebags, where it was clasped over his plaid at his chest. She smiled as her fingers traced the lines of the jewelry, over the golden head of the stag and the thistle and swords crossed beneath that.

Ross had no doubts, no misgivings at all about taking Caitrin to wife, but when she slid her hand down his chest and away, setting her hand into his and folding her fingers around his, his certainty that he wanted Caitrin at his side always only intensified.

It was an improvised and at times irreverent handfasting, in which John served as the officiant.

"In days gone by," John said to the assemblage, "if the laird were to wed, I'd wager the chosen bride would no' be so bonny as this one here. Aye, and we'd fill the hall with family and guests from outside our own beloved Westcairn. They'd come from far and wide—earls and barons and mormaers, mayhap even the Lord of the Isles or the king himself. We would feast upon succulent roasted boar with all the trimmings, puddings and sweetbreads, pickled herrings and so much more. We'd sing and dance, be lively well into the night. The bridegroom would likely have to kick out guests after three days of feasting." He nodded, considering his next words. "As you ken, we canna have that here. But it dinna take away from the significance of the vows. It dinna make the marriage any less sacred." Smirking, he raised his voice a bit to say, "Likely, it dinna even mean we'll ken any reprieve from the manner in which these two make eyes at each other, as if all the rest of us are blind in one eye and canna see out the other." John paused, waiting for the chortling and guffawing to settle. "Aye, but a fine day for Westcairn, for all of us who live under her wide bough. Our laird is strong and true, needs a mate who can match him ounce for ounce in courage and wit. I ken we all might agree she's every bit as brave and then leagues above him for her cleverness," he said, having to finish the last part over the ensuing laughter, "but we'll hang onto her 'fore she figures it out, that she got the short end of that stick."

"Is there more?" Ross interjected, a good-natured grin evident. "Or might we get on with the actual ceremony?"

"That's more words you spoke now than all year long, son," charged Arailt to John through a chuckle. "I'm thinking now is no' the time to be garrulous."

John gave a bittersweet grin. "It's no' everyday I get to see my brother wed. There will be only this one time, for I ken he has chosen well." He moved his regard away from Ross and Caitrin to encompass all those gathered. "Leave it to those who dinna care about love and loyalty and courage, to arrange their marriages around land and power and coin. We will join our laird and Caitrin together this day, and their union will outlast all others, for they have faith in each other, and love, as you ken, is eternal."

John produced a strip of cloth, which was not only linen torn from an unused fabric or garment, but was a sleeve of finished cloth, with neat seams sewn all along the edges and more embroidery, in earthen hues, depicting a stag's head and swords and thistle, just as Ross's brooch.

John explained to Caitrin, "The late mistress of Westcairn, our own dear mother, gifted each of her sons with this cloth, so that we would always carry Westcairn with us and ken that home is where love begins. This one belongs to Ross, and it will be used to bind your hands in marriage."

Ross lifted his arm up and out, his elbow bent only slightly and looked to Caitrin, who did the same, laying her hand atop his. John then wrapped their hands in the soft cotton strip and wound the ends around and around their joined hands.

Ross spoke then, said very clearly in a firm voice, "I take thee, Caitrin, to be my wedded wife and to hold from this day forward. In fair or foul, in sickness and in health, to cherish as only mine. Not only for one year but for all of our days, until death does part us, according to God's holy ordinance and thereunto, I pledge to thee my troth."

He watched her while she gave her own vow, which was similar to his own. Her voice was softer, but just as sure. "I take thee, Ross Kildare, to be my wedded husband, to have and to cherish as my own and hold through fair or foul, sickness as well as health. For all the rest of our lives, according to God's plan for us, I pledge my heart to thee."

He smiled proudly at her, brimming with confidence for this union and was pleased to receive her answering smile, filled with a wee hint of adoration that he fell instantly in love with. They continued to give their attention only to each other, while John gave more words to conclude the rite. Later, Ross would not recall what came after her vow, he would recall naught but her smile and how his heart swelled with joy.

He did, however, hear his brother say, "I ken they normally conclude these things with a kiss, to seal your fate together."

Turning his entwined hand palm up, Ross clasped his fingers around Caitrin's and pulled her to him. With one forward motion, he'd yanked her into his arms, their matching laughter silenced when his mouth crashed down on hers. 'Twas no chaste kiss the groom gave the bride. His lips were persuasive and demanding and Caitrin responded eagerly, wrapping her free arm around Ross's middle. His mouth did not become softer as the kiss lengthened. Instead he used his left hand and arm to crush her to him while he feasted on her lips and tongue.

The cheer that went up was initially as loud as Ross's pounding heart, until Samuel and Arailt hissed at the same time, "Shh!" and "Hush!" to the happy revelers. This served as well to break the kiss, and Caitrin and Ross were then besieged by their family and all their well wishes.

Chapter Sixteen

It was nothing like the feast that would have accompanied their handfasting if they'd traded vows inside Westcairn, but justice was certainly done to the occasion, made joyous by lively moods and laughter rather than streaming ribbons and bonfires and other decorations. The village had been raided once more, so that two chairs, mismatched, sat in the center of the site, where Ross and Caitrin had sat and consumed their bridal meal. This was only more of the same fare, venison and baked fish and more flatbreads, but was enhanced by the addition of sweet breads. Someone must have raided the stores of sugar and almonds that had been purchased near Glasgow upon the army's return from the siege at Caerlaverock months ago. That stock had been meant for the larder at Westcairn and was not squandered now but welcomed for the sweetness given to those nutty cakes.

By necessity, there could be no large and clamorous celebration, but this did not deter some from making their own music, humming gaily while they danced about before their laird and mistress. As it was, some soldiers did miss parts of the handfasting itself or the quiet feast that followed, as Ross had instructed that at least two watches must hold their positions, those that kept an eye on the comings and goings at the front and rear of Westcairn.

Ross did not wait for darkness to fall to claim his bride and remove her from the celebration. He had plans for her, one of the few things he had predetermined, that he wanted to love her in daylight, wanted to see all the emotions cross her bonny face, wanted to be able to explore with his eyes and not only his hands.

He found her talking to Arailt and Mercer, or rather listening kindly to those two go on about the old days, both likely assuming that she was not only polite but actually interested in their tales of days gone by.

"...and then this one here," Arailt was saying, tossing a thumb over toward Mercer, "says to the innkeep, *Aye, I'll marry yer daughter, but only if my wife gives her blessing.*"

Approaching from behind, Ross slid his fingers up Caitrin's spine, into the loose hair at the middle of her back. Under his warm fingers he received her reacting shiver, a response to his touch. Coming to her side, he lifted his arm and hand, draping them casually over her shoulder, as if he'd done so a thousand times before. To his increasing joy, Caitrin raised her hand, bending it at the elbow, so that her fingers reached his near her shoulder, and she twined theirs together.

"You dinna get all her attention, all evening long," Ross interjected, giving fair warning to Arailt and Mercer.

Mercer, who rarely spoke without eloquence or somberness, said quickly, "We were only keeping her company while she steadfastly avoided yours." And he and Arailt broke out into riotous laughter, fueled more by their lively moods than by too much ale, Ross hoped.

So it was, when only a few hours had passed since he'd pledged his troth to her and she to him, Ross took Caitrin's hand

and led her deeper into the forest, to where he'd moved their tent for just this night.

This spot, chosen with care, had taken him some time to locate today. He'd wanted it far enough away from Little Westcairn so they would not be disturbed though also near water, but not so far that they couldn't be found if needed. Only John knew of its exact location. Or so he thought. When they reached the tent, he saw that the v of the front flaps was decorated with a garland of greenery and more of the dried autumn heather. A small torch had been struck into the ground several feet away from the tent. It was unlit now, surely meant to be used throughout the night if desired.

Caitrin gasped with delight. "Did you do this?" She asked, her eyes shining with gratefulness.

Ross grinned. "I did naught but move our bedchamber, such as it is. I have a feeling this is the work of Aggie's girls." They must have wheedled the location out of his brother.

With her hand still in his, Ross stopped in front of the tent and turned to face his bride.

'Twas extraordinarily green at this site, in brush and pine needles and vines, while a slice of late-day sunlight slanted in from the direction of the water, presenting a shaft of golden light to the emerald of the forest.

For a moment, all the world was gone and only Ross and Caitrin stood upon the earth.

She might well be shy now, her cheeks tinted pink, but she held Ross's adoring gaze.

"I will no' hurt you," he thought to tell her.

"I know."

Simple words, naught but a statement of the faith she placed in him. They should not warm him or stir him as they did. But he was a man, a leader of men, and aye, some of his worth was tied up in that, what he was able to provide to his people, and what they believed of him.

With a gentle tug of his hand, she was drawn closer. His heart lurched inside his chest when her gaze shifted to his mouth, knowing a kiss would come, and her own lips parted, either in wonder or in readiness. When his mouth covered hers, he found that she needed little coaxing. She opened to him immediately and her tongue met his, dancing and twining with his, both tasting of sweet cakes and honey ale.

Releasing her hand, Ross took her face in both of his, felt her hands slide along his forearms, and deepened the kiss.

He paused only briefly, to promise against her lips, "Though it will torture me, I will go slowly. But I mean to begin as we shall proceed: giving and taking freely, open and honest in this loving." When she nodded against his lips, he said with some hoarseness, "I want to be naked with you, lass, and touching every inch of you."

GOOSEFLESH ROSE OVER all of her body at his titillating words, eliciting a breathy gasp.

Ross returned to her lips, collecting that sound, and kissed her as he had before, though gently this time as if *slowly* would begin now. Tentatively, Caitrin touched a hand to his shoulder, pressing her fingers into the flexed muscles under his plaid and tunic. His tongue teased her lips, until her next sigh opened them, and she joined her own with his. Again, he covered her mouth fully, slanting above her while one hand traced a tantalizing line from under her arm, down the side of her, smoothly along the velvet of her wedding gown, and over her hip. The journey of his hand continued, sliding around to her back and lower, cupping her bottom to bring her closer to him. Caitrin basked in the feel of him, how solid and hard he was, from head to toe.

"I wanted to love you first in sunlight, Caitrin," he whispered as he kissed a path down her neck, leaving heat in its wake. "I want to see all of you. Later, when darkness comes, we will use our hands to see."

Caitrin's skin prickled again with excitement at the very idea.

Cupping her face in his palms, Ross returned his lips to hers, almost unmoving, inviting her, it seemed—daring her—to forward their union. Caitrin could not resist, tilting her face up, opening her mouth to him. She wrapped her arms tightly around him, threading her fingers into his soft and thick hair and showed him everything he had taught her about kissing. She gave herself freely, thrusting her tongue into the recesses of his mouth and heard him groan as he responded and fitted himself more intimately against her, pressing a hardness into her stomach. She kissed him with a calmness that belied all the screaming inside that begged her to climb into him and greedily take all of him.

Soon, she understood that aside from the delicious things his kiss was doing to her body, that a joy welled within her for the little grunts he put out, making his pleasure known.

Ross's hands were everywhere, his gentle massage sending currents of heightened desire through her, until his hands were on her arms and pushing her away. *No*, her brain cried out.

"I need this gone, Caitrin," he said roughly, fisting his fingers into the fabric of her sleeves.

She knew no shyness then, only need, to give him what he wanted, to know this with him. She bent her head and used her trembling fingers to unknot the strings that held the bodice in place. At the same time, and while he watched her undress, Ross unfolded his plaid from over his shoulder and dropped that to the ground. He paused in the action of gathering his tunic at the hem to pull over his head when Caitrin untied the inner knot and opened the entire front of the clever gown, allowing it to fall off her shoulders and down her arms until it fell away completely, pooling at her feet.

Ross's lips parted as he stared at her breasts, where her nipples poked through the fabric of her shift. Absently, he pulled his tunic from where it was tucked into his breeches, but all the while his attention stayed on her, and her skin tingled under the contact of his heady gaze.

And then she was in his arms again, crushed against him, and her shift was pushed away from her shoulder, and his lips touched all the skin that was exposed. This drew a shaky breath from Caitrin, and she closed her eyes and tipped her head back, the exhilarating sensation of his wet mouth on her bare flesh overtaking everything else.

While he continued to trail kisses along her shoulder and collarbone, his hand rose up between them and cupped her breast. His hand was large and firm upon her, cupping and lifting, her breast filling it. His thumb grazed over her nipple and Caitrin marveled at the wonder of this, so much uproar in those previously unused, unknown parts of her body.

Only the feel of his warm, solid flesh under her roving hands thrilled her more. He was hard and contoured spectacularly, her fingers adoring his body.

"More," he growled suddenly, his voice rough and breathless.

Caitrin gasped, tortured by the removal of his warmth and heat as he put space between them once more. Her torment was short-lived then, as his intent now seemed to be removing the rest of their clothing. When he toed off his boots, Caitrin did the same with her mismatched leather shoes. And then, neither swiftly nor with aching slowness, Ross lifted her kirtle up and over her head, tossing it away onto the forest floor. He might well have been surprised that she wore no hose—there were none to be had, and Fiona had winked at her and promised her Ross would not mind—but all she saw was delight in his hungry gaze.

She stood naked before him inside a streak of light from the setting sun. When he didn't touch her immediately but let his gaze rake over her in such a way as to suggest a reverence she did not deserve, Caitrin shifted her weight from one leg to the other, breathing starkly through her nose.

And then Ross lifted her hand and touched it to his chest before directing it downward, specifically putting it on to the bottom of his shirt. Of her own accord, understanding that he desired that she undress him, Caitrin applied her other hand as well and took up the hem at the opposite side. Taking one step closer she raised the hem and the shirt just as Ross lifted his arms. Her fingers grazed the underside of his arms as she pushed the linen up and away until Ross took hold of it and discarded this in the same careless manner as he had other pieces. He faced her, and because she burned with a heretofore unknown curiosity, Caitrin set one hand high on his sun-bronzed, muscular chest. He stiffened beneath her, his pectoral muscles shifting with a tantalizing motion. He was hard and smooth. A carnal wonder bade her touch him with both hands, skimming them over his bare skin, in a harmonized motion, out and away, over his shoulders, at the same time.

"*Jesu*," he breathed hoarsely and attacked her again, crushing her to him, shattering her brief composure with the feel of her naked breasts so magnificently pressed to his chest. He wrapped a hand around her neck, held her firmly, close to him while his mouth devoured her, and he ground his hips against her.

Caitrin panted into his kiss, overcome and enlivened at the same time, understanding what the hardness he pushed against her represented, and aware of her tremulous response, gathering between her legs. Passion ignited further boldness in her that her hands found the top of his breeches, held still at his hips. She had bare knowledge of men's clothing, save for what wash day had shown her at the Lorne home, and reached for the ties in the front, some urgent whisper inside her telling her she needed him naked now as well. She needed to feel all of him against her, stoking the fire he'd started.

Ross gave aid to her efforts, deftly loosening the strings and removing his breeches. His broad chest tapered down to lean hips, paler than the top of him, having rarely seen the sun. His manhood jutted out from a thatch of light brown hair, thick and proud. The lingering daylight showed the magnificent size and shape of him, creating both reservations and questions about how, precisely, this worked. But Ross granted no time for either to manifest, stepping closer again as he settled his hands on her hips, kissing her again into a fine frenzy.

He did not hold her close again though, which left Caitrin wondering if he thought to spare her sensibilities, with his new nakedness. And just as a certain wantonness induced her to reach for him, to discover him, he intercepted her hand, whispering, "Not yet," against her lips.

Caitrin moaned, refusing to be denied completely, molding herself against his hard cock and his hard thighs, moving her hands freely over his back and arms. Ross groaned, the sound coming from deep within his chest, and squeezed his fingers into the flesh of her backside, urging her even tighter against his hips and erection.

"Get inside that tent, love," he ordered gruffly against her lips, smoothly pivoting her around so that she faced the opening. Never before had Caitrin been aware of her body, or nervous about a heated gaze upon her figure, not even moments ago when Ross had eaten her alive with his hot gaze. But now she suffered a moment's pang of unease, assuming his blue eyes were trained heatedly upon her backside now as she entered the tent. A moment only though, as Ross joined her in the next second, his hand skimming up along her leg as he fitted himself on the mattress with her.

He greeted her now with another open-mouthed, sensuous kiss, stirring her anew. But he was not still, and not only satisfied with her mouth. He slowly kissed a trail down her chin and neck, and palmed her naked breast with his huge hand, leaning down to take the nipple into his mouth. Caitrin stiffened, her nails digging into his shoulder, frozen with delight, her mouth gaping in awe. At this unexpected touch, Caitrin sank into the mattress, trying to halt the wild and unexpected rush of excitement stirred by his mouth covering her breasts, his tongue licking at her nipples. Soon though, she was arching her back and holding his head close as he brought each nipple to perfect arousal. He showed her the connection between different parts of her, how the attention given to her breasts created a swirling, wanton heat between her legs.

He knew of it, she suspected, that his fingers went where the heat and fire were, at the juncture of her thighs. His clever fingers slid down her soft belly and lower, and a gravelly noise escaped him when his fingers delved into the hair between her legs.

"I want you wet for me," he murmured, nipping at her breast, pressing his fingers deeper into the folds, where she was indeed wet.

Caitrin opened her mouth against his shoulder but could make no sound. The folds hidden beneath the soft curls were slick and unbelievably hot. His thumb brushed across the delicate nub at the same time one long finger penetrated her. Another gasp, another shiver, an ache inside for more of this, his hands and his mouth.

"Ross, I..." she began but stopped when he withdrew his finger only to stroke it forward, inside her again. "Oh." Something inside her begged her to move in concert with him, and she lifted her hips when he caressed deep and let them fall when he withdrew. "Oh, my...."

The chuckle this generated in him was a gorgeous noise, husky and satisfied, she thought. He worked his finger inside her for a wee bit longer and lavished attention upon her breasts at the same time. Caitrin was inundated with sensations, mostly in response to his touch, but at the same time knew she wanted him to feel as she did. Once again, she tried to reach for him, for the hard shaft that leaned against her thigh.

"Nae, lass," he breathed against her. "For this time, the first time, I need to be in control."

She wasn't sure of the complete meaning behind these words but knew a wee bit of a thrill that anything she might do could possibly make him lose control.

He shifted then, rolling on top of her, settling between her legs, consuming her with another hot kiss at the same time she felt his erection stroking just where their fingers had, and she heard herself moan again with need.

The head of his cock met with the very center of her, and Caitrin somehow knew this would complete her and deliver to her what her untutored body craved right now. She moved her hips to draw him inside her, heard him growl, suggesting he liked this, and she shifted again. Ross stilled, his lips returning to hers as he flexed his hips and answered her want of more, entering her slowly. With his elbows and forearms on either side of her head, pressing into the flat mattress, he watched her as he pushed further inside her. Caitrin stared back, her fingers digging into his sides with this new sensation and wished now for so much more light inside the tent to see him, to see if he felt what she did, how beautiful and perfect and right this was. She saw only that his eyes were shiny in the lengthening dusk and that he breathed through his mouth as he watched her.

Caitrin did the same, her lips forming a little *o* to force even breaths, even as her hips continued to move against him. He surged forward then, stopping at the resistance within.

Ross dropped his forehead to hers. "The very last thing I want to do is hurt you, lass. But I—it needs to be done."

Caitrin had some vague notion of what he spoke, having been informed by more than Ross that there would be pain. She nodded, hearing his words again. *The very last thing I want to do is hurt you*, uttered with a tortured and sorrowful tone. Ross rose, planting his palms on either side of her, being high above her and pulled himself out almost all the way before pushing back in to the point he'd reached before. He did this several times while Caitrin acquainted herself with his chest, running her hands over the solid muscles, liking the way they bulged and shifted as he rocked in and out of her. And then he surged forward with a great thrust, filling her completely, bringing forth a startled cry. Tears pooled for the surprising extent of the pain and Ross stopped moving altogether, poised above her, waiting.

Breathing raggedly, slightly worried now that she might not enjoy what else might follow, she nodded again, giving him an encouraging smile, having some inkling that they weren't done yet.

He began to move again, just as slowly and as tortuously as he had before, sliding in and out of her, soon enough making her forget the pain and feel only him. She cried in earnest now, but only on the inside, so in love with the idea that she belonged wholly and truly to Ross now.

And all that he'd aroused in her only moments ago returned, announcing itself as a fire coursing through her, lighting and searing many parts of her. He moved faster, wedging a hand under her bottom to show her how to meet his thrusts. Slick, wet noises accompanied their bumping and scraping, arousing Caitrin yet more, until every sensation surged and swelled and roared inside her.

This, she had not expected. Her eyes widened, looking to Ross for confirmation that it should be like this, so overwhelming, so shattering. But she was unable to keep her eyes open so that they shuttered close, her lids twitching, her toes curling as her orgasm crashed over her. At one point she lifted herself off the mattress while it rolled over her, her fingers clawing at the linen cover. What she felt was nearly indescribable, something she hadn't imagined existed, and while it ravaged her, heightening every nerve and tingling so many places within, she tried desperately to know and feel and claim each part of it, having some belief that surely it must be short-lived, lest it consume her.

Her husband continued to pump, faster and faster still, even while Caitrin was spent and amazed, until he lunged one last time against her and went still with a low grunt and a drawn out, brutal sigh.

They were motionless, Caitrin spent, her legs limp now against the bed, Ross between her thighs, his breath so choppy now while he held himself perfectly unmoving inside her. Caitrin was acutely aware of him throbbing within her and moved again, just a bare shifting of her hips. He shook his head, side to side, though could not lift it, even as he seemed to beg, "Be still, love." Caitrin sighed and settled, her body melting into their tiny bed, while she considered all these naked and perspiring entwined limbs, and what they had done, and how she felt so splendidly spent. She smiled and closed her eyes again.

HE MIGHT HAVE GUESSED that making love with Caitrin was only going to appease him briefly, that it would actually whet his appetite for more, not quench it at all.

They might have slept for an hour, mayhap more, he did not know. That had been after he'd made a run to the creek to wet a cloth he'd had the foresight to stash in the tent. Caitrin had giggled at his dashing about in the early twilight without a stitch of clothing upon him. And ah, how sweet and shy she'd been when he'd returned and had washed between her legs. If there had been any daylight left, surely he'd have seen her cheeks blistered red with her embarrassment. 'Twas not his intent, to make her uneasy. He said as much. She bore it well and allowed him to hold her close when it was done.

And now he woke, supposing it was not yet midnight, and his first thought was of her, warm and secure in his arms. Smiling at his own good fortune, having met earlier the full promise of Caitrin's passion, Ross pivoted on his hip, which rolled Caitrin onto her side. He fit himself against her back and bottom and moved his hand around the front of her. His sleepiness faded quickly while he let his hand roam, testing her wakefulness. He kneaded her breast and she purred, sleepy but definitely not sleeping. And then she wiggled her bottom against his waking cock and that was all it needed that Ross lifted up and over her, turning her onto her back. He plundered her mouth in a stirring kiss before putting another concern into words. "You're probably too sore yet," he imagined. He'd not ever had a virgin but had heard there should be some time allowed for recovery.

"I am tender, yes," she breathed against his mouth. "But I want to know all of that again."

"Tomorrow might be better though," he said, in love with the way she opened her legs to him, how perfect it was to settle in the space between her thighs. He kissed her nose but did not grind his hips against her as he wanted to, needing to be sure she was agreeable.

And his fabulous bride, who'd likely not ever moved her hips so provocatively as she had earlier, did so again just now, thrusting against him that his erection surged.

"Kiss me, husband," she asked, "and make me feel all that raging fire as you did."

Aye, he was going to love this wife of his.

Chapter Seventeen

When two more days had passed and the English did not emerge from behind the safety of the curtained wall of Westcairn, Ross decided that he had waited long enough, and he had done all that might be done to prepare this army right now for battle. It was time to take the fight to Westcairn, to take back what belonged to him.

Never before had he been anxious that he might not survive. Aye, he realized straight away the reason behind his current concern. 'Twas not a debilitating fear, not one that would see him suddenly inept, but it was strong enough that he had to consider whether or not he would be as courageous, if he would take valiant chances with little care for his own skin. And his worry was not about Caitrin, wondering if she would be cared for and embraced by Westcairn's people for all her life. The fear was mostly rooted in what bitterness he would know, should he now not survive, that he'd met her and had wed her, and had loved her, but that now he might die, and have no more days with her. Upon reflection, he decided he'd be furious with this circumstance, should it come to be. Enraged at the unfairness of it.

Still, he could not let it incapacitate him. He just could not.

And first he wanted more of Caitrin. He advised John to gather the men in one hour, that he would address them at that time. And then he sought out his wife.

He found her with Samuel, down upon the banks of the closer loch.

Later, he would give Samuel some grief for not having discerned his presence, though not too much. Ross was a natural silent stalker, known for his ability to sneak up upon an enemy. Also, he knew how distracting Caitrin could be. The sky was clear blue, which meant that the midday sun would make her eyes a perfect shade of bright green, a diversion in and of itself. And when she laughed, well there wasn't much a man could do to turn his attention from that.

He stopped at the edge of the woods, before he might have revealed himself, and listened to their conversation. He didn't consider that he was creeping up on her. And he certainly wasn't spying with any hint of jealousy, wondering what she was up to with Samuel. Instead, he liked to watch and listen to her interact with others, so different now than how reserved and aloof she'd been weeks ago.

"He's no' without resources," Samuel was saying, "either friends or kin further about. We'd no' be homeless."

"But what will that do to him, if he cannot recover Westcairn?" Caitrin wanted to know.

Samuel hesitated a wee bit, and Ross had to wonder how much of the truth—which Samuel would know of Ross—his friend would give to Caitrin.

Apparently, all of it. When Samuel's answer came, it was similar to one Ross would have given if he'd been asked directly. "Lass, ye ken failure would no' affect the laird, no' at all; he'd no' be here to ken it. He'll succeed or he'll die trying, that's all there is to him."

"I was afraid you might say that, Samuel," Caitrin said in response to this. She got to her feet and stared out over the glistening water of the loch. After a moment, she turned her face to Samuel. "Will you promise me that you won't let him die?"

Samuel shook his head and stared only at the ground. "Ye ken it dinna work like that, lass."

"But promise me all the same, Samuel," she implored. "I—I cannot lose him, too."

Samuel deftly avoided making such a promise. Like Ross, he did not make loose with any vow. "I came down here to keep company with ye, lass," he said instead, "was hoping for a wee bit of conversation that dinna have anything to do with our current circumstance." He chuckled a bit, something the big man rarely did. "If I were looking for whingeing, I'd have stayed up there with Arailt, and listened to his."

Caitrin laughed at this and stared down Samuel. "Very well, Samuel. And very clever, to avoid giving me that promise. Fine then, tell me about yourself, Samuel."

Ross used this moment to announce his presence. "There's some whingeing you dinna want, lass."

Samuel and Caitrin turned at the same time. Ross first gave Samuel a critical look, silently letting him know he was not pleased that Samuel had not been aware of his coming. Approaching the pair, he then said to his lieutenant, "We're gathering at the ridge in one hour."

Samuel understood what this meant and nodded solemnly. "Aye then, I best get moving." With a nod toward Caitrin, he took his leave.

As he departed, Ross met and held Caitrin's gaze. There was no panic in her clear green eyes, but she clearly had an inkling that something was afoot. "Today it is, then?" She asked.

"The beginning of it, aye," Ross answered. He moved closer and kissed her brow quickly, taking her hand at the same time. "But you'll no' worry, lass."

At this, she smiled grimly. "Of course not."

"Aye then," Ross acknowledged the unlikelihood of this, "but you'll wait until I'm out of sight?"

Caitrin tilted her head, causing the sun to glint off her flaxen hair. "This is my role then? To put on a brave face and convince you that I have no fear?"

"Nae, lass. Emotion should be honest, I ken." He grinned then. "Mayhap only temper it a bit." At her somber nod, he said next, "Caitrin, it is no' only about recovering Westcairn. I dinna only wed ye to give you the protection of my name. I took you to wife because I perceived a fine future with you, at my side as the mistress of Westcairn. I need to give you that home."

"I understand that you are responsible for all these people, and that there is more at stake than only Westcairn or vengeance or anything related to it. But Ross, I need only you."

His chest expanded at these words—with pride or joy or love, he wasn't sure; mayhap all of them. He might then have requested a kiss to see him off, but before he could, Caitrin leaned into him, sliding her arms around his middle, over the leather breastplate he'd donned, holding him tight, her cheek pressed against his chest. Ross closed his eyes and returned her embrace, his chin set upon her hair.

"Come back to me, Ross."

"Always."

CAITRIN WAS NOT AWARE, until she returned to Little Westcairn with Ross, that the entire small civilian population was moving up into the hills today. While Ross and his soldiers brought the fight to his keep.

Upon spying all the dismantled tents and one smaller mare being loaded as a pack horse, she turned a quizzical frown upon her husband.

"Up to the cairn at the top of the mountain, lass," he advised. There was a bit of a wince to his stoic expression, as if he expected an argument, sending her and the others further away.

But Caitrin nodded instead and tried once more to smile for her husband's sake. He did not need her petulance right now. He was anxious to get on with his plans for Westcairn, she could see—in his tightened jaw and fisted hand; in the way his eyes scanned the area, looking with some impatience upon Agnes trying to herd her brood. He wanted them all gone and settled, and soon.

Pretending it might not be the last time she saw him, Caitrin stood on her toes and kissed his lips, letting it linger. She covered his clenched hand and squeezed it and told him she would be fine, and before worry got the better of her, before she showed him her fear, she pivoted and went to give aid to Agnes. She scooped up the giggling Isaac, and took Marion's hand, and they followed Hamish and Arailt and the column of twenty other souls who marched through the forest to the mountain at the southeast side.

The mountain they climbed was not so very high, but parts of it were decidedly steep. They trudged along for twenty minutes and still, when Caitrin lifted her gaze, she felt as if they still had so far to go. Carrying Isaac, she struggled as much as Agnes, who cradled her youngest child in her arms, which put them at the end of the line, the stragglers. Marion stayed with them, but Rachel and Mildred had gone on ahead with Ida and Fiona. When they came upon an old trail that cut a flat path along the side of the mountain, Agnes begged to stop.

"Will no' make a difference," Agnes huffed, trying to catch her breath, "if we get there in five minutes or if it takes twenty more."

Caitrin was game to rest a few minutes as well. "What's a cairn doing at the top of the mountain?" she wondered, shifting Isaac onto her other hip.

Agnes shrugged, making a show of panting slowly through pursed lips. "Been here longer than any living man, I ken. There's a cave up there as well, that's why we're headed there." She gulped another breath and chastised Isaac, who was squirming in Caitrin's arms. "Be still, love. We're almost there."

Caitrin wondered but did not ask why they didn't employ the cave over the last few weeks, as a safer, less accessible camp. Agnes must have read her mind that she added, "Cave is no' big enough for all of us, the army included. And it's colder up there, and there's no water. We canna stay long."

The next persons ahead of them, Ida and Fiona and Agnes's two girls, were already out of sight, as they had not stopped, but continued up the hill. Caitrin glanced left and right along the path, which must have been used regularly at some point, as it was worn down to hard packed earth in many sections; no trees or brush grew from the narrow lane that wound around the mountain.

"Ready?" She asked Agnes, who adjusted the bairn in her arms and nodded, her cheeks flushed with her exertions. "Come on, lass," she said to Marion, who'd plunked down in the middle of the trail, reaching her hand to her. She jerked her head left, her attention drawn by a sudden flurry of noise coming around the bend in the trail. Before she saw anything, she yanked Marion to her feet and shoved her upward, where the incline began again, into the brush and trees. "Go!" She urged and waved her hand at Agnes to go ahead of her, pushing at the woman's plump behind to urge her up the hill.

"Hold!" Was called behind her.

Caitrin did, pausing and turning to the riders that appeared on the path, six of them, but only because that lone directive had not been uttered in English but in Gaelic. She faced the coming party, huge men upon huge beasts, crowded upon the narrow trail. And though she'd never in her life defended herself with a weapon, instinct saw her pulling the knife Ross had given her from the makeshift sheath and belt she wore. The tartan plaids, indicative of Scotsmen, only gave her tiny relief. 'Twas not the Kildare tartan and these men did not look to be the friendly sort.

Thrusting the knife out toward them, while Isaac whimpered in her arms, Caitrin warned them, "I will slice you stem to stern if you come any closer."

"Hold, lass. We mean no harm," said the forward man, whose green eyes said that might be true, even as his frown was heavy. "This is Kildare land. What are you about?"

Caitrin jabbed the knife at him. "This *is* Kildare land," she threw back at him, "and what are you about?"

The one behind the green-eyed man dismounted, his great size and the menace of his features forcing Caitrin back a step or two. "We're bound for Westcairn, lass. But you can no' be out here. There are English in these parts."

"Bound for Westcairn?" Agnes said from within the trees, bringing many gazes to her. "The English are already there!"

The man now on foot stopped in his approach, turning to exchange a look with the mounted, green-eyed man. When he turned back, he leveled Caitrin with his stark, gray gaze, to which she responded by lifting the knife higher.

"We come for Ross Kildare," he said.

She did not lower the knife, but her shoulders drooped with some relief. Tears welled. "Are you friend or foe? And what would you be wanting with Westcairn's laird?"

In response to this, the green-eyed man, with his hand folded casually over the pommel, said, "If there's English at Westcairn, then we'll be looking to help him expel them."

She did not lower the knife, not trusting them completely yet, as they were strangers still. But she said, "Then go on. You do not want me and these. Go to Ross, on the ridge at the edge of the forest, overlooking Westcairn. He's about to sack his own keep."

Both men frowned, confused, possibly wondering who she was to be giving them orders.

Caitrin's eyes widened. Why did they dawdle? Thrusting the knife at the man in front of her, she commanded brusquely, "Go! Go to Ross!"

He grinned at this, the gray-eyed man, and gave a shrug before turning to gain the saddle again.

"As you wish, lass."

EIGHTY-SEVEN MEN WAITED for Ross at the ridge overlooking Westcairn, standing just below the sightline so that the enemy did not see the army congregating. When Ross left his home in the spring to join Lord Comyn's forces in the south, he'd marched with almost double that number. He was not made of stone that he bemoaned the loss of good men only for what detriment it created now, but then he was the leader of the army that this weighed heavily upon him, that he wouldn't have the numbers needed to outwit, outfight, and outlast the English who'd taken his home.

It was a crisp fall day with a light breeze aiding the trees in shedding what remained of their leaves. If the wind kicked up any more, they would be forced to delay their attack, as they could not firmly attest to the ability of the stone-tipped arrows in windier conditions. The same sun that had shown him the mesmerizing green of Caitrin's eyes only a few minutes ago now highlighted the resolute expressions of his army. To a man, they were somber and alert, imbued with a sense of do-or-die, but needing still to see and hear the clear authority of Ross's devotion to his plan, to be compelled to give more than they had at any other time.

A trebuchet might have served them well, and Ross would not have regretted the damage it would have caused to Westcairn. But they had neither the time nor the full resources to engineer a workable machine such as that, certainly not with Raynor gone earlier this year. Raynor had not been lost to battle or any wound, but from some disease that had struck only him and quickly, that he was upright and clear-headed one day, and then immobilized and twitching incoherently the next, perishing not long after whatever claimed him had smacked him. Thus, they had only the bulk of their archers and a wee bit of subterfuge as elements of the first component of attack.

As he walked his giant steed back and forth at the fore of the assembled army, Ross pointed his drawn sword to the dozen men dressed in the confiscated English togs. "Once you've gained entry at that postern gate and subdued all you can, doff that garb right quick, lest we mistake you for any miserable Englishman when we come."

John was among those dressed as the hated enemy. He reminded his unit. "We've one objective, lads. Leave the back door open and unlock the front."

Gruff chants of "Aye!" followed this.

Ross stopped, front and center, and provoked his army to war. "We've done all that can be done in preparation for what must come. This, now, my friends, is the greatest fight of our lives," he called out in a strong and steady voice so that all would hear him. "Whether or no' we triumph, we must resist our enemy in any and every way. Should we no' prevail, should it turn that way, our goal then is to take the bastards with us, to take all the evil away from here. We must leave to those who survive us and those who come after us a Scotland as great as it ever was, or greater still." As this was akin to any of the crucial battles in which they'd engaged, Ross rallied them with words he'd uttered at Falkirk and Stirling and even more recently, at the River Cree: "You ken, as always, that I am resolved to live or die amongst you, to give all my blood for my Scotland and for my honor," he called, "and for my freedom." He could have roared all of it, could have stirred them to an even greater and instant passion, but he knew well his army, and they were a beastly lot when the fight was on. The English would have heard their answering war cries, but they should not just yet. "Godspeed, my friends," Ross offered with a resolute nod to his warriors.

"'Tis a fine speech there, lad," someone called out.

"I've heard better," another voice said loudly.

Ross narrowed his eyes at the faces before him. Those nearest to him turned around, looking for the giver of this mild, nearly offensive praise. Bodies at the rear of the formation began to move and shift as two men walked among them, cleaving a path with their very presence.

Gabriel Jamison and Calum MacKinnon, with whom Ross and the Kildares had fought alongside only recently. It was at Gabriel Jamison's Blackwood that Ross had spent some time, aiding that laird in the recovery of his kidnapped wife, before Ross had ridden away and had come upon Caitrin only days later.

The two men, impressive in stature as well as reputation, strode through the troops, making their way toward Ross upon his steed. Gabriel Jamison was as fierce a warrior as Ross had ever known, but a person might well mistake the easy smiles and friendly green eyes of the man for softness, a mistake that person might only make once. Calum MacKinnon had renounced his own uncle after a betrayal and made his place with the Jamisons now. He was as hulking and intimidating as Samuel, with a temper to match; his sword arm was strong and swift, and Ross had seen him fight aplenty, always pleased that he would never have cause to come up against so sure and steady a combatant as Calum.

But what were they about, here at Westcairn?

Gabriel stopped in front of Ross, who then dismounted to greet his friends. A man should not ever greet his equals from a loftier position. He clasped Gabriel's arm firmly when it was offered, and then Calum's.

Their timing was either breathtaking or regrettable, depending upon their purpose. "What are you doing here?" He asked.

"Wondering why the hell your missive made no mention that Westcairn was taken, that you only thought to advise that some English had come this far north," Gabriel said, his eye keen upon Ross. "We had more than one notice, from different parts of this region about English come, laying sieges hereabouts. But my own friend's message says naught about his keep being seized."

"Aye," Ross acknowledged. "They've taken Westcairn." He was yet in battle form and could not afford a grin, even as he said, "You might want to excuse me and the lads for a wee bit, while we see about getting it back."

At any rate, neither Gabriel nor Calum were amused.

Gabriel had a few years on Ross, but not enough to lay claim to the frustrated, paternal admonishment that came next. "Why the bluidy hell did you no' send for us? Why only advise and no' request assistance? We might have been here a week ago with a full and competent army."

"Vengeance is my own," Ross said simply. Of course he'd considered such a scheme. But he'd discarded it just as quickly. The fight was his. And this was not an argument he wanted to have, not now. He'd done all that was required of him when he alerted others of the local threat.

"God's bluid, Kildare! We've one bluidy enemy! 'Tis the same one!" Calum's rage was blistering, not anything Ross hadn't witnessed a time or two over the long months he spent fighting at that man's side.

"And you just lent aid to me to recover my wife!" Gabriel added. "Did you no' ken I would—"

"It is no' the same!" Ross returned hotly. He got right up in Gabriel's face, pointing his finger at him. "Your wife was stolen, that was no' something to be ignored and I and my army were *right there*. This is different. This is vengeance. My wife is no' in danger. She is safe. This is for me and mine. My brother died at their hands. They will die by mine."

Gabriel seethed at being challenged, his teeth clenched. He seemed to fight against spewing more angry words, because Ross had not sent for him.

Ross said next, with only half as much bluster, "You had just returned to Blackwood, you had just gotten your wife back. I could no' ask you to—"

"Wait," Calum interjected sharply, holding up his hand. "Did you say your *wife* is no' in danger?"

Gabriel looked at Calum, considering the query. "He has a wife?"

"He just said as much," Calum said, shrugging, losing a bit of his furious steam as well.

And just like that, their moods improved. Gabriel grinned, his green eyes crinkling at the corners. "Where'd you find the time to collect a wife along the way?"

Ross was relieved they were here. He wouldn't have asked it of them—it was *his* fight—but he knew they weren't going away now. Thus, his entire mood was lightened as well. "I rather stumbled upon her," he said with a crooked grin.

"And no one," Gabriel questioned, spinning around to point his finger at all the watching soldiers, "not one of these fine men thought to advise the poor lass against taking on such a millstone?"

"She dinna talk so much at first," Samuel stated, at Ross's flank, "by the time she did, it was too late."

John added, "She'll catch on and then we'll see the tail of her, running in some other direction. God help her."

"She wouldn't happen to be a green-eyed, flaxen hair lass, would she?"

Ross whirled on Calum, his fist clenching on the hilt of his sword, all good humor gone.

Sensing Ross's revived aggression, Calum held up his hands defensively. "We met her up the side of the mountain. She is well and safe. We sent a unit up there with her and the others."

Ross relaxed once again, his nostrils flaring with his exhale.

"We ken you chose well," Gabriel said, slapping Ross on the shoulder, "soon as she threatened Calum with a blade that would no' even slice his thick skin. She never blinked, showed no' an ounce of fear. We thought she just might mean it, that she'd cut him."

Calum grinned, as he so rarely did. "Which begs the question: what's a fine mate such as she doing with you?"

Ross nearly rolled his eyes. "Are we done, then?" He asked, only partially amused. "Did you come all this way only to harangue me, or shall we get to the fight?"

Gabriel glanced up at the sky, noting the sun's position. "Aye, let's get on with it. We left a day ago. I told Meggie I'd be home for the evening meal tomorrow."

Shaking his head, Ross returned Gabriel's smirk. He never had known a more congenial man, one who was often so delighted to engage in warfare.

Chapter Eighteen

The west side offered the greatest protection and cover to get closest to the wall. But the wall there was straight up, with nothing to scale or climb, so it was not a place from which they could launch their offensive. It was, however, a place to needle the English inside his keep. Ross planted two archers inside the woods within two hundred yards of the wall and advised that their only job was to dispatch any man on that side. If a man was visible atop the western wall, he should be shot down.

Those men dressed as English would not only trot up to the rear gate of Westcairn and hope they might be received and admitted. They did not want the English to have time to see through their ploy. Instead Gabriel offered to send a troop of his men chasing those supposed English to Westcairn, which should see the small postern gate opened in a hurry. But this could not be done until all the companies were in place. Gabriel and Calum had arrived with an army of almost one hundred, which at first gave Ross pause, that he should have left Blackwood vulnerable.

"Nae," Gabriel assured his friend. "Harry is there, with another hundred strong, sent down from Calum's cousin at Caerhayes, to keep watch while we were gone."

His mind set at ease that Blackwood was not in any danger while he enjoyed the benefit of the Jamison numbers, Ross discussed his basic strategy with Gabriel and Calum so that their army did not walk blindly into the fray. Shortly after that, not more than thirty minutes after the arrival of Gabriel and Calum, the order was given for John and Gideon and the others garbed in the English rags to begin their march along the elevated road that led to the backside of Westcairn and that smaller gate. When there was still a few hundred yards between the fake Englishmen and the gate, Gabriel gave the command for a troop of twenty men to pretend to give chase upon the rarely used road.

The timing had to be precise, so that only seconds would pass between that rear gate being opened to admit those men, seemingly running for their lives, and the beginning of the assault at the face of Westcairn. To the English behind the curtain wall, everything did rather happen all at once. No sooner had the postern gate been unlocked and their racing comrades admitted than the west side of the wall was bombarded with a barrage of missiles. Screams sounded all around: on the western wall, where two men were felled straight away; and at the rear gate, where three more true English were attacked by those coming. And then there was a fight to control the gate, John and his unit quickly subduing enough of the enemy that Gabriel's men following were able to gain access. And just like that, more than two dozen Scotsmen were inside the walls of Westcairn.

The next move had only been provisional, predicated on whether the back door ruse was successful or not. When it was, Ross led the next unit, he and forty men racing for the now open gate at the north side of the keep.

At the same time, Gabriel and Calum led the charge directed at the front of Westcairn, which was more a diversion than anything else, until the imposing larger gate could be opened from within.

Two things almost instantly became apparent as Ross set foot inside the courtyard of Westcairn for the first time in almost a year. First, the English—for whatever reason—truly were surprised by the attack. At times, it seemed they didn't know where to look, or who to fight. Next, quickly known to almost every man in any segment of Ross's siege, the English inside Westcairn had nowhere near the numbers, not even the low estimates that Ross and John had supposed. This was evidenced by how subdued was their defense and then by how swiftly entry had been gained. Ross needed only to engage one or two of the enemy before he was only standing at the side yard near the bakehouse, looking around for any other that required his fight. There was none, and he was not the only Kildare man standing around without an enemy to engage.

He saw his brother, John, upon the low stairs of the rear wall, pleased that he looked none the worse for wear, less so now since he had, as instructed, rid himself of the English togs. Inclining his head toward the front of Westcairn, Ross directed, "To the gate!" and the brothers and several others made their way around the keep, intent on opening the front portal to the rest of the combined Kildare and Jamison armies awaiting entry at the fore.

Ross and John took on what few Englishmen defended the gatehouse while several others cranked the arm and the rigging to lift the outer portcullis while three more Kildare men released the thick wooden beam that held the gate closed.

And everything that had been easy—that had seemed *too* effortless—was gone with the wind that blew stiffly through the bailey and along the stout curtain wall. The doors to the keep itself, which led directly to the hall, burst open as if blown apart from within. Noisy war cries sounded as Englishmen poured out, dozens and dozens of them, having only waited until Ross's army was within the wall. The fight was on then. Ross's adrenaline kicked in with no small amount of thrill to finally get at these English.

And as he clanged swords with one intrepid foe near the gatehouse, Ross realized what the whole of the English plan was. In his periphery, he saw that Gabriel's army and the rest of the Kildares, who'd been charged with breeching the front of Westcairn, were engaged with more English outside the gates. Ah, so they'd planned to let them in, and then had expected to surround them, contain them, and slaughter them.

Ross had always imagined that man for man, the English were not strong enough or brutal enough to hold their own against any Scots army. Aye, and maybe if Ross had only his Kildare army, they'd have been trapped within these walls, might well have met their end. 'Twas a sound plan, for the numbers the English supposed Ross controlled and because mayhap the English had imagined that since the Kildares were familiar with their own keep, they'd have greater success storming it and would not be denied entry for long. Likely the strategy would have worked had it not been for the addition of the Jamison army.

Thus a vicious battle raged, sword against sword, all the cavalry outside the wall, while within every man had only his agility and brute strength to aid him. Samuel swung an axe in one hand and wielded his long sword in another. John grunted with rage with each thrust of his blade. Gideon somersaulted beneath the swinging blade of the enemy, gaining his feet at the man's back, his blade impaling the enemy in its next stroke. Ross kicked the latest dead man off his sword and pivoted just in time to dodge the assault from another contender. And on it went, until more bodies littered the ground inside the bailey than the number that remained standing, until Gabriel and Calum could be seen bringing the fight to the gates, getting closer, the dried autumn grass outside the wall colored red and strewn with more corpses.

Ross knew only a moment of panic, when he saw his brother clubbed upside the head and felled, landing face first in the dirt of the yard. He roared John's name, too far away to stop John's attacker from completing the kill. The leggy Englishman used two hands to lift his sword to bring down the killing blow. It never came. An arrow struck him in the face, spilling him onto the ground next to John. Ross spared a glance to the wall, from where the killing arrow had come and found one of Gabriel's men smirking for his perfect shot.

Intent on reaching his brother, Ross lifted his sword to the next closest Englishman, bewildered then when that man tossed his weapon aside and lifted his hands in supplication. Looking around, he saw that any remaining, standing Englishman—only about a dozen—had done the same.

Gabriel, still mounted, had breached the gate, forcing some of those surrendering men to walk backwards, into the center of the courtyard. More Jamison's, mounted as well, formed a perimeter around the prisoners. Seeing that Gabriel had the yard well in hand, Ross sheathed his sword and went to his brother.

John moved, groaning, before Ross had reached his side. He turned his brother onto his back, to find the entire left side of his head and face covered in blood. But John's eyes were clear and focused.

"And this is why I've petitioned for helms, Laird," John said, his voice strong enough that Ross's fear abated, and he slumped, wasted, onto his knees. Wearily, John let his arm flop out onto the ground at his side.

"Your noggin is hard enough," Ross said, relief overcoming him.

Helping his brother to sit, both Kildares raised their faces when a shadow fell over them.

Gabriel and Calum stood nearby.

The four men surveyed the carnage around the once beautiful courtyard of Westcairn. Ross winced when he spied Mercer, twenty yards away, lifeless upon the ground. And there was Martin and Oliver as well, among the many felled Kildares, who would fight no more battles.

His chest constricted and his throat burned while he pursed his lips with anguish.

"I take no life for granted," Gabriel said evenly, "but I ken every man gone today is proud to have stood against tyranny and injustice."

While this was true, it gave Ross no peace. John lifted a hand and patted his shoulder and Ross nodded, his head bent.

Ross stood and helped his brother to his feet, intent on entering the keep.

Calum stopped him with a hand on his arm. "You dinna want to see anything they may have left for you to find. Let us clear it first."

Ross wanted to argue.

Gabriel spoke up. "Go collect your bride, lad. We'll clear the keep and yard in the meantime."

"Westcairn is yours, Ross," Calum said.

FROM THE GATE OF WESTCAIRN, the climb to the top of the mountain took nearly half an hour and depleted what little stores of energy Ross had retained after the fight. But he wanted Caitrin, wanted his wife in his arms, to know she was safe.

When he came close to the cairns it was quiet, too quiet, that he knew they hid, that they were watching.

"Caitrin!" he called out.

A flurry of sound erupted, and he would have grinned had he the strength, when several heads popped out from behind trees and brush. Swiftly, he scanned the faces: Fiona, wielding a dull-bladed axe, with Marion tucked behind her stood to his left, further up the incline; Agnes and her two sons peeked out from behind a sturdy thicket of pines; Hamish was closest, with Ida and another of Agnes's girls with him, his lone hand holding his well-loved hatchet; and there was Caitrin, with Daniel and Rachel, stepping out from the backside of another tree. Her fingers were white-knuckling the blade he'd given her weeks ago, which she'd apparently put to good use against Calum earlier.

As soon as she saw that it was Ross, she dropped the knife to the ground and raced downhill toward him. He caught her around the waist and swept her up in his arms, neither of them caring about what blood and gore crusted his padded armor or hands. Relief washed over him, warm and sweet—sweet enough that he allowed a grin for how tightly she held him, how strong were her arms around his neck. He tugged at one arm. "You are in love with me," he challenged. "That's all that makes sense, to hold me so tight now."

Though it had no sound, Ross felt her answering laughter in his chest and neck and against his cheek.

Caitrin did not demur. "I must be. And you as well, for how strong your arm is around me."

"Seems so." He pressed a kiss against the side of her head. "Come. I want to take you home."

FOLLOWING ROSS AND the others, Caitrin stepped through the gates of Westcairn. Inside, the packed earth and loose gravel of the courtyard was spotted here and there with bloodshed, some puddles larger and more grotesque than others. 'Twas eerily quiet, all of it. Not a sound could be heard, not from within the low-ceiling stables or from the bakehouse, where a thin plume of smoke said a fire burned yet in an oven; not in the stiff wind that blew through the bailey nor even from any object it moved; not even from a thick woven chain that hung from an arm inside the smithy's shed and swayed without noise.

They came, one by one, all of Westcairn's inhabitants, and each must have known their own bittersweet joy, to be returned finally where so many had been lost in the original siege and many more today. Agnes hugged her smallest bairn and held the hand of her other son and cared not that any saw that she wept openly. But even that was silent, Aggie's usual volume muted with her awe. Fiona and Gideon stood together, lifting their gazes to the shredded and half-charred remnants of an English flag that hung over the inner wall. John stood three feet from his brother, likely thinking of Robert. He lowered his gaze to the ground and punched his hands onto his hips and struggled, it seemed, to keep his lips from quivering.

Caitrin strode toward Ross, pausing only long enough to set her hand on John's arm. He did not look up but nodded curtly, and she pursued nothing with him, let him have this moment.

Ross, too, wore his hands on his hips. But he did not struggle with tears as did John. His face was tipped upward, his gaze proud upon the pale stone keep. Sidling next to him, she rubbed her hand down his bare upper arm.

Ignoring everyone but him, she felt her own tears rise. "You are home, Ross."

And now he reacted, his jaw tightening while his eyes watered. Gruffly, he pulled her against him, wrapping both arms tightly around her. Eagerly, she wrapped her arms around him, her fingers splayed out upon his back. Ross breathed raggedly, weeping mayhap. After a moment, he whispered fiercely against her hair, "*We* are home, lass. We are home."

HE WAS BOTH ANXIOUS and then afraid to enter the keep itself, not entirely sure what he might find. With Caitrin's hand in his, he entered first, before any other.

The great hall was dim, no candles lit on either of the hanging candelabras. He began to survey the room even before his eyes adjusted to the light.

Mayhap this was exactly what he'd expected, the disarray, the lack of care, the destruction, shown in the filthy rushes and soot-crusted hearth, in the English armor and standards and crest high upon the wall above the family's table, the Kildare ornaments nowhere to be found. A long dagger had been thrust into the once fine wood of the main table, left there purposefully as a memento, he was sure. The gorgeous carved wood screen of the minstrels gallery, which ran the length of the long wall opposite the door, upon the second floor, had been attacked with an axe or sword or some other weapon, and lay in fractured shambles, very few panels left standing. The stone of the arched doorways—the entrance to the corridor that led to the kitchens behind the keep—had likewise met with destruction, so much of it chipped away, crumbled on the floor. If this hadn't only just been attacked today, those chunks of stone and that dust had laid there and had been walked over for some time.

He'd have done the same—or worse—if he'd known defeat was imminent. Whether his own keep or a stolen one, if he knew he was about to forfeit it, or die trying, he'd have razed the thing to the ground. Mayhap they'd enjoyed the keep while they'd occupied it and had no plans to make their own quarters either unsightly or unusable. It was more an afterthought, he surmised, some aggression taken out on the keep today or very recently, when they supposed they might be ousted from it.

He moved further within, forgetting for a moment that Caitrin's hand was still within his grasp, until their arms were tugged as he moved but she had not. Turning, Ross considered her expression.

Her gaze was more sorrowful than even his, at the devastation left behind.

This was a sorry shadow of the home to which he'd wanted to bring her.

It dawned on him then and enlivened his whole mood, that Caitrin was not only someone that you brought home with you. She was someone around whom you built your home. He knew that, possibly had known that for a long time, that home would be where ever she was.

He was neither shy, nor often stingy with his words, but he hadn't told her that. He needed to.

He waited until she pulled her gaze from her examination of the hall and looked at him. She wrinkled her nose and mouth and gave him a mournful look, expecting that his rage or his own misery must be great, mayhap that the joy they should have known with their victory was tempered by the state of Westcairn, the very fact that it was a tomb to so many, his brother included.

But she smiled at him, which was meant to be reassuring even as it was laced in heartache. Her smile—whatever its objective at any given occasion—still and always was the most beautiful thing in the world to him.

"It will be home again, Ross. It will."

He closed the distance between them and lifted his palm to her cheek. He kissed her forehead and promised, "It will be whatever we make of it."

Two months later

CAITRIN SIGHED AS SHE entered the pitch-dark chamber she shared with Ross.

'Twas a fine chamber these days, so different from what they'd encountered initially upon their return. Thankfully, at that time it required little more than a thorough scrubbing, the bed and tall bureau and other pieces of furniture intact. The bedcovers had been sacrificed, the mattress too. Caitrin had tried to wash them but could never quite get past the idea that in all probability, the man who had killed Robert or at least was responsible for his death, might well have lain upon those linens or that cushion. Without telling Ross, she'd burned them one afternoon while the laundry's fire smoldered. And then she'd sewn a new mattress cover and had filled it with fresh straw until she could purchase or amass enough of the downy geese feathers that she'd forfeited.

With her back against the door, she closed her eyes briefly and considered her long day. Much had been done. Everyday was the same in that regard, that there was much to do and consider and arrange. While Ross was busy with the exterior of the keep, specifically seeing to repairs and in the last few weeks, upgrading the defenses of Westcairn, Caitrin had assumed control of the keep itself. Hamish and Aggie had been pleased to take charge of the kitchen. Fiona and Ida donated several hours a day to the cleaning and upkeep. Arailt had eagerly hung up his sword, at Caitrin's request, and would now serve as Westcairn's steward, in charge of the bookkeeping and the coin going in and out, and for now, the larder, the pantry, and the buttery. She'd known it almost from the start, that the people of Westcairn, whether Kildares by blood or marriage or only proximity, living within her boundaries, were a tight-knit and generous tribe. They did and would always work well together.

When she opened her eyes, they'd by now adjusted to the gloom of the chamber, and Caitrin smiled, seeing Ross asleep on their bed. She thought he might have only sat at the end of the bed to remove his boots but had collapsed backwards instead. He was fully dressed, and his feet were still on the floor while his sword was separated from his belt but still in his hand, next to him upon the mattress.

Thoughtfully, she pushed away from the door and first peeled his fingers away from the sheath of his sword. He slept on and she set the weapon aside. Next, she knelt at his feet and worked at the laces of his boots. He woke while she did this, warming her heart because his first words, at realizing the service she provided him, were, "I love you." When she'd removed his boots completely, he murmured, "Come lie beside me."

Weary herself, she was happy to oblige, and to leave off changing into her nightclothes for a little while. She climbed into the bed as he improved his position, moving further up the mattress, near the exquisitely carved headboard. His eyes were heavily-lidded when he opened his arm to her, and Caitrin went willingly into his sleepy embrace.

They neither spoke nor bothered to fight against closing their eyes, so exhausted were they, until several minutes had gone by and Ross's arm flexed, as if he'd just been jerked awake.

"I made Samuel my captain," he said then, his groggy voice nearly disguising his startling news.

"Why? Oh, gosh—but John?"

"Will be laird of his own keep."

More wakeful now than she had been, Caitrin wondered, "But how? Why?"

"It's no' unheard, that a laird gifts his son with his own land and manse," Ross explained. "Aye, he's no' my son, but why should I—by right of birth order alone—hold all the Kildare power? Actually, my da had considered it years ago, building smaller keeps upon Westcairn land. Greater defense then, family stays close, and we can work more land, either with sheep or crops."

"Where?"

"Opposite the stream where you had a bath one time, naught but a mile and a quarter away. We can erect a temporary building while his keep is being constructed. It'll take a few years to see it well-built, with good defenses."

"Can...you afford this?"

"Aye, *we* can. Westcairn is no' so rich as an earl's holdings, but we do well here, export thousands of pounds of wool every year. And praise to my da, who was a great man but trusted few, and always kept a hidden cache of coins, buried under the stone floor of the steward's office. The English did no' discover that."

How...amazing and wonderful and right. Caitrin raised herself on her elbow to consider her husband. "I think you are a very great man, Ross Kildare."

He was weary but smiled, nevertheless. "My mam used to enjoy telling my da that the greatest of men were usually supported by a strong and capable woman."

Caitrin chuckled. "Was your father not so keen to let her know that she was valued—wonderful even—that she needed to instruct him on this?"

His eyes were closed yet. The smile returned. "Let's just say that it was from my mother that I learned to not be stingy with either my words in general or any praise that should be given."

"I wish I could have known her, all your family—your brother, Robert, your father."

"They'd have approved. Heartily. Da' would want to ken your pedigree, how you felt about giving me a score of sons.

Mam would want to feed you, fatten you up. You'd have been Robert's confidante, I imagine. He was a thinker, no' a fighter."

Grinning, Caitrin laid down again in his arms. "I want sons—many children—but Ross, I do not think I would have the energy for a score of them."

"Nor I, truth be told."

"We'll start with one," she said mildly, rubbing her hand over her flat belly, staring at the timber ceiling with a serene smile about her. "Next summer, I should imagine."

She felt the plump mattress shift as her husband jerked to attention at her revelation. Opening her eyes, Caitrin met Ross's wondrous smile, as his face hovered close above her.

"Really? A babe?"

"Aye, if Agnes is right."

His grin improved. "She would ken, aye?" He stared at her, awe and wonder lighting his beloved features. A short chuckle emerged, raising Caitrin's brows.

"Every day, love, I swear I canna love you more. And every day, you prove me wrong."

Her brows remained lifted. "I hope, sir, that my worth—that indeed the degree of your love—is not based solely on my ability to reproduce."

Ross shook his head slowly and said with some tenderness, "Your attempts at reproduction, aye, but never only your actual ability." He grinned, feigning a wince when she clapped him on his shoulder for that ribald jest.

Risen above her, he turned and passed his gaze over her form, and then laid his hand over her belly, where the first of many children lived right now.

"I was afraid to love you, Ross, afraid that you would be snatched away from me or I from you. But oh, how glad am I that I ignored that worry." She snorted a wee tiny laugh. "As if I had a choice in the matter. I knew—somehow—that it would be right and good, and rewarding and honest. That it would be everything to me. It is that, Ross."

He grinned sleepily and gave her a lingering kiss. "It is as I said, love: Mayhap I should try to love you more, but I dinna ken that I could."

Pretending an affront, she showed him a pout. "You *should* try, though."

"Aye, I will, love." His hand skimmed down over her hip and thigh. "Hike up that skirt, I'll give a good effort right now."

Epilogue

*Westcairn,
Spring, 1332*

"YOU LOOK LIKE A MAN with the weight of the world on his shoulders."

Seated in the laird's chair behind the family table in the great hall, Ross glanced up to see his wife on the stairs, second step from the bottom, her shoulder leaned against the stone wall there, as if she'd watched him for a while.

He nodded and gave her a weary smile. "Aye, love."

Caitrin moved then, coming into the dimly lit hall. It was late, well after midnight. Today's feast was done, quieted now for almost an hour. The bride and groom had been ushered up the stairs to what would be the wedding suite tonight, that had been many hours ago. A lone taper sat upon the table in front of Ross, lighting only a circle of space around him and the tabletop, where a few goblets and pewter mugs still sat. There were crumbs and stains upon the fine linen tablecloth, one that Caitrin herself had embroidered for the wedding feast of her lastborn son. She and Aggie would spend much time tomorrow—later today—scrubbing viciously, trying to rescue the linen to save for future use.

Caitrin sat in the chair next to his as she had done for decades now. Their hands found each other's across that small expanse of space that could never separate them, their fingers entwining as if by unspoken command.

"It was a beautiful celebration," she said.

"Aye, it was."

"I think they will do well together. He is perfect, of course," she said, turning her head on the high-backed chair to grin at her husband. "And she is lovely, quiet and clever, a great complement to his sometimes riotous ways."

"He gets that from you," they said at the same time, a long-standing jest between them, one that had been uttered mayhap a hundred times by now, having raised five sons.

Ross chuckled softly and Caitrin grinned serenely.

When she laughed nowadays, deeper wrinkles crinkled around her eyes and mouth. If the wind caught her hair, pulling it out of her neat chignon or braid, the fingers that pushed it away from her face were no longer straight and smooth, but aged with bends and lines, and the hair itself was liberally gray, the beautiful flaxen blonde gone so many years now.

Likewise, the face she had smiled at every morning for so many decades, the one she had loved for so long, was neither smooth nor spotless; his once dark blond and thick hair had given over to thinner and white; the hands that held her, though still strong, were dotted with age and damage from the sun.

"What has you pensive then?" She wondered.

"Joy, I guess it is," he said, his voice still low-timbred but without the depth it had known in his youth.

"We are blessed."

"*I* am blessed," he clarified. "None of this would be—who can begin to fathom what might have been?—if no' for you."

"Ah. Then you're still in love with me?"

"Always." He swallowed, thoughtful, his mind churning. "What do you call it, that I stumbled upon you after such tragedy but knew almost immediately that I couldn't be without you?"

"Fate might be the word you are looking for, but if I remember correctly, you first refused to escort me."

"But that's what has me pensive—what if you'd gone away, what if Calasraid hadn't been attacked? You might have only stayed all your life with that woman—what was her name?"

"Eskaline."

"Aye. I might have gone on to Westcairn, found her sieged and might have forgotten all about the sorrowful lass with the clear green eyes."

"What has you now thinking about this? That was so long ago." A hint of concern tainted her question.

Sighing, Ross rubbed his hand over his mouth and jaw. "I dinna ken. I'm getting maudlin in my old age."

"Ah. Is that it then? You've married off the last of your sons, and are now considering your own age and mortality?"

She'd asked in a light tone, but his answer came with some urgency, a wee bit of panic creeping in. "I want more, Caitrin. I'll always want more. That brat you raised, Henry, jested only this morning that I've more yesterdays than tomorrows—"

"I will scold him sharply."

"I'm no' done with you, Caitrin—with us. I want more years, or all of them returned to me so that I can live them all again with you."

"You're beginning to scare me, Ross."

"Dinna be scared, love. I'm no' unwell. But it sits sorely with me, to no' have a lifetime ahead of us, but mostly behind us."

Softly, she reminded him, "But oh, what a glorious life we've had, Ross. And there's more to come yet."

"But what is it, then, that it's no' enough? That I want it to last forever."

She laughed. It was a mother's laugh, given to a child who asked a question whose answer was obvious. "That is love, dear, as well you know."

Recovering himself, made uneasy by his own mawkish grumbling, he said, "But you dinna seem burdened by so much grief that we've more yesterdays than tomorrows."

"He really is a brat," she said with a grin, referring to her middle child, now a man and a father himself. Standing, she pushed back her chair so that it was well out of the way and went to her knees at Ross's side, taking his hand in hers. "What life can compare to this, love? To ours? My heart is yours, Ross, all my life, in this one and the next. We shall never be parted."

He smiled down at her, laying his hand against her cheek. They'd known too much, joy and sorrow, for him to have been shamed by his misty eyes.

"I am only more in love with you, Ross, after all these years. They've not all been easy or kind. We've lost loved ones, too many to count even after we finally came to Westcairn all those years ago. We've buried two of our own children, we've seen you gone to fight more wars, we've fought over things small and large—I once didn't speak to you for an entire three days, so angry with you wanting to send our boy off to foster with the Jamison. I've been angry and sad and sometimes I truly believed my heart was broken, demolished, never to be recovered. But through all of that, one thing has always been constant: my love for you. Likewise, I never doubted your love." Her expression softened, as did her voice. "Will you promise me then, love, that you will wait for me or come to me, where ever we go next? I can bear anything if you promise me that. I will vow the same. I cannot be without you."

Ross nodded, his eyes shining yet. "I vow, love. But you're right. We've this life first, and it's no' done yet."

Caitrin laid her own hand over his. "Come to bed, love. The next of our many tomorrows will come soon enough, likely with the grandchildren bounding into our chamber in only a few hours."

Nodding, he stood from his chair, pushing it back as he did. He would hold his wife in his arms tonight and not be tortured with things he could not control. He would dwell on what was his, how fortunate he was.

He glanced down and held out his hand at the same time Caitrin grinned and said, "You need to help me up, though. I think I'm stuck."

Ross chuckled, the sound as rich and young as it ever had been and pulled his wife to her feet and into his arms.

The End

Other Books by Rebecca Ruger

Highlander: The Legends
The Beast of Lismore Abbey
The Lion of Blacklaw Tower
The Scoundrel of Beauly Glen
The Wolf of Carnoch Cross
The Blackguard of Windless Woods
The Devil of Helburn by the Sea
The Knave of Elmwood Keep
The Dragon of Lochlan Hall
The Maverick of Leslie House
The Brute of Mearley Hold
The Rebel of Lochaber Forest
The Avenger of Castle Wick

Heart of a Highlander Series
Heart of Shadows
Heart of Stone
Heart of Fire
Heart of Iron
Heart of Winter
Heart of Ice

Far From Home: A Scottish Time-Travel Romance
And Be My Love

Eternal Summer
Crazy In Love
Beyond Dreams
Only The Brave
When & Where
Get the Free Novella (Nicol and Eloise's story) by signing up to my Newsletter
A Year of Days
And! coming 2024
Beloved Enemy
Winter Longing
Hearts on Fire
Here in Your Arms

The Highlander Heroes Series
The Touch of Her Hand
The Memory of Her Kiss
The Shadow of Her Smile
The Depths of Her Soul
The Truth of Her Heart
The Love of Her Life

Sign-Up for My Newsletter and hear about all the upcoming books.
Stay Up To Date!
www.rebeccaruger.com

Printed in Great Britain
by Amazon